Sara Jo Cluff

TAYLOR'S OUTRAGEOUS VOW

For Disneyland

CONTENTS

CHAPTER ONE

*B*oys were basically the worst creation of all time. They couldn't be trusted. They'd shower you with love and promises of the future, give you pretty much the hottest and most spontaneous year of your life, and then rip that fire from your heart with absolutely *no* warning.

I snatched the silver frame covered in rhinestones from my nightstand and rolled my eyes. When I bought the thing, I thought it sexy and elegant. Now it looked cheap and trashy, just like the guy standing next to me in the picture.

Growling, I shook the frame in my hands, gripping it tightly, wishing I could do the same to Zander. I'd spent so much time trying to find the perfect prom dress, wanting to be as hot as I could for Zander without causing my dad and six older brothers to have a heart attack.

It was such a special night. In addition to looking totally adorable together, we won prom king and queen, and we celebrated our one-year anniversary.

"A year? I gave *a year* of my life to this loser?" I stomped over to the window, flicked it unlocked, and then tried to lift it. The window barely made it an inch before it wobbled to the side and jammed. With one hand, I slammed my palm against the metal window frame, trying to get it unstuck. The window didn't budge.

I needed both hands.

Letting the frame fall to the ground, I rolled out my neck and shoulders like I was preparing for battle with one of my older brothers, and then tried again, pressing both my palms against the lip of the window. With a great heave of effort, I threw everything I had into it, my feet digging into the carpet as I used all my arm strength.

"What are you doing?" My brother's voice sounded from somewhere behind me, probably in the doorway of my room.

"What does it look like I'm doing?" The window jerked, teetered to the opposite side, and jammed again.

Samson appeared at my side, a mixture of humor and pity in his brown eyes. "Can I try?"

I rounded on him, hating that I had to look up. Why were all my brothers so tall? "I'm perfectly capable of opening a window myself, Six!"

He scratched at the scruff on his chin, the only facial hair he'd been able to grow after going to college. "Oh, the angry brother numbers. So didn't miss that while I was gone." He folded one arm against his chest and held up his other hand. "Hear me out. I know it's by order of age, but I'm thinking you should go youngest to oldest, not oldest to youngest. I should be One. Give Neo Six. You know him the least."

Ignoring him—something I was normally exceptionally good at—I stepped back, took a deep breath, and threw myself at the window. My body ricocheted off the glass, sending me stumbling backward.

As I rubbed my arm and held in all the swears that wanted to fly, Samson went to the window, shimmied it out of its stuck position, and lifted it easily. The intense summer heat blew in, reminding me how grateful I was for air conditioning.

Trying to ignore my brother's smirking face, I bent down, snatched up the frame, and tossed it out the window, only to have it bounce off the screen and onto the floor.

I huffed, motioning to the screen. "Why is that there?" And why was nothing working for me? Everything always worked. Everything.

"To keep flies and boys out," Samson said, amusement painting his face.

I pushed my palms against the screen, but nothing happened. "How does it come out?"

He motioned to the bottom of the screen with his hand. "Those black tabs. Lift them up."

Thankfully, the screen came out smoothly, ending my humiliation.

"It's actually kind of comforting that you didn't know how to do that," Samson said. "Means you've never escaped your room that way."

I tossed the screen out the window, not bothering to see where it landed, and went to grab the picture frame once again.

Samson stuck his head out the window, leaning a hand on the windowsill as he looked down. "Uh, you were supposed to bring the screen inside, not throw it on the ground."

Glaring at him, I held my arm out the window, letting the frame dangle from the tip of my fingers with dramatic flair before dropping it.

Samson sighed. "You're lucky there's grass down there and not concrete." He grimaced. "Or a car."

"Why are you here again?"

He grinned, holding out his arms. "Aww, come on, lil sis. You know you're glad to have me home for the summer."

I slapped his arms away. "Nope."

I went to the bed, scooping up more of Zander's items into my arms. His black hoodie he always let me wear, saying I was sexy when I wore it. Out the window. A box of dried-up flowers from the bouquet of red roses he'd given me after our first fight. Out the window. All the cheap jewelry he'd spontaneously bought me. Out. The. Window.

"Hey, Tay?" Samson's tone hitched up. He pressed a finger into the indented crescent-shaped scar next to his right eye. His contemplative gesture. "Are you sure this is healthy?"

I shook a box of love letters at him, the smell from Zander's musky cologne wafting out. The cologne I got him for our six-month anniversary because I thought it would make him smell how I imagined Matthew McConaughey smelled. "It's either this, or I kill him."

Samson moved to rubbing the back of his long neck. "Yeah, we should probably go with this. Orange isn't your color."

I pointed at him with the box. "I can totally rock the color orange."

I chucked the box out the window, watching as the lid flew off and at least a hundred letters rained down on our lawn, the sight warming my frustrated heart more than I thought it would. Too bad I couldn't throw Zander out the window.

I turned away, but then heard a song playing from somewhere outside. Leaning my palms on the windowsill, I stuck my head out, looking around until I saw my two best friends, Daphne and Veronica, standing in the middle of our curved driveway.

Daphne had on her Cheer Bear onesie, even though it was crazy hot. She held her phone above her head, dancing around to some song about raining men.

Veronica must have seen the scowl on my face because she jumped up, snatched the phone from Daphne's hand, and quickly shut off the song. At least Veronica was in a tank and a short cotton skirt, something sensible for the heatwave we were experiencing.

"What are you doing?" Daphne asked, her hands on her hips.

"You really think *that's* the best song to be playing right now?" Veronica asked, her sarcasm cranked high.

"Uh, stuff is raining down from her window," Daphne said, "and it's Zander's things, so…"

Samson pushed me to the right so he could lean out the window, too. "Plus, it's catchy. Who doesn't love 'It's Raining Men?'"

Daphne waved up at my brother. "Hey, Six! When did you get home?" She'd taken my angry brother numbers and turned them into endearing nicknames for her own use. She said it was easier to keep track of all of them that way.

"Last night. During the grand finale, too." He put his arm around my shoulder and side-hugged me. "Good thing I came home when I did. Zander was able to walk away alive."

I squirmed from his grasp and looked down at my friends. "I'm not accepting visitors at this time."

I shoved Samson out of the way and slammed the window closed, letting out a satisfied breath. For a fraction of a second, I felt better, thinking of all those things now gone from my life. Then I pictured Zander's gorgeous face, and everything came rushing back, and, boy, was he lucky he wasn't standing in front of me, because I probably really would have thrown him out the window.

"You know that won't stop your friends, right?" Samson said.

Seconds later, the doorbell rang off the hook. With a grunt of frustration, I ran out of my room and to the banister, slapping my hands against it and leaning over so I could see the entryway.

My super sweet sister-in-law waddled toward the front door, one hand on her lower back, the other on her very pregnant belly.

"Don't you dare answer it, Aria!" I growled, harsher than I

meant to, but there was no going back. My words echoed around the large entryway, amplifying the sound.

Aria paused under the chandelier and looked up at me, her red eyebrows furrowed. "I ordered takeout."

"It's my friends, not your food." I tried to sound at least a little nicer. She didn't deserve my anger.

Brother number four—and Aria's lesser half—ambled into the entryway sporting his goofy smile. He joined Aria, towering next to her small frame. He towered over a lot of people. Like all my brothers did. "Mom's making spaghetti tonight."

Aria stuck out her tongue. "That's why I ordered takeout."

Quinn chuckled before bending down and kissing her on the forehead, making Aria do her squishy-I'm-so-in-love-with-you face that I once found adorable but now made me gag.

The doorbell rang again.

Daphne Richards and Veronica Rodriguez are at the front door, our automated system rang out.

"Daphne and Veronica?" Quinn grinned widely, making his already large mouth look gigantic. His long legs had him at the door in seconds, and he opened it before I could stop him.

Daphne burst into the entryway, pulling down the hoodie of her onesie and fanning her face. Her dirty-blonde hair fell around her, sticking to the sweat on her cheeks and neck. "Dude, it's hot out there."

Aria fanned her face as well, using both hands. "I'm hot just looking at you. Why are you wearing that?"

"I wanted to cheer up Tay-Tay." Daphne pointed to the rainbow on her belly as if it was obvious.

"It's not working." I squashed down the relief at the sight of my friends. I needed to remain mad and not let the sorrow take over. Zander wasn't getting any more of my tears after what he did to me.

Seriously, how could *he* break up with *me*? I do the breaking up in relationships. Always.

Veronica came in, shutting the door behind her before hugging Quinn and Aria. Sweeping her bangs back from her eyes, she bent down so her face was level with Aria's stomach. "Listen, kid, if you want to survive in this family, you'll need a name chart."

Aria rubbed her stomach. "That's actually not a bad idea."

Quinn frowned, a hand on his cleanly-shaved jaw. "Why? We don't have *that* many people in our family."

"Sure, Four." Daphne zipped down the front of her onesie. "How many siblings do you have again? Oh, that's right. Six. Not to mention three of them are married. And some have rugrats." She let the rest of her onesie fall to the ground, then she stepped out of it. She wore her favorite Cherry Coke shirt and red shorts that fit nicely around her slightly curvy frame. "You know how many siblings I have?" She made an '0' with her hand. "Zero. Zilch. Nada."

Quinn stared at the onesie on the floor and leaned over to Aria, his quiet voice far from quiet. "I know she's still dressed, but I still don't feel right for witnessing that."

Aria laughed, pressing the back of her dainty hand to her mouth.

Veronica pushed Daphne on the arm. "After having you, can you blame your parents for stopping?"

Daphne grinned as she brushed off her shoulders. "True. Why mess with *perfection*?" She sang the last word.

Veronica rolled her eyes and turned her attention to me as she tightened her high ponytail, which meant business. "Taylor, we're coming up. Don't you dare lock us out."

She trotted up the curved stairs, her long ponytail swishing side to side. Daphne scooped up her onesie from the floor and shuffled up behind her, looking a lot less graceful than Veronica.

Samson stood at the top of the stairs, leaning against the

wall, and folding his arms. He jerked his head toward me. "Good luck. She's in a mood."

I snarled at him. "No, I'm not!" Silence permeated the air, thick and heavy. I sighed. "Whatever." I motioned to my open bedroom door. "Come on in."

Veronica paused and stared at Samson, drawing an air circle around his chin. "What is this?"

Samson rubbed his scruff. "Trying something new."

Veronica shook her head. "Don't." She pointed at his scar. "And you have an eyelash hanging out in there again."

Samson wiped it away, laughing.

Veronica and Daphne came up to me, kissed me on either cheek at the same time, then went into my room. I had to hold back the smile that wanted to erupt on my face.

Samson moved to follow, but I held up my palm. "You're not invited."

He frowned. "I just want to run interference in case you start throwing other things out the window. Like your friends."

I waggled my finger at him. "Oh, no. This is a no-boy-zone for the unforeseeable future."

"I'm your brother," he said, a hand on his chest.

"I actually like the sound of that," Quinn said from the bottom of the stairs. "No boys in Taylor's room. Ever."

Samson moved toward my room, so I wrapped my arms around his middle and threw him to the ground like I did when we wrestled, getting out some of the stress eating away at me. Samson groaned on the floor as I stretched out my arms and neck, smiling at how good that had felt.

The front door opened, and my dad strolled in, pausing when he saw everyone.

"Why is there stuff scattered all over the lawn?" Dad asked, pointing his thumb out the door and glancing at everyone.

Ryker, brother number five, slowly trekked in behind Dad, setting down his duffle bag in the entryway. His resident leopard gecko, Spencer, sat perched on his shoulder. "Not the first impression I wanted to make for my roommate."

"What roommate?" I asked.

Samson rolled onto his stomach and tried to get up, so I set my foot on his back and pushed him back down.

Ryker looked up at me, his gecko doing the same. "My friend. We're sharing a dorm. He'll be here with us for the summer."

"*Him?*" I threw up my hands. "Why are there so many boys here?"

Ryker's confused gaze swept over to Aria and Quinn as he pointed up at me. "What's wrong with her?"

"Zander broke up with her." Quinn once again used his "quiet" voice.

Ryker let out a breath of relief as he tucked his long hair around his ear. "It's about time. I thought this day would never come." He looked over his shoulder and out the front door right as a scuffed brown military boot crossed over the threshold. "Everyone, this is—"

"NO BOYS!" I stormed into my bedroom and slammed the door.

CHAPTER TWO

I flopped down on my bed, frustration rolling through me. Zander had made me officially hate boys, and now my house was full of them.

"Alexa," Daphne said, taking a seat on the bed next to me, "play the album *SOUR* by Olivia Rodrigo."

Perfect choice.

Daphne slid the red scrunchie from her wrist and tied back her sweaty hair.

Veronica sat down on the other side of me, taking her long ponytail and resting it over her shoulder. She had her eyebrows perfectly drawn on, long fake eyelashes, and her skin so creamy smooth it looked soft to the touch. Flawless, as always.

"Maybe we should try something uplifting, Daphne," Veronica said.

I reached for a pillow, not wanting Veronica to change the music, but Daphne beat me to it and smacked Veronica across the head.

"Read the room, Veronica," Daphne said. "She's in a sour mood."

Veronica yanked the pillow from Daphne's hands and

started whacking her with it. "I'm trying." *Whack.* "To be." *Whack.* "Positive!" *Whack.*

Daphne curled into the fetal position, covering her head with her arms. "I surrender!"

Veronica finally stopped, tossing my pillow back to the top of the bed. "Good. What should we play instead?"

Daphne peeked through her arms, and when she was satisfied that she wouldn't be hit again, rolled onto her stomach and grinned at us as she cupped her chin in her hands. "Oh, I'm not changing the music. I just wanted you to stop hitting me."

Veronica opened her mouth, but I held up a hand. "Daphne's right. Let me play the mood out. Once it's gone, we'll switch."

Daphne stuck her tongue out at Veronica. With narrowed eyes, Veronica lunged for the pillow at the same time Daphne rolled off the bed and landed on the floor with a loud thud.

"I'm raising my white flag!" Daphne bellowed from the floor, her arm waving frantically above her head like a wild woman.

A laugh rumbled inside me, and I tried to keep it at bay, but I couldn't. It busted out, drowning out all other sounds. The muscles in my stomach clenched as tears pooled in the corners of my eyes. My laugh came out in a wheeze as I struggled for air.

I hadn't laughed like this in the longest time. Not since Zander—

My laughter cut off. I wiped the tears from my eyes and stared at the ceiling, trying to hold back the sobs. I'd shed enough of *those* kinds of tears last night when he broke up with me. I'd woken up with the urge to drive over to his house and beat him up, which was when I finally told my friends what happened, knowing they were always my voice of reason.

I felt Veronica and Daphne both lie down on either side of me, each taking one of my hands.

I sniffed. "I hate boys."

Daphne scoffed. "They're the *worst*. Forget about them." She added a mob boss flare to her words. "Who needs 'em, am I right?"

My laugh came out strained. "Says the girl with the perfect boyfriend."

Daphne squeezed my hand. "Weston isn't a *boy*. He's a man. He's my manfriend."

"Why doesn't that sound right?" Veronica asked.

"I really needed this right now." My voice came out in a whisper. They always cheered me up, and they didn't have to try. They just had to be themselves, letting me know I picked the perfect friends.

Daphne rolled onto her side, facing me. "Listen, what Weston and I have is rare, so we're taking our relationship out of the equation. Love is hard to find. And true love? *Pft.* Good luck with that."

I opened my mouth to argue because she so wasn't the person to be handing out this advice, but she pressed her finger against my lips.

"Hush, my darling Tay-Tay." Daphne practically cooed the words. "There's no point in trying to correct my logic."

Veronica rolled on to her side as well so she could face us, straightening her skirt in the process. "Correct your logic? Who talks like that?"

Daphne pointed a finger into her chest. "Me. I just said it." She reached across me and placed her palm against Veronica's forehead. "Are you feeling well? You seem to be missing the obvious today."

Veronica opened her mouth to talk.

I slapped my palms over both their mouths. "I'm done with boys."

Daphne blew a raspberry against my hand, so I lowered it, wiping my hand on my shirt.

"I'm serious," I said. "I'm making a vow right here, right now. No. More. Boys."

Veronica pulled my hand away from her mouth. "That's the most outrageous thing you've ever said."

Daphne patted my arm. "And trust us when we say you've said *a lot* of outrageous things."

"They're too much drama," I folded my arms. "They break your heart. They're selfish jerks." They break up with you out of the blue with no reason.

How had I not seen it coming? Had I completely overlooked the warning signs? Or had there been none and Zander was just a complete jerk? Probably the latter.

"You can't compare Zander to every guy out there." Veronica tugged on her ponytail, a newfound habit. "There are good guys, we just have to find them."

Daphne arched an eyebrow. "*We* have to find them?"

Veronica rolled her eyes. "We already know you found your Prince Charming, okay?"

"I was referring to you," Daphne said. "Is everything okay with DeShawn?"

"Don't try to change the subject." Veronica placed her hand on my arm. "We're focused on Taylor right now."

I sat up. "*Is* everything okay with DeShawn?"

They hadn't been dating too long, but I thought things had been going well. Not on the #Daphton level of well, but the normal level.

Veronica sighed, rubbing her temple that was pulled taut with her tight ponytail. "I really don't want to talk about it right now, okay? We're still together, so don't go jumping to any conclusions."

"It's too late," Daphne said. "The possibilities are running through my mind. He's a serial killer, isn't he? Runs a drug cartel?" Her eyes went wide. "He's dead. That makes so much sense. That's why he went from a total loser to someone

Veronica would want to date in the blink of an eye." Her voice dropped to a whisper as she stared at Veronica. "You're dating a ghost."

Veronica just glared at Daphne, not blinking for the longest time.

I sighed, wrapping my arms around my legs and pulling them against my chest, setting my chin on my knee. "I know you both think I'm crazy, but I'm swearing off guys until college. I don't need the distraction."

"That's not a terrible idea," Daphne said. "Focus on you." She pumped her arm. "Become the Taylor you've always wanted to be."

"It's a little extreme," Veronica said, "but if that's what you want, I'll support you."

Daphne blocked her mouth with her hand so I couldn't see her lips and looked at Veronica, but her whisper was loud and clear. "I give it two weeks."

Veronica mimicked Daphne's action. "Five."

Daphne stuck out her hand. "Deal."

Veronica shook her hand, then frowned. "We didn't just make a bet, did we?"

Daphne shrugged. "What's wrong with making a bet?"

Both Veronica and I narrowed our eyes at Daphne.

"Oh, come on," Daphne said. "That was *so* three months ago."

"How are Bentley and Sierra doing, anyway?" Veronica asked.

"Nope!" I shook my head. "No relationship talk around me."

Daphne saluted me. "Aye, aye, Captain."

"What a man, what a man, what a man, what a mighty good man," rang out from Daphne's phone, telling her of an incoming text from Weston.

Daphne smiled sheepishly, pulling her phone from the back

pocket of her shorts. "Just gonna silence this really quick." She tucked her phone back away and waved her hand. "Message from a friend. No big deal."

I rolled my eyes. "We know it's from Weston."

"You know what sounds good?" Daphne blatantly tried to change the subject. "A big ol' Cherry Coke. Let's go get one."

I lay back down on the bed. "You know I drink Dr Pepper. And I'm not leaving my room tonight. I'm on a strike until all the guys in this house clear out."

Veronica ran her fingers through the ponytail hanging over her shoulder. "Um, you want your brothers and dad to move out?"

"There's too much testosterone!" I swore I could feel it oozing through the crack under my door. "Why did they all have to move back home?"

"Wait, they *all* moved back in?" Daphne asked. "Yeesh, you guys are going to have to build another wing to this place."

I shook my head. "Well, no, but there's a lot staying for the summer or while their house is being built. It's too many."

Daphne patted my arm. "Should have thought about that before you had six brothers."

"Didn't really have a say in the matter, Daph," I said. "Besides, they were all here by the time I was born."

"What about The Hideout?" Daphne asked. "Is your dad done fixing it up?"

"Almost," I said.

Dad built me a treehouse when I was a little girl so I had a space to run to when I needed to get away from all my brothers. As they slowly moved out of the house, my need to use it dwindled until I stopped using it altogether.

With all my brothers coming home this summer to celebrate Dad's sixtieth birthday, Dad said he'd fix it back up for me so I could sleep there when brother number two, Ollie, and his family showed up, since they would be using my room.

We were only a couple of weeks away from then, and it still wasn't finished. But it would be the perfect place to get away.

Veronica pulled out her phone, twirling her ponytail around her fingers. "Should we order pizza? If we're stuck here all summer, I gotta eat."

I looked up at her. "You're staying here?"

Daphne patted my cheek. "We're all yours until you kick us out."

Veronica chuckled. "Please. We all know she'd have to drag you out of the house, Daphne."

"Yeah, she'd have to kick me out," Daphne said. "Literally." She got up and grabbed my laptop from my desk. "What should we binge-watch?"

"Nothing romantic," I said. "Or dramatic."

Daphne nodded. "Good call. Maybe something with action, like blowing things up and such."

I rolled on to my stomach. "What about crime shows?"

Veronica set her phone down. "So you can learn how to get away with murder? I don't think so. Also, the pizza is on the way. I got cheesy garlic bread as well."

Daphne danced where she stood. "Happy Death Day. That's what we're watching."

"Perfect." I grinned at her. "Now, go get me that Dr Pepper you promised."

CHAPTER THREE

I don't remember falling asleep, but when I woke, it was dark out, and both Veronica and Daphne were sound asleep on either side of me. Veronica was curled on the edge of the bed, taking up the least amount of space. Daphne, on the other hand, was sprawled out, one leg perched on top of Veronica and an arm draped over me.

As carefully as I could, I lifted Daphne's arm, rolled out of the bed, and crept out of the room. Yes, I'd said I was on strike and wouldn't leave my room, but I had to at some point. Besides, I was the only one awake.

I was welcomed to an eerie silence in the hallway, despite how many people were sleeping under our roof. With my friends, family, and a guest, there were ten people currently in our home. It wouldn't be long until my entire family was here —all my brothers, their spouses, and kids. I mean, that had to be a fire hazard of some sort.

It wasn't like I minded being around my family, but with all my brothers gone, I'd grown accustomed to the quiet house. Growing up, it was always so loud. With all the tile and large living spaces, their shouts echoed. There was never a quiet moment, never a time to reflect or collect your thoughts. I *needed* those moments right now so I could get over Zander.

It would be near impossible with everyone back home.

I padded into the kitchen, needing a drink. When I opened the fridge, I stared inside, wondering what to get. Water was the smart middle-of-the-night-choice. But the Dr Pepper called my name, wanting to quench my sorrow. Yeah, the caffeine would make it difficult to fall back asleep, but sometimes I needed a hug from the inside.

Pushing logic aside, I snatched a can of Dr Pepper and closed the fridge. I was about to pop it open when I heard a noise behind me. I whipped around to find a figure looming in the darkness, facing me. By the squared shoulders, it was definitely a guy, which ruled out all the girls in the house, and he was too short to be any of my brothers or my dad.

Instinct took over, and I chucked my can of soda as hard as I could, hitting his face. On the way back down, two loud thunks echoed around the kitchen as the can ricocheted off the counter and onto the ground. Carbonated soda shot everywhere like a geyser from the can.

As the person doubled over and cried out in pain, I frantically searched for something I could use as a weapon. My hands fumbled over something large. The metal paper towel dispenser. Without much thought, I flung that in the general direction of the intruder. By the yell that followed, I connected. Served him right for breaking into our home.

Wait. Someone had broken into our home. I needed to call the police. My cell was in my bedroom, and my parents canceled our home phone forever ago.

"Alexa, call the police!" I yelled as loud as I could.

Alexa: *"Hmm, I can't help you with that."*

I let out a growl of frustration.

No matter which way I went around the island, I had to go past the intruder to get to a phone. Or to my dad or one of my brothers. They were big and tough. Their massive size alone should scare anyone.

Through the dark, I stumbled over to the knife drawer and grabbed the biggest handle I could find, hoping the blade attached was big as well.

Bracing myself, I turned toward the intruder, trying to figure out the best route. The guy was spewing Spanish out of his mouth in rapid succession. From the limited Spanish I knew, I recognized some not-so-nice words.

I glanced at the island. Going to the left would give me the largest distance from the guy, but he could still catch up in the living room.

I spotted a pile of what appeared to be pots, pans, and dishes. My brothers hadn't cleaned up after dinner like they were supposed to, for once their lazy selves coming in handy.

I could use a pot as a weapon. Or a shield. I quickly snatched one up, flinching as a bunch of other pots clanged onto the tiled floor. Then I smiled. All that ruckus had to have woken up the nine other people in the house, despite how big it was. Sound carried in this place. This guy chose the wrong home to break into.

Steeling myself, I held the pot close to my chest and ran toward the intruder, knife extended.

Before I could get to him, lights suddenly came on, practically blinding me. I stumbled to a stop, holding my arm up to block some of the light shining in my eyes.

"What's going on?" Mom demanded as she finished yanking on some basketball shorts so she wasn't just in one of dad's old T-shirts. "Why is there soda all over the place?"

"Huntley, are you okay?" Ryker tugged a shirt over his head and then tucking his shaggy hair behind his ears, the ends curling around his lobes.

Huntley. Who in the world was Huntley?

A warrior cry bounded down the stairs, and suddenly

Daphne came into view, wearing her pink Care Bear onesie and holding a lamp from my bedroom. Veronica was at her heels, holding my other lamp, a fierce growl on her face.

"Are you making potatoes?" Dad squinted like his eyes were adjusting to the light. He was in a tee and cotton pants, his brown hair a disheveled mess. "You should have just come down at dinner time, Tay."

I turned to him, totally confused. I motioned to the guy hunched over near the counter. For some odd reason, Ryker had a hand on his back, leaning toward him and whispering like they were friends.

"He broke into our home!" I yelled, pointing my knife at the guy. Wait. It wasn't a knife. It was a potato masher. I briefly closed my eyes and sighed. Wrong drawer.

Quinn and Aria appeared from one of the bedrooms down the hall, both in their pajamas and shuffling like zombies rising from the dead.

Daphne lowered the lamp, a frown on her lips. "I thought you were in danger."

I shook the pan toward the intruder. "I was!"

Daphne tilted her head to the side, the hood of her onesie moving with the motion. "Huntley?"

"Who's Huntley?" I asked.

The intruder slowly raised his arm, almost in a surrender.

I looked at Daphne. "How do *you* know him?"

She pulled down the hood of her onesie. "Met him in the hallway earlier when I had to tinkle. Nice guy. He's studying to become a podiatrist." She grimaced. "Which is disgusting because, feet, but whatever."

"What's wrong with feet?" Veronica asked.

"*Everything*," Daphne whispered-shouted.

Ryker brushed past me, a glare in his hazel eyes that made me slink back. He whipped open the freezer, grabbed a bag of frozen corn, and then snatched a towel hanging over the oven handle. "What is wrong with you, Taylor?" He stormed back over to … Huntley, I guess … and handed him both items.

Huntley pressed the towel against his nose—which was bleeding profusely—and then put the frozen corn over his left eye.

Mom had moved over to Huntley as well, using a towel to wipe at the blood falling down his chin and dripping onto his bare—and very toned—chest. Why wasn't this guy wearing a shirt?

"Do we need to take you to the hospital?" Dad crouched in front of Huntley.

Huntley shook his head. "I'm fine. Just a bloody nose." His good eye flickered toward me, a mix of rage and amusement battling behind it.

Heat rose in my neck and cheeks. I slowly set the pot and potato masher back onto the counter. "Would someone please tell me what's going on?"

Ryker motioned to Huntley. "This is my roommate, Huntley Esposito. Huntley, this is Taylor, my annoying little sister I told you about."

Huntley nodded his head toward me. "I'd say it was nice to meet you, but it's really not."

Aria waddled into the kitchen with one hand on the small of her back, stepping around the mess on the floor. She squeezed my arm and softly smiled at me before she went to the pantry and pulled out some crackers.

Everyone else was staring at me. The only person who hadn't woken up was Samson, but that boy could sleep through anything.

I leaned against the counter. "How was I supposed to know that? All I saw was a dark figure looming there, and I panicked."

Quinn squeaked out a laugh. "Man, you really must have gotten used to all of us being gone. You see a person in our home and your mind immediately goes to a stranger, not one of the many people who live here?"

The heat in my cheeks expanded to every piece of my body. "He's too short to be any of you!"

Aria sucked in a sharp breath at the same time Veronica said, "She should really stop talking."

Daphne held up her phone, "Despacito" playing from it.

Veronica slapped Daphne's arm. "What are you doing?"

Daphne took a large step away from Veronica. "He said Esposito, which made me think 'Despacito,' which made me think we could really use some music up in here to break the tension."

Aria danced near the pantry, munching on some crackers. Quinn joined her, taking her hand, and twirling her around, surprisingly smooth on his feet for being such a goofball.

Dad sighed. "This isn't a time for a dance party."

"Oh, Mr. Thomas." Daphne shook her head in sheer disappointment. "It's always time for a dance party."

Veronica pounced on Daphne, grabbed her phone, and ran into the other room. She held the phone high and tried to turn off the song while pressing her other palm into Daphne's face to keep her at bay.

It was silent for a moment before Huntley suddenly busted out laughing, causing all attention to turn to him. After he composed himself, he turned to Ryker. "You weren't kidding about your home being utter chaos."

Mom put her hand on her hip, her eyes narrowed at Ryker. "You told him our house was chaos?"

Ryker swept out his long arms. "Tell me I'm wrong."

Mom opened her mouth but then quickly shut it, rubbing the back of her neck as she nodded.

Dad clapped his hands. "All right, show's over. Everyone back to bed. Taylor, clean up this mess." He looked at Huntley. "Do you need any ibuprofen?"

"That would be appreciated." Huntley's gaze swept to me once again.

I normally didn't mind people looking at me, but with the curiosity behind his eyes, I felt uncomfortable, unsure of what to do with myself. I quickly grabbed some towels from the drawer and began mopping up all the soda on the floor. What a waste of a Dr Pepper.

Daphne trotted back into the room and wiggled her phone. "Got it back. What song do you need?"

Dad pointed at the stairs. "Daphne, Veronica, back to bed."

They both hung their heads and said, "Yes, Mr. Taylor," before sprinting up the stairs. Daphne shoved Veronica so she could beat her to the top.

Quinn took the box of crackers from Aria and set them back in the pantry. He put his hand on the small of her back. "Let's go, sweetie."

Aria wiped at the corner of her mouth. "Grab me some milk." She stood on her tiptoes and kissed Quinn's jaw, winked at me—her soft green eyes melting some tension—and then waddled back to their bedroom.

Once Quinn had the milk, he lifted it toward me in a salute and joined his wife in their room.

That left Ryker, Mom, Dad, and Huntley all staring at me with different expressions. Mom was pure disappointment. Dad switched between amusement and exasperation. Ryker was fuming, more upset than the time when we were kids and I told him about all the presents Mom and Dad had gotten him for Christmas.

Huntley still wore his intrigue, and I found myself clutching my arms close to my chest. I needed to end this moment.

After throwing the soiled towels in the laundry room, I grabbed a few ibuprofens from the cupboard next to the sink, plus a glass of water, and brought them to Huntley. Squashing down my embarrassment, I set the items on the table in front of him.

I cleared my throat. "I'm sorry, Huntley. I may have over-reacted."

"May have?" Ryker shook his head. "You could have caused some serious damage."

My gaze wandered to the potato masher on the kitchen counter. Even if it had been a knife like I'd intended, I wouldn't have actually used it on the guy. I just wanted protection in case *he* tried to attack *me*.

"It's fine," Huntley said. "Now I know to make my presence known when I walk into any room in this home."

"Just don't walk into my room, and you'll be fine." I went to the fridge to grab another can of Dr Pepper.

"Why would he go into your room?" Ryker asked.

"That's a good question." Dad folded his arms and lifted his chin a little.

I scoffed. "Now who's overreacting?"

I popped the top of the can and was about to take a sip when suddenly Samson's blurry form came into view as he charged at Ryker, grabbed him around the middle, and threw him to the ground.

I quickly downed my soda, praying for the night to be over.

"Sneak attack!" Samson panted as he put his hands on his hips and looked around at us. Getting a sneak attack on Ryker was rare, mostly because we had a rule that we couldn't attack him when he had Spencer on his shoulder, which was pretty much all the time.

Samson's ginormous smile faded when he saw Huntley's banged-up face. "What happened to you?"

Huntley raised his hand again, his eyes on me. "Can I have Dr Pepper, too? Handed, not thrown. Also, you might want to look into setting up Alexa to call the police. Could come in handy if I had been an actual intruder."

"She can do that?" Mom looked at the white Echo Show sitting on the counter.

I fished another can out of the fridge and brought it to Huntley. When our hands brushed each other, a weird, tingling sensation shot through me, and I suddenly needed another drink.

CHAPTER FOUR

*D*aphne and Veronica were already asleep by the time I went back upstairs. I was wired, thanks to the whole Huntley incident plus the three cans of Dr Pepper I ended up drinking.

I sat down on the floor in front of my bed, using the bed as back support. Pulling my legs into my chest, I tried to think of anything and everything *not* Zander. But my mind wouldn't cooperate.

Why did he break up with me? He hadn't given me a real reason, just that it was 'time to move on with our lives.' Lamest excuse ever.

Did he miss me? Did he think about me? Was he regretting his decision to call it quits?

Against better judgment, I pulled up his social media profile on my phone, taking in his new profile pic. He was looking off to the right, a warm smile on his face, his black hair slicked back, wearing his favorite aviator shades, and the ocean behind him. He captioned it with, "Time for the next chapter in my life. Exciting things are coming. #optimistic #thingsarelookingup."

What was he talking about? What exciting things were happening? And things were looking up? Was life with me *really* that bad? I mean, he always seemed so happy and content in our relationship. The break-up had come out of the clear blue. He'd given no indication that he wanted to end things until he showed up at my door.

The way he had spoken to me made my blood boil. It was like he was this wise, older guy with so much knowledge about life that my tiny brain couldn't possibly comprehend. He spoke in a sweet, soft tone, like he was talking to a child.

The fact that he had the audacity to step onto my turf and rip the rug out from under me was mind-blowing, and so not like him.

My fist clenched, and I wished I would have punched him instead of slapped him. I mean, the red mark I left behind on his cheek was nice, but a broken nose or black eye would have been so much more satisfying.

I cringed, thinking about Huntley and the black eye I'd probably given him. Poor guy. Now that things had simmered down, I was starting to feel *really* bad. I don't know what had come over me. Instinct to protect myself took over the second I saw an unknown figure in my kitchen.

My phone screen flashed. I looked down to see someone had commented on Zander's photo.

No, not some*one*. Some *girl*. I pulled up her profile. Simone. Ugh. She was strikingly beautiful with raven black hair and piercing blue eyes. She had to have been wearing colored contacts. No way her eyes were naturally that color.

I went back to Zander's picture.

Simone: *So glad I snapped this pic. U r so hot.*

She had taken the picture? Was his natural smile because of her? And why was she on his page at three in the morning? Who does that?

The bed shifted behind me, and I suddenly felt a presence

over my left shoulder. Since she was humming "good 4 u" by Olivia Rodrigo, I knew it was Daphne.

Daphne pointed at Simone's comment. "Is it really that difficult to write out 'you are'? Man, teenagers are so lazy these days."

"She's hot, isn't she?" I whispered.

"I need to see a better picture than that tiny one next to her comment if you really want me to answer that question."

I pulled up her account again and clicked on her picture. Simone was in a bathroom—probably hers—taking a selfie through the mirror, head kinked to the side. Her arm rested over her head, and her make-up was way over-the-top. Naturally, her shoulders were bare, and she was wearing a ridiculous, sultry smile.

Daphne whistled. "Uh, yeah, she's gorgeous."

I tried to swat her, but she rolled out of the way, went too far, and thumped onto the floor, letting out a strained, "Ow."

She crawled over and sat next to me. "I meant that in the 'if you're into stunningly gorgeous people, then, yeah, she's hot' kinda way."

"Was that supposed to make me feel better?" I asked.

Daphne linked her arm through mine. "I'm not here to make you feel better. I'm here to shine light on the situation. If Zander dumped you out of the blue, and then has girls like this creeping in his life, maybe he's not the guy you thought he was."

"What do you mean, 'girls like this'?"

"Girls who take photos of themselves through bathroom mirrors, showing off their bare shoulders so you'll think she's naked." Daphne shrugged. "I mean, I guess she could be, but what message is she sending?"

I snorted out a laugh. "You sound like an old person sometimes."

Daphne grinned. "Thanks." She patted my arm. "Looks like

we need to do some investigating and figure out what's really going on with Zander."

It wasn't a bad idea. I needed some answers.

"That's a terrible idea." Veronica's groggy voice came from over my right shoulder. "Don't you remember when you and Taylor tried to spy on Bentley and Sierra? That was a disaster."

Daphne shook her head. "It was a great idea. We stopped a kiss from happening and stopped Sierra from taking the lead."

"This isn't a bet," Veronica said. "This isn't Taylor and whatever her name is—"

"Simone," I said.

"—both vying for Zander's attention," Veronica finished. "If anything, she needs to be letting go and moving on."

Daphne held up a palm. "That's true, but sometimes moving on means getting someone fully out of your system. If you just ignore it and pretend they don't exist anymore, it will drag out the process."

Veronica hopped off the bed and sat on the other side of me, crossing her feet at her ankles. Her hair flowed around her shoulders. Much better than the tight ponytail look she'd recently adopted. "Yeah, she needs to rip off the Band-Aid, throw it in the trash, and let the wound heal. Naturally."

Daphne turned so she was facing Veronica and me. "Some wounds can't just heal like magic. In fact, if they get too much air, they can get infected, or you could open the scab again."

I set down my phone and slapped my palms over their mouths. "This is starting to make zero sense. You two suck at analogies."

Daphne tried to speak, her lips vibrating my skin and making me giggle. I quickly removed my hand from her mouth.

"The point I'm trying to make is that you need to flush the grief out of your system by whatever means necessary," Daphne said. "For some people, that means walking away and never looking back. That's not you, Tay. You're going to let this fester and eat you alive. So, let's listen to some angry ex-girlfriend music, get vengeance, and *then* you can move on with your life."

Veronica pulled my hand away from her mouth and rested it against her chin. "Vengeance? What do you have in mind?"

Daphne suddenly shot up, flicked on the light switch, and ran to my desk in the corner of the room.

I put a hand over my eyes for a second. "Yeesh, warn a girl before you go turning on lights."

Daphne rummaged through my desk until she found a notepad and a pen, then rejoined us on the ground. Her smile grew as she wrote something on the top of the paper. "Swearing off boys isn't enough. You need a bigger vow. Something outrageous." She flipped the pad around so we could read, her sparkling green eyes peering over the top.

Taylor's Vow of Vengeance.

My smile matched hers. "I love it."

Veronica sighed. "I'm so gonna regret this." She interlocked her fingers and stretched out her arms as she rolled her neck. "Let's do this."

CHAPTER FIVE

*M*y Vow of Vengeance was super simple: GET EVEN.

I'd been blindsided by the break-up, which went against everything my brothers had taught me growing up. They drilled into me the importance of always knowing your surroundings, which was how the sneak attacks started among all the siblings. It always made us on high alert. And it made the payback attack more intense and probably slightly dangerous.

Zander's sneak-attack break up had left me stunned and confused in the moment—hence the slap and not a full beat-down. Now it was time to roll up my sleeves and get to work making Zander pay for what he did by whatever means necessary. He wouldn't get the last word.

I opened the door to my room, peered out to make sure no one was in the hall, then slinked across the hallway and into the bathroom. I was in desperate need of a shower. I couldn't make Zander regret his decision if I looked and smelled gross.

I paused in front of the bathroom mirror. Dark rings sat under my eyes. It was going to take a gallon of concealer to cover them up. Maybe Veronica could help. She worked wonders with make-up.

I was just so unbelievably tired. I couldn't sleep after finding out about that Simone girl. Had Zander already moved on? It had only been a day. Had I meant nothing to him? Had all those love letters and the long middle-of-the-night video chats where we whispered in the quiet of our bedrooms so we wouldn't wake up our families meant nothing to him?

After a long, hot shower, I slipped into my robe and wrapped my hair in a towel before heading out into the hall.

The moment I opened the door and stepped out, I ran into something hard.

A round of Spanish expletives were thrown at me—second time within twenty-four hours—and I wondered if it was starting to become a thing.

Huntley rubbed his arm, but my focus was pulled to his massive black eye and swollen nose.

I placed my hand over my mouth in pure shock. I knew I had chucked that can of Dr Pepper pretty hard, but I didn't think it had caused *this* much damage.

I lowered my hand. "I'm so sorry, Huntley."

Huntley shook out his arm. "Don't worry about it. Last night's beating was worse."

I furrowed my eyebrows. "What? Oh! No! I meant about last night. You look terrible."

"That's the sweetest thing anyone has ever said to me." He gently pressed his fingers against his cheek as a smirk pulled across his lips. "So you don't feel bad about running into me?"

"Of course I do!" Biting my lip, I lightly traced the bottom of his bruise with my finger, his skin surprisingly warm. "How bad does it hurt?"

Huntley shrugged. "Believe it or not, I've had worse. This is nothing."

My gaze traveled from his swollen eye to his good eye, which were both level with mine. They were deep brown with tiny golden flecks. "Wow. Your eyes are *ah-mazing*."

"So, you can say nice things. I was beginning to think you only handed out insults." His good eye smiled at me, making me realize how unbelievably close I was to him. I couldn't get a good look at his mouth to see his actual smile.

I tried to move my body back, but it was like I was frozen, tethered to this guy and his entrancing gaze.

"Uh, Taylor," Huntley said, the smile in his eye switching to sheer amusement.

"Hmm?" Seriously, those little gold flecks were intoxicating. I was seconds away from getting a DUI from staring into them.

"You're kind of in my space," he said, almost in a whisper. A sexy whisper.

With a gasp, I jumped back, hitting the wall. I was openly— like no hint of discreetness whatsoever—checking out my brother's roommate.

College roommate. This guy had to be what? About twenty-one? That's how old Ryker was. Talk about being illegal.

The crisp sound of someone biting into something came from behind Huntley. I gazed past him to see Samson leaning against the wall, laughter in his eyes as he ate an apple.

Daphne's head came into view as she leaned close to Samson. "This is the greatest moment of my life."

"Same," Samson said.

Huntley casually turned around and stepped back, which brought a smirking Veronica into the scene as well.

Daphne's eyes went wide. "Holy massive bruise, Batman!"

Veronica whistled under her breath. "You really did a number on the guy, didn't you?"

"What are you guys doing?" I asked, not able to hide the horror in my voice.

Samson grinned. "Watching this all unfold. It's beautiful, really." He glanced over his shoulder. "Good thing Ryker wasn't here to see. He'd be ticked."

Daphne set her hand on her hip. "He should be happy. It's like she's all, 'Zander who? I've got a sexy Despacito in front of me.'"

Huntley furrowed his non-swollen eyebrow. "Who's Zander? And it's Esposito."

Daphne nodded. "I know. And Zander is her ex as of a day ago." She started humming "Despacito," doing a little dance in the hallway.

Huntley ran a hand over his close-cropped hair. "I haven't even been here twenty-four hours, and this the most bizarre experience I've ever had."

"Oh, the fun is just getting started." Samson took another bite of his apple, winking at me.

I clasped the top of my robe and shrank into the wall, wishing I could disappear.

"Here you are." Mom popped up on the other side of me, making me jump into the air. She didn't even flinch. "I need you guys to go check out a venue for your dad's party." She handed me a paper with an address scribbled on it.

"Why can't you go?" I asked. Though I absolutely loved parties, and seeing the venue could be fun.

"I'm taking Ryker to the dentist." She rolled her eyes. "I should make him take the bus. I don't know why he won't just get a license."

"Because he's Ryker," I said at the same time as Samson.

The guy had an unexplainable and unhealthy fear of driving. Samson and I took the driver's test on our sixteenth birthdays. I thought having his two younger siblings get their licenses would make Ryker give in, but it only gave him two other reasons to *not* do it: he had two new drivers at his disposal.

Huntley chuckled. "I honestly think that's the only reason he invited me here this summer. So I could drive him here."

"Wouldn't surprise me." I smiled at him.

A set of keys appeared in front of my face, jingling together. "You can take *the shuttle*."

With a grimace, I snatched the keys from Mom, then tossed them to Samson as quickly as I could. "He can drive."

Samson barely caught the keys against his chest. "Oh, come on. You know I hate driving the thing."

"You guys have a shuttle?" Huntley asked.

Veronica shook her head. "It's just a really big van to hold their really big family."

"All I did for fifteen years straight was shuttle the kids around," Mom said as she rummaged through her purse. She finally pulled out her wallet and handed me a credit card. "Grab some lunch while you're out." Then she handed me another piece of paper. "Also, I need you to get everything on that list for the barbecue tonight, so you'll need all the spare room in *the shuttle*."

Daphne shimmied. "We're having a barbecue?"

Mom grinned at her. "Yep. Bring your swimsuit, too." She lightly kissed my forehead, right under my towel, reminding me that I still had my hair wrapped in it. "Just make sure to be back by five so you can help set up."

Samson snatched the list from my hands. "Five? How long is this list?"

Mom backed down the hallway, taking the fob to her BMW out of her pocket. "Thanks kids, you're the best." She blew air kisses before she disappeared down the hall, yelling for Ryker that it was time to leave.

Daphne smiled sheepishly at me. "Uhm, I have to go as well. But we'll start the V of V tonight. Gotta start with a little recon."

"What's the V of V?" Samson asked.

"Vow of Ven—" Veronica started.

"Nothing!" I cleared my throat. "It's nothing." I wasn't sure why I didn't want anyone to know, but I didn't. Well, I didn't want Huntley to know.

Samson arched an eyebrow at me but dropped it and showed Daphne the list. "We need your help, Daph."

She started backing away. "Sorry, Six, but I have about a billion bag orders to fulfill for my business. Can't get cranky customers. So sorry."

Veronica tilted her head to the side, a hand going to her hip, her long ponytail swaying with the motion. "Let me guess, Weston is going to help you?"

"Uh, yeah," Daphne said. "So what?"

"That means you're going to make out for the next few hours instead of helping me," I said.

"Bow-chicka-wow-wow." Daphne wiggled her eyebrows. "You know it. But you kids have fun. Weston and I will be here tonight for the barbecue." She blew us all kisses with her hand and then ran after my mom. "Can I get a ride, Mrs. T?"

Mom's reply was muffled, but I did hear her say loud and clear, "Ryker, you are *not* bringing Spencer to the dentist."

Samson sighed. "Looks like it's just the four of us." He tapped Veronica's arm. "Unless you have to leave, too? What's his name? Shawn or something?"

"DeShawn," Veronica said, "and he's working all day, so I'm all yours."

Samson held out his fist for her to bump. "Good. We better get started."

I patted the towel on my head. "Give me ten minutes."

Samson pulled his phone out of his pocket and checked the time. "Ten minutes, starting now."

With a squeal, I rushed past all of them and ran into my bedroom.

With six brothers, I had a strict time allotment for getting ready. If I wasn't ready when the timer went off, my whole family would leave me at home alone, which I hated.

Though, that was mighty tempting so I wouldn't have to spend the day making a fool of myself in front of Huntley. But I could never turn down the challenge.

CHAPTER SIX

In record time, I rolled my hair into two buns on top of my head, threw on some makeup, and found my favorite red skirt. Without a minute to lose, I slipped into my heeled booties, and bounded down the stairs. I would have worn my black leather jacket if it weren't so hot out.

Quinn meandered out from the kitchen, whistling while holding a plate with a delicious-looking grilled cheese sandwich. He paused when he saw me, his whistle going flat. "Oh, no you don't. Back upstairs, young lady."

I put my hand on my hip. "Why?"

He pointed at my skirt with his plate. "That's way too short. Dad will kill you if he sees you in it."

"Along with your brother, apparently." Veronica tugged on her ponytail. "Seriously, why do guys feel the need to tell a girl what to wear?" There was an edge to her voice that made me think she was talking about more than my skirt.

Quinn opened his large mouth and then snapped it shut, a frown forming on his lips.

Aria came out from the bedroom and worked her pregnant

self over to Quinn. She took the plate from his hands and smiled at me. "You look gorgeous, Tay."

Quinn switched to his not-so-whisper whisper. "But look how short it is."

Aria took a bite of the sandwich, swallowed it, and looked up at Quinn. "First of all, if I had long legs like hers, I'd be showing them off, too. And don't get me started on how hard it is for tall women to find clothes. As a short girl, I know exactly how much it sucks."

I smiled at Aria. "Thanks, sis." I guess the good thing about having so many brothers was I finally ended up with some sisters.

She winked at me. "You're welcome, sis." Her eyes suddenly went wide, and she jumped into the air, sending the grilled cheese flying.

I looked down to see Spencer, Ryker's leopard gecko, wandering across the tile, headed for the kitchen like he needed a snack. Too bad we didn't keep live crickets in the kitchen, which were his favorite. I shuddered at the thought.

"Shouldn't he be in his cage?" Quinn picked the grilled cheese off the ground.

"Can we go now?" Samson asked with a bored voice.

I looked over my shoulder to find him and Huntley standing next to the front door. Huntley was watching the whole thing like it was the most entertaining show he'd ever seen. He had to think our family was crazy.

Samson and I ended up doing rock, paper, scissors to see who'd have to drive *the shuttle*. I lost.

Samson immediately went to the back of the van so he could be my eyes back there. I expected Veronica to ride shotgun, but she hopped in the middle of the van, letting Huntley take the passenger seat.

I tried to scold her with my eyes, but she just shrugged, pulled out her phone, and typed something.

My smartwatch and phone buzzed seconds later, alerting me of an incoming text.

Veronica: *He's hot, Tay, and totally your type. Good distraction.*

Me: *I'm not looking for another relationship right now! And, eww, he's old!*

Through the rearview mirror, I saw Veronica roll her eyes as she responded.

Veronica: *I'm not saying get together with the guy, I'm saying continue to gawk at him until you get the other guy out of your head.*

Me: *I so did not gawk.*

Veronica: *It was gawk city up in there, and you know it.*

My phone was suddenly ripped from my hands.

"You shouldn't text and drive." Huntley set my phone in the center console. Hopefully, he hadn't seen any of the texts.

I scoffed. "Thanks, *Dad*."

Huntley flinched as he buckled his seatbelt, then turned his attention to the window. I'd somehow struck a nerve, and a twinge of regret flitted in my heart.

This guy was going to hate me by the end of the summer. The thought shouldn't have bothered me, but it did.

My hands tightened around the steering wheel. Hormones were *the worst*. Why couldn't I break-up with *them*? Send those hormones packing.

"You're clear back here!" Samson yelled from the backseat.

Closing my eyes, I took a long, deep breath, trying to relax my nerves.

"What music do you like?" Huntley asked.

I turned to him. "Uh, classic rock. Why?"

He turned the knob for the radio, finding a station that happened to be my favorite before settling back in his seat. "Best radio station out there."

"Right?" I said.

He smiled over at me. "You have good taste." He softly

touched his swollen cheek. "And good taste in beverages. Love Dr Pepper. Except when it's being chucked at me."

"I'm really sorry, Huntley," I said.

"Let's go, Tay!" Samson shouted. "We don't have all day!"

"I know!" I yelled back, glaring at him in the rearview mirror.

He flipped me off, making me roll my eyes.

Why did I have so many brothers?

"You Give Love a Bad Name" by Bon Jovi came on the radio, so I cranked up the music, a smile finding its way to my face.

It wasn't long until Huntley and I were singing at the top of our lungs, Huntley even playing the air guitar. I caught Veronica's smirk in the rearview mirror, but I didn't let it stop me. It wasn't like Zander stripped me of everything. I could still have fun.

When we got to the venue, I felt the lightest I had since the break-up. Daphne was right. Music and singing were totally therapeutic.

Veronica came to my side once we got out of *the shuttle*. "You're welcome."

"For what?" I asked.

My watch vibrated with an incoming notification. Veronica had posted something on social media. I pulled my phone out of my skirt pocket and checked her page. She'd posted a picture of Huntley and me at a stoplight, both facing each other and singing, looking like we were having the time of our lives. Veronica had captioned it with #optimistic #thingsarelookingup. Same hashtags Zander had used on his picture.

I bumped her with my hip. "Genius."

Veronica tossed her long ponytail over her shoulder. "Girl, you know I got you. Always."

"I know," I said.

She paused, twisting her lips to the side, and picking at her skin with her teeth. She was worried about something.

"Now what?" I asked.

She came close and showed me her phone. Zander had officially updated his status to "in a relationship" with Simone listed as his girlfriend.

Unbelievable.

He'd basically left me for another girl. It was better than cheating on me, but still. It had been less than two days.

I quickly texted him: *I should have punched your traitorous face. Better watch out for karma.*

"Uh, we should probably go inside," Samson said.

Veronica squeezed my arm. "We'll get vengeance, I promise."

I shook the anger brewing inside me out of my system. I had more important matters, and I would not let Zander ruin my day. With a lift of my chin, I silenced my phone and tucked it in my pocket.

A short lady welcomed us at the doors to the event center, her short brown hair in an A-frame. I took in her floral jumper with a smile on my face.

"Love your outfit," I said at the same time Samson offered the lady his hand and said, "Samson Thomas. My mom, Maggie, sent—"

"Follow me." The lady spun around and headed into the center at a brisk pace.

Samson quirked an eyebrow at me, but I just shrugged and hurried to catch up with her. I was amazed at how quickly the lady walked. Coming from a family of tall people, I was used to walking fast because their strides were so long. But all of us were having to semi-run to keep up with her.

She led us up a flight of marble stairs and into a humongous banquet room, stopping abruptly. We all piled to a stop behind her, bumping into each other.

"This is the Cascade Ballroom, the biggest we have, as Maggie requested." Her large brown eyes swept the room.

Veronica huffed and puffed next to me, clinging onto my arm. I'd never seen her so winded before.

I glanced down at her. "You okay?"

She wiped away some sweat above her lip. "No one told me we'd be participating in the Olympics today."

The lady continued, her focus everywhere but us. "You can comfortably fit well over a thousand guests. We offer catering and decorations, which I mentioned to Maggie over the phone."

"A thousand guests?" Huntley's eyes—well, eye—was wide. "You guys know that many people?"

I choked back a laugh. "No, but—"

"We can easily make the place look like a basketball arena, no problem." The lady typed something on her phone as she spoke. "I'm not sure how far your mom wants to take it, but I can introduce you to Francisco and our design team. They can help make your dreams a reality."

Veronica leaned toward me, finally breathing at a normal rate. "Uh, if your mom wanted it to look like a basketball court, why isn't she using an actual basketball court?"

The lady's piercing eyes swept over Veronica, making Veronica shrink into me and let out a small squeak. She stared at Veronica for a few moments, total silence filling the vast room.

Samson finally cleared his throat. "Did you already discuss prices with my mom?"

The lady stared at Veronica but spoke to Samson. "She has everything in the email I sent. You'll find we're quite affordable and offer the best services in the area." Her eyes snapped to me, and Veronica let out an audible sigh of relief. "I can send her the contract this afternoon."

Huntley leaned toward the lady, causing her gaze to fly to

him. He kept a smile on his face, all charm and showing no signs of intimidation.

"Do you mind if we have a moment to look around?" Huntley asked.

The lady's demeanor softened—barely—and she nodded briskly. "Of course. I'll send Francisco up to talk set-up." She left without a backward glance.

Samson watched her leave with his jaw hanging open.

"Set-up?" I moved toward the center of the ballroom. "I thought Mom just wanted us to check it out. Not plan the thing."

"Same," Samson said, his focus still on the door the lady had gone through.

Huntley came up next to me. "There really is a lot of room to work with. You could do some fun things if it's in the budget." He looked at me. "Did your mom give you a budget?"

I shook my head. "I have the same information you have. What she handed me this morning."

Huntley smirked. "Guess that means you can do what you want."

"Oh, the damage we could do." A smile broke out on my face. "We should switch the theme. Paw Patrol?"

"How old is your dad turning?" he asked.

"Sixty," I said.

His grin expanded, reaching up to his eyes. "Golden Girls."

"Brilliant." I bumped my hip with his.

Looking around the massive room, all the plans started forming in my head. We could set-up bleachers—or better yet, folding seats like they have in arenas—along with basketball hoops and a scoreboard.

Out in the hallway, a shouting match started, all of it in Spanish. Veronica looked over at Huntley, and their eyes widened as the yelling went on.

"This isn't good." Veronica looked at the open door and

tugging on her ponytail.

"What are they saying?" Samson asked.

"Uh, let's just say Francisco isn't digging the basketball theme." Huntley folded his arms. "Apparently, it's insulting."

"What's insulting about basketball?" Samson rubbed the crescent-shaped scar near his eye.

Veronica moved toward the door. "It's about artistic design." She looked over her shoulder at us, her tone snooty. "It's beneath him."

Huntley briefly set his hand on my arm. "Let me go talk to him."

I shot a skeptical look at Samson, but five minutes later, Huntley was walking through the doors with a smiling, chatty Francisco.

The man looked sharp in his blue plaid suit and tie with his black hair cropped close to his head. He smiled at me, showing off a dazzling set of white teeth. "I'm Francisco, your party planner extraordinaire. Anything your little heart desires, I can do."

Samson came forward and held out his hand to Francisco. "I'm Samson."

Francisco's gaze flitted over to Samson, his smile not faltering for even a second. "I don't do that." He turned back to me. "I have a party to oversee downstairs at the moment, but I can meet on Tuesday to discuss all the details." His tone went a little strained on the last word, like he still wasn't sure about hosting a party for us.

"Well, I need to talk to my mom to make sure she wants to go with this venue," I said, "but—"

Francisco waved his hand. "Trust me, honey, there's nowhere else for your mom to go to get this kind of service for such a value. She'd be *insane* to turn it down." He moved toward the door. "Seven a.m. Tuesday morning. Don't be late."

"Seven?" I squeaked out, but he was already out the door

and gone.

Veronica looked at me. "Yeah, so not going to be coming with you then. I have a date with my bed."

"Let Mom do it," Samson said. "We were just told to come today." He glanced at the time on his phone. "Let's get some lunch."

"What about that new Thai place in Yorba Linda?" Veronica said.

Samson's eyes lit up. "That sounds perfect."

The two of them walked out, chatting about their favorite Thai food.

I turned to Huntley. "What did you say to Francisco to make him change his mind?"

Huntley shrugged, then slipped his hands into his pockets. "Told him your dad used to play for the Lakers, and if he threw a party for him, maybe other players might want to use this venue."

I choked on a laugh. "That was eons ago for like, a year, and Dad was a benchwarmer."

"Francisco doesn't need to know that." Huntley smiled, then grimaced, like it had hurt. He gently touched his nose. "I think you owe me another Dr Pepper. One wasn't enough."

"I think I owe you a lot more than that." I smiled sheepishly.

"We can start with one and go from there." He bumped my arm.

I pulled my mom's credit card out of my pocket and waved it at him, happy to finally be having a decent moment with Huntley. "How about lunch as well?" I looked down, noticing his scuffed brown military boots. "Love your shoes, by the way."

His smile dissipated. "They were my dad's." He walked out of the room without looking back.

And just like that, the moment was over.

CHAPTER SEVEN

$\mathcal{I}$ sat on the edge of the pool, swirling my feet in the warm water. Daphne and Weston were lying stomachs-down on a round watermelon float, their arms linked together as they chatted away. Weston wore a set of blue trunks, plus a Captain America water shirt and probably a gallon of sunscreen Daphne had lathered on him, thanks to his super-sensitive skin.

Daphne had a cherry-red retro bathing suit and a pair of Mickey ears she'd made with the Cheer Bear rainbow on them. It was her new alternative to the Care Bear onesies, which were way too hot for the summer. She had a set of ears for every bear so she could reflect her mood. Ever since she and Weston had gotten together, it pretty much alternated between Cheer Bear, Love-A-Lot, and Tenderheart, with random appearances by Funshine Bear.

Watching them interact with such ease, like they'd known each other for years, sometimes yanked at my heartstrings so hard I was afraid they'd snap.

"It's adorably sickening, isn't it?" Veronica took a seat next to me. "I wasn't even sure if true love was possible until I saw the two of them together."

"Two seeds in a watermelon." I grimaced at my choice of words. "That was awful."

"Terrible," Veronica said through her laugh.

I turned to her, seeing she was in a baggy shirt and shorts. "Aren't you going swimming?"

She pulled at her shirt like it was too tight, though it wasn't. "I need a new bathing suit. My other ones don't fit anymore."

Veronica had gained a little bit of weight over the past few months, but not enough that she'd outgrow her bathing suits.

"Who cares if they're a little snug?" I said. "There's no judgment here." I bit off the last words, thinking of my brothers and all their comments. I rubbed her arm. "Veronica, don't worry about my brothers. They're idiots."

She turned to me, a frown on her lips. "I don't care what your brothers think."

"Then why not put your swimsuit on and jump in?" I slipped into the water and motioned for her to join me. "You know you wanna."

Her eyes flickered over to where DeShawn was talking to Huntley, Ryker, and Samson near the grill. Spencer was sleeping on Ryker's shoulder. Dad and Quinn were working on the hamburgers, in a very serious discussion about something probably entirely stupid.

"I'm fine." Veronica's unfocused gaze went to the water in the pool as she ran her hand down her ponytail.

I swam over to her, folding my arms and setting them on the edge of the pool. "What's going on, Veronica?"

She quickly shook her head. "Nothing." She pulled her phone out of her pocket. "We need to plan our first move with Zander."

"I still can't believe he's already moved on. He wasted no

time." My stomach sank to the bottom of the pool. "Do you think there was something going on before he dumped me?"

"It's probably best not to think about that." Veronica's eyes lit up. "We should tail him. See where he's going."

I rested my chin on my arms. "We can't use any of our vehicles. He knows what we all drive."

Veronica looked back over at the guys, and a grin broke out on her face. "He doesn't know Huntley's car."

"Why would Huntley let us borrow his car?" My eyes sought him out. He laughed at something Samson had said. Ryker had rolled his eyes at the same time, which was so typically him. Always the skeptic.

The water behind me rippled, and suddenly Daphne and Weston floated into view.

"What are we talking about?" Daphne asked in a conspiratorial whisper.

"We're going to borrow Huntley's car and stalk Zander tonight." Veronica leaned toward us, more excitement on her face than I'd seen in a while.

"Huntley's okay with you borrowing his car?" Weston asked. He moved his finger so it was just above his nose, doing an air scratch above his sunscreen-covered nose.

"What are you doing?" I pushed away from the side of the pool so I could see them better.

"I have an itch but don't want to scratch the sunscreen off." Weston's eyes crossed as he tried to look at his nose. "I thought maybe if I mimed it, my mind would think it was scratching it and it would help."

Veronica choked back a laugh. "Is it working?"

Weston sighed. "No."

"Oh!" Daphne shouted. "Huntley is approaching. I repeat, Huntley is approaching."

I pressed a hand to my ear and grimaced at her. "Yeah, we heard you the first time."

"I think the neighbors heard you the first time," Veronica said.

DeShawn and Huntley walked up to us, both laughing. DeShawn slapped Huntley on the shoulder. "I like this guy. He's funny." He looked over his shoulder at my brothers. "Unlike Ryker. That kid is wound tight."

Huntley rubbed the back of his neck. "He's interesting to room with, that's for sure."

I looked up at Huntley, who had crouched down to be more level with us. "Out of all my brothers, you drew the short end of the straw."

Daphne waved a hand. "Five's not *that* bad. He's just set in his ways."

"And they're the *only* ways," I said.

"What's with the lizard?" DeShawn asked. "Is it one of those emotional support pets or something?"

I looked over at Ryker, who had wandered over to Dad and Quinn. "It's a gecko. Ryker's had him for years." I'd never really thought too much about it. Ryker and Spencer were a package deal.

"Huh." DeShawn took off his shirt, showing off his ripped abs. I expected Veronica to do her swoony-eye thing she always did around DeShawn, but instead, she looked at the water, squirming like she was uncomfortable.

DeShawn jumped into the pool, creating a huge splash, getting water everywhere. Veronica had lifted her arms, trying to block herself from getting wet, but it did little good. DeShawn proceeded to do laps, leaving our little group alone.

"So," Daphne said, smiling up at Huntley. "Can we borrow your car tonight?"

Huntley jerked his head back in surprise. "Why?"

Daphne's voice dipped low. "We have a situation to take care of that requires the utmost discretion."

Huntley's swollen eye widened to the point where it actually looked normal. "Color me intrigued."

Daphne turned to me. "Yeah, okay, I totally like this guy."

For some reason, I found myself blushing. I didn't know why Daphne felt the need to even tell me that. I lowered the bottom part of my face into the pool in hopes to cool myself off.

"So, we have this vow of v—" Veronica started.

I popped back up and hissed at her, causing all eyes to turn to me. "He really doesn't need to know the details."

Huntley sat down next to Veronica on the edge of the pool, dipping his feet into the water. "If it involves borrowing my car, I kinda do."

I sighed. When Daphne had first brought up the Vow of Vengeance, I thought it sounded brilliant. But now with Huntley here, it sounded juvenile. He was going to think we were some stupid high schoolers, which, I guess we were.

"I'll give you the condensed version," Weston said. "Taylor's long-term boyfriend dumped her out of the blue, now she wants vengeance, which requires some stalking, which requires a vehicle—"

"That her boyfriend wouldn't recognize," Huntley finished, nodding. "Makes sense. But here's the thing: I don't let people borrow my car."

Daphne adjusted the ears on her head. "Trust issues?"

Huntley leaned back, resting his weight on his palms. "You want to use my car to stalk someone."

"Touché." Daphne pointed to the ears. "I'll make you one of these bad boys. Though it doesn't have to have a rainbow on them. Anything you want. Pick your poison."

"Why would he want Mickey ears?" I wished I could dip under the water and never resurface. What must Huntley think of us?

"Why *wouldn't* I want Mickey ears?" Huntley pointed at Daphne. "Can you make them in guitar shape?"

Daphne's eyes lit up. "Oh, I do love a challenge."

"Yes, you do," Weston, Veronica, and I all said at the same time. Then we busted out laughing.

"Why a guitar?" Daphne asked.

Huntley lifted one shoulder in a shrug. "It's a hobby of mine."

"You any good?" Veronica asked through her calming laughter.

Huntley twisted his hand back and forth. "Let's just say I don't totally suck."

"How would your mom rank you?" I asked. "That might help us get a gauge."

He stared off into the sky for a moment, squinting his good eye. "Not sure."

I dipped down until the water covered my mouth and nose, wondering if I should just go completely under. Both times I'd mentioned parents, Huntley had gotten all weird about it. What if he didn't have a family? What if he was a foster kid or something? Or maybe his whole family died in a horrific house fire, and he was the only one who survived.

Okay, Daphne's morbid sense of reality was starting to rub off on me.

"Does this mean you'll let us borrow your car?" Weston asked, not missing a beat, and clearly not noticing how uncomfortable I was, thank goodness.

Huntley looked over at Ryker, then turned his attention back to us. "Fine. But I'm driving."

"Woot, woot!" Daphne tried to "raise the roof" which was difficult with her lying on her stomach and one arm still linked with Weston's.

Served her right for trying to "raise the roof." Her young,

nineties-raised mom was sometimes the worst influence on her.

There was a commotion on the back patio, and I turned just in time to see Quinn barrel into Samson, throwing him to the ground with a battle roar. Quinn straightened, a wicked grin on his face. "Sneak attack!"

Samson had only been back two days, and the sneak attacks were already in high gear. With the rest of my brothers coming, I had a feeling that number would skyrocket. Samson could end up with another scar, which was how he got his crescent-shaped one next to his eye.

"Hamburgers are ready!" Dad shouted from the grill.

Everyone but me—and Samson, who groaned on the patio floor—practically scrambled out of the pool and to Dad. I was too worried about Huntley, hoping I hadn't once again hurt his feelings when I mentioned his mom.

I swam to the edge of the pool and Huntley offered me a hand.

With a little bit of reluctance, I let him help me out of the pool until we were standing face to face.

"Huntley, I'm sorry if I upset you." I kept my voice low. "I'm guessing family is a sensitive topic?"

"Understatement of the year," Huntley said, those golden flecks in his eyes driving me wild yet again.

"Want to talk about it?" I asked.

He shook his head. "Not right now. Maybe someday, though, over a Dr Pepper?"

I smiled. "Deal."

"Taylor!" Mom yelled over at me, wiggling my cell phone. "Your screen keeps lighting up with notifications."

I jogged over and took my phone from her before she joined the others around the grill.

I had some missed texts.

Zander: *What are you talking about?*

Zander: *Why am I a traitor?*

I'd almost forgotten I'd texted him earlier.

Zander: *Your slap was more than enough, and uncalled for.*

Zander: *I'm not a traitor.*

Zander: *I've done nothing wrong.*

Then why was he so wound up about it?

Zander: *Are you ignoring me?*

Zander: *Very mature, Taylor.*

My thumbs pounded across the screen of my phone. *Sorry I haven't been sitting by my phone all day long waiting for your response. I have a life, you know.*

Zander: *Why am I a traitor?*

Me: *You already know the answer to that.*

I turned off my phone, my patience spent.

CHAPTER EIGHT

I rummaged through my closet until I found the black romper Daphne had made me for my birthday. The girl had turned her bag-making skills into clothes and other accessory-making skills, and I swear she'd have her own clothing line someday. It fit me perfectly, and even though it was a tad longer than I'd wanted and had sleeves, I absolutely loved it.

I made sure to wear my black booties, wanting to blend into the dark as much as possible. It reminded me of the time Daphne and I spied on Sierra and Bentley back when Daphne had made that questionable bet with Sierra—who could get Bentley to ask her to prom. I worried for a second, flashbacks of falling out of the tree invading my mind, but then remembered it had all worked out in the end. Both girls got the guy they wanted and had become friends instead of enemies.

My insides boiled as Simone's sultry face flashed into my mind. I was *so* not becoming friends with her. Ever.

"Why do you look like you're about to murder someone?" Daphne stepped into my room. She was wearing a red and white gingham romper with cherries on it, an outfit she'd made herself. Her Mickey ears had the Cherry Coke logo on them. She used a red hair tie to pull her wavy blonde hair back into a ponytail. Her eyes went wide. "Wait, *are* we murdering someone tonight? I thought we were just going to spy." She clutched a hand to her throat. "I'm so not ready for this."

I motioned to her totally adorable red outfit. "You wore the wrong color, Daph."

She waggled a finger at me. "I wore the *right* color. If someone catches us and we are all wearing black, how suspicious would that be? But if we're all in our normal get-up, we can be like, what? We were just hanging out. Complete coincidence that Zander happens to be here with Simone."

I slipped a black leather bracelet onto my wrist. "You really think he's going to be with *her*?" Yeah, they were social-media-official, but I still had this naïve hope it was some sort of a joke.

"Eh." Daphne tilted her head to the side. "I'm only about one-hundred and twenty percent certain."

Veronica bounded into the room, a bright smile lighting up her face. She wore an olive-green romper with cut-off sleeves and a tie that cinched the waist. "Isn't this amazing?" She slipped her hands into the pockets. "It even has pockets. POCKETS."

"Everything should have pockets." Daphne held up a finger. "Everything."

Veronica swished her hips side to side. "Daphne made me a new one since the last one was too small." She went up to my mirror and checked herself out. "I haven't felt this good about myself in the longest time."

I joined her, putting an arm around her shoulders. "Amazing what the right piece of clothing can do, isn't it?"

"And not having someone questioning your weight," Veronica said so quietly I almost didn't hear her.

"Who's been questioning your weight?" I asked, lowering my arm.

Her wide eyes shot up to mine as she tugged on her ponytail. "What? Nothing. No one."

Daphne interlocked her fingers and stretched out her arms. "Who do we have to beat up?" She lowered her arms and pointed a thumb at me. "Scratch that. Who does Taylor need to beat up? She's better at that kind of stuff than me."

I bent forward, sweeping my arms into a circle and putting on my fierce growl I used before wrestling matches with my brothers, my voice coming out low and throaty. "Give me a name."

Veronica choked back a laugh. "It's nothing. Forget I said anything." She went to tighten her high ponytail, so I beat her to it, pulling out the tie and letting her hair fall around her shoulders.

"There." I combed through her hair with my fingers. "Much better."

"What's with the new ponytail obsession anyway?" Daphne asked.

Veronica shrugged. "DeShawn says it makes me look like Ariana Grande." She put her hand on her hip and looked back into the mirror. "Daphne, I could kiss you, this romper is so perfect."

"Aww, come here." Daphne wrapped her arms around Veronica and repeatedly kissing her on the cheek.

I joined them, kissing Veronica's other cheek.

"I thought we were leaving?" Huntley asked from the doorway to my room.

Weston popped his head in, shaking it when he saw us hugging Veronica. "I swear, I can't leave you gals alone for two seconds." He patted Huntley on the shoulder. "Get used to it. These three are as thick as thieves."

"And way more trouble," Samson said from the hallway. He put his head between Huntley's and Weston's. "You girls ready?"

I finally released Veronica. "You're coming with us?"

Samson frowned. "Geez, sis, don't sound so disappointed. Don't worry, I won't tell them about the time Quinn and I found you trying on our jockstraps." He slapped a hand to his mouth, a fake look of surprise in his eyes. "Oops."

"Okay." Daphne smiled at Samson. "I guess I can see the perks of having a sibling."

"Maybe you'll get one," Samson said. "Isn't your mom getting pretty serious with that Cody guy?"

Daphne pursed her lips. "I really don't want to think about Mom and Cody making babies, so never bring that up again."

"You'd be a terrible older sister anyway," Veronica said

Daphne's jaw dropped before she huffed. "I would be the *best* sister ever. That baby would be lucky to have me in their life."

I motioned to my outfit. "Just think of the cute little rompers you can make the baby."

"What if it's a boy?" Huntley asked.

"Baby boys can wear rompers, too," I said.

Weston grinned. "Now I'm picturing a baby in a little Care Bear onesie."

"I could make one for each bear!" Daphne's smile faded. "Wait. No! I'm not supposed to like this situation. No Care Bear onesies for babies!"

"Are we going to leave sometime tonight," Samson asked, a bored look in his eyes, "or should I go pop some popcorn and we can just watch a movie?"

I checked myself in the mirror, making sure my hair and make-up were flawless. "We have a mission to do. Let's go."

When we got outside, I stopped next to Huntley's sedan. "Um, there's six of us, and this seats five." I looked over my shoulder at Samson. "Sorry, bro, guess you can't go."

Huntley went to the driver's side and unlocked the door.

"Actually, this is a six-seater, so we're good." He opened the door and unlocked the rest of the doors.

Veronica, Daphne, and Weston quickly piled into the back. Samson opened the front passenger door and motioned for me to go in.

"After you, sis," Samson said.

I leaned down and looked at the bench in the front. "Um, how old is this car?"

Huntley patted the dashboard. "This beauty is still in great condition, I'll have you know. My dad got it the day I was born. Once I was old enough, he showed me all the ropes about taking care of a car." He leaned toward me. "You'll be fine. Get in."

When I didn't move, Daphne leaned forward from the back and honked the horn, making Huntley laugh.

"Let's go, woman!" Daphne said.

"Why do I have a feeling I'm going to regret this?" I asked Samson.

He grinned. "Oh, I have no doubt you'll regret your entire Vow of Vengeance."

"Then why are you coming?" I asked.

His eyes sparkled. "I'd never miss this show for anything in the entire world."

I poked his chest. "You better not do anything to interfere. You know I'm capable of winning a wrestling match now."

He grimaced, rubbing his lower back. "Don't remind me."

The horn honked again.

With a sigh, I slid into the car, taking my position in the middle front seat. I suddenly had flashbacks to my childhood days. Before we had *the shuttle*, my family had a three-row Suburban. All six boys would take the back two rows, leaving me sandwiched between Mom and Dad up front.

Daphne stuck her head between mine and Huntley's. "The

nice thing about a bench upfront is that you can make out up there. No need to crawl into the back."

"I like the way you think." Huntley smiled at her.

"So does my boyfriend." Daphne arched an eyebrow, then slowly disappeared into the back.

Once again, I found myself wanting to shrink into hiding, but Huntley just laughed. "I like your friends." He started up the car, and the radio came on, playing "Highway to Hell" by AC/DC.

Samson leaned toward me. "Kind of fitting, isn't it?"

I set my palm on his forehead and pushed him away. I glanced in the rearview mirror to see Daphne doing the air drums while Weston did the air guitar. I leaned a little to the left so I could catch a glimpse of Veronica using her fist as a microphone and singing along.

"I love this song," Huntley said.

I turned to find I was unbelievably close to him. I hadn't realized I'd leaned over so much.

He faced forward, a small smile tugging at the corner of his mouth. "AC/DC is one of the greatest bands of all time."

Okay, this guy liked old bands, which confirmed he was old like my brothers, so why did I keep checking him out? Even if I were looking to start something—which I *so* wasn't—he wouldn't be interested in some teenager.

I mean, I guess *I* liked the band as well, but that was thanks to my dad and all my older brothers.

"Uh, Taylor?" Huntley asked, the smile still pulling at his lips.

"Yeah?"

"Personal space."

"Oh!" I shot to the right, smacking into my brother.

Samson rubbed his arm. "What are you doing, Tay?"

"Nothing!" I looked in the rearview mirror to see Daphne

mouth, *"bow-chicka-wow-wow,"* and by the way Huntley laughed-slash-coughed next to me, he'd seen her as well.

I sank into the seat the lowest I could possibly manage, which wasn't much.

"So, where exactly are we going?" Huntley asked.

"Wherever Zander is," Daphne said from behind me.

"Which," Veronica said, "from looking at his social media, is down in Newport Beach."

"With Simone," Daphne whisper-shouted.

"Prime vengeance time." I looked at Huntley. "Take the 91 to the 5 and that will drop us off in Newport."

"I know how to get to Newport," Huntley said.

I threw up a hand. "How was I supposed to know that?"

He looked over his shoulder at Veronica. "You're positive he's still in Newport?"

"Well, Simone just posted a picture of the two of them outside some restaurant off PCH in Newport saying they were about to get dinner—because we totally care what they're up to —so, yeah, I'd say I'm pretty positive."

I rubbed my hands together. "That will give us plenty of time to drive down there before they leave."

Huntley seemed a little hesitant, but he finally pulled away from the curb and headed toward the freeway.

CHAPTER NINE

*H*untley found his way to PCH with ease, like he'd driven the route a million times. As we neared the street that would take us toward Balboa Island, I spotted Zander's car in the parking lot outside a Mexican restaurant.

I leaned over Samson. "There's his car!"

"Good," Veronica said from the back seat. "That means they're still there."

Keeping my eyes on Zander's car, I patted Huntley's arm. "Find a place to park."

"You know that's practically impossible down here, right?" Huntley turned off PCH and onto a side street. "Especially this time of night."

I almost made another comment about him sounding like my dad, but I bit my tongue. Last time he hadn't reacted very well.

"Then just pull over and let us out," I said.

Daphne suddenly appeared between Huntley and me, her arm extended as she pointed out the window. "Pull in there! That lady in the really expensive-looking car is leaving!"

I slapped Huntley's arm repeatedly. "Go, go, go!"

"I'm going!" Huntley quickly pulled into the parking lot. "Which car?"

"That one," Daphne said, still pointing. "The expensive one."

Huntley rolled his eyes. "They're all expensive. This is Newport Beach."

I squeezed Huntley's arm, and wow, was it firm. "That yellow Porsche."

He drove over and turned on his blinker, signaling that he wanted to take the lady's spot.

Problem was, there was another car—a Mercedes by the look of it—coming from the other way that also had their blinker on. The driver of that car and Huntley had a glare-down, and I wasn't sure who would win.

"I've got this," Daphne practically hissed into our ears. She climbed over Weston, opened the door, and flew out of the car toward the Mercedes.

As the Porsche backed out, Daphne maneuvered herself in a way that made the lady back toward us, giving us the advantage. As soon as the Porsche cleared the spot, Daphne moved in front of the Mercedes and began dancing, really working her arms and legs, making it impossible for the car to move. Her Cherry Coke Mickey ears brought another level to the spectacle.

"She's so hot," Weston whispered from the back seat.

I shared a brief smile with Huntley before he pulled into the parking spot. We all piled out of Huntley's car in time to see the driver of the Mercedes flipping off Daphne as he sped away.

Daphne's wide grin faded.

"I can't believe you just did that." Veronica shook her head at Daphne.

"Strangest experience ever," Huntley said under his breath next to me.

Daphne straightened out her romper. "Wait. I just really did that, didn't I?"

"Yeah," Weston said. "And it helped us get the spot we needed." He tried to put an arm around Daphne's shoulders, but she bent down, pressing her palms to the top of her knees.

"What was I thinking?" Daphne asked. "I just danced in a parking lot with people watching, and what must that guy think of me?"

"That you're a crazy teenager?" Samson said.

I elbowed him in the stomach. "Not helping."

Veronica rubbed Daphne's back. "It's fine. He's probably forgotten about it already. No big deal."

Daphne breathed deeply like she was on the verge of a panic attack. "It's a huge deal. He's going to be telling people that story for the rest of his life to everyone he meets." She crouched down until she was sitting on the asphalt, her arms wrapped around her legs. "What if I ruined his night? What if he *needed* that spot? He was probably about to propose to his girlfriend, and it was his only chance because she's leaving on a red-eye flight to see her dying mother, and now he'll never get the chance, and I'm seriously starting to regret all my life choices."

Weston and Veronica bent down next to her, wrapping their arms around her.

"Happy thoughts," Veronica said.

Huntley leaned toward me, his voice low. "What's happening?"

I tugged him off to the side. "Daphne deals with major anxiety. She tends to overthink things when she does something she deems embarrassing. She'll probably relive that moment in her head for the rest of the week."

Huntley's concerned gaze went to her. "That's awful. What do we do?"

"Talking calmly helps," I said. "Remind her of all the things that make her smile. Try to get her focus elsewhere." I watched as Daphne leaned into Weston, clinging on to his shirt. "Water helps, too. Maybe there's a convenience store nearby."

Huntley popped the trunk of his car and pulled out a bottle of water.

I took it from him with a small smile, then bent down in front of Daphne and handed her the water. She greedily took it, ripped off the lid, and drank.

I stood back up and went to where Huntley leaned against the back of his car.

He bent toward me, keeping his voice low. "I'm just kinda surprised. She seems so outgoing and sure of herself."

"It really depends on where she is and who she is with," I said, my voice hushed as well. "In known territory, and with close friends and family, she's fine." I squeezed his arm. "The fact that she's so casual around you means she's comfortable being around you. Total compliment."

After a few more minutes, Daphne calmed back to her normal self. We helped her stand and did the best thing for her in those situations: moved on like it hadn't happened.

"So, what do we do now?" Samson asked.

"We need eyes on the target." Veronica squinted at the restaurant.

Huntley scratched his forearm, a faraway look in his eyes. "No windows up front, and it backs up to the water, so the only way to see them would be to go inside. Once you do, though, you'll pretty much be exposed unless you hide behind the bar. Getting there without being seen would be tricky."

We all paused, looking at him. It took him a moment to realize we were all staring. Then he just stood there, smiling sheepishly.

"Have you been here before?" Veronica finally asked.

Huntley cleared his throat. "A few times, yeah."

I put a hand to my throat, horrified that I'd once again made

Huntley uncomfortable without trying. He seemed to have a history with the place, and not necessarily a good one. "You used to take an ex here, didn't you?"

He stuffed a hand in his pocket. "Something like that."

"And I'm taking it didn't work out?" Daphne nodded like she'd caught on to something.

"Something like that," Huntley said again.

"Good to know." Daphne winked at me. "This restaurant is a curse upon relationships. Zander and Simone don't stand a chance."

"Well, if we can't go inside, what can we do?" Samson asked.

"We need to ruin his night," I said. "I'm just not sure how."

Daphne held out a hand, counting things off with her finger. "We could pay a waiter to spill food on them. We could let a rat loose in the restaurant. Pull the fire alarm and hope the sprinklers turn on. Take all the air out of his tires so they can't go anywhere else and will have to call a tow truck."

Veronica put a hand on her hip. "Where are you going to find a rat?"

"Alley?" Daphne and Weston said it at the same time, almost in the same pitch. They fist-bumped then flung out their fingers, making an explosion sound as they did.

Huntley tapped my arm. "You could let the air out of his tires. It would ruin their night."

"I'm not slashing anyone's tires," I said. "I mean, I hate the guy, but not enough to commit a crime."

Huntley backed toward his car. "You don't need to slash them to let the air out. It's actually pretty simple." He opened the trunk and rifled through the back until he came out with a pair of needle-nose pliers. "We can use this."

"You keep pliers in your car?" Samson looked inside the trunk.

What *didn't* this guy have in his car?

"I keep tools with me," Huntley said, like it was totally normal. "Always need to be prepared for the unknown." His words hitched at the end, like the phrase meant something personal to him.

I really needed to get him a Dr Pepper and ask him what was going on in his life. Except he probably wouldn't open up to me. We just met.

What was I thinking that for anyway?

"What do we need to do?" Daphne asked.

Huntley pointed at her with the pliers. "You four are on watch-out. Surround the perimeter." He turned his attention to me. "Take me to his car."

Daphne jumped in the air a couple of times, sweeping out her arms. "I feel like I've prepared my entire life for this moment."

"Uh, Daph," I said.

"Yeah?"

"Maybe you should ditch the Mickey ears?" I said. "Kind of makes you stand out."

Daphne blinked at me a few times before she spoke. "I'm just going to pretend like you didn't say that." She took off toward the restaurant, the others not far behind.

I led Huntley to Zander's car. A lump formed in my throat at the sight of it, remembering all the times Zander had driven me places. All the times he'd held the door open for me. All the times we'd shared a kiss in the front seat. I smirked. All the times my dad or one of my brothers pounded on the window, making us break it up.

"Do you care what tire?" Huntley asked.

I shook the memories from my mind. "Let's do the front driver's side so he'll see it when he gets in the car."

"Smart." Huntley held the pliers out to me. "Want to do the honor?"

I took them from him, opening and closing them a few times. "What do I do?"

He motioned with his head for me to follow. We crouched down next to the tire. Huntley twisted the cap off the air valve. "Simple really. See that pin?" He pointed to the pin inside the valve. "Grab it with the pliers and twist to the left."

Using the pliers, I gripped the pin and twisted it as instructed. Soon, a whoosh of air came from the valve, followed by a continuous flow of air as I kept twisting. The pin popped out so unexpectedly that I fell backward, my butt landing on the hard asphalt.

Huntley smiled at me. "Yeah, it can fly out like that."

"You couldn't warn me?" I went back to crouching.

He pointed to his black eye. "You didn't warn me."

I couldn't help but smile. "True."

A couple of voices came toward us, causing us both to turn in their direction. It didn't sound like anyone I knew. They were both speaking Spanish, having what seemed like a heated conversation.

A warm hand clamped over my mouth at the same time an arm wrapped around my middle. I got carried off to the front of the car.

Huntley turned me toward him and pressed a finger to his lips. He still hadn't taken his hand off my mouth. His eyes searched mine, and I realized he was waiting for me to give him a signal that I wouldn't make a sound.

I jerked my head in a nod.

Huntley lowered his hand and peered over the hood of the car. I mimicked his movement, trying to follow his line of sight. A couple stood in the parking lot, not far from us. The man was a tall, overbearing white dude who took the word beer-belly to a whole new level. He had to be housing triplets in there. The shorter, slender Hispanic woman kept poking the man in the stomach, yelling things at him in Spanish that I couldn't understand. The man seemed to speak Spanish as well, though not as fluently.

"Why are we hiding from them?" I whispered to Huntley.

He shook his head at me, his eyes telling me to be quiet.

Behind us on PCH, a car horn blared, making Huntley and me whip around, standing a little out of instinct. Two drivers at a stoplight shouted something at each other, then drove away.

My gaze traveled back to the fighting couple, only to find them staring at us.

"Huntley?" The lady came toward us.

With a deep breath, Huntley stood all the way up and smiled at her. "Hey, Mom."

I shot up. "Mom?" I looked at the lady, seeing a little bit of a resemblance between mother and son.

"What happened?" His mom hustled over, placing her hands on his cheeks and taking in his bruised face.

"Still getting in fights, huh?" The man approached us, his voice gravelly like he sucked on rocks daily. "I knew college wouldn't fix ya."

"Shut it, Ron," Huntley said through clenched teeth.

Huntley's mom finally looked at me. "Oh, hello. I'm Rosa."

"Taylor Thomas." I tried my best to smile even though the whole situation was completely uncomfortable.

Her brown eyes lit up. "Thomas?" She looked at Huntley. "Is she related to Ryker?"

"He's my older brother," I said. "But I assure you, we're nothing alike."

Rosa chuckled, so warm and inviting that I relaxed a little. I just needed to keep my focus on her, not Ron.

"He's quite the interesting boy from everything Huntley has told me." She whacked Huntley's chest. "Why didn't you tell me you were coming down to visit? We would have made up the guest room—"

"He's not staying with us." Ron's voice was awfully close. So was his presence. I could feel the heat radiating from him.

Huntley moved so he was between Ron and me, keeping me a little bit behind him, almost in a protective way.

"No, I'm not." Huntley's voice was sharp. He looked at his mom. "I'm staying with the Thomas family."

Hurt flashed across her eyes, so brief I wondered if I had been wrong.

Footsteps pounded toward us, and we were suddenly surrounded by my friends.

"We gotta go." Daphne bounced on her feet like she had to pee.

"They're coming." Weston bounced in rhythm with Daphne.

"I think they might have spotted us," Veronica said, a sheepish look on her face.

"Think?" Samson looked at her incredulously. "He said your name."

Veronica slapped Samson on the arm. "If you hadn't told me to go inside, this wouldn't have happened!"

"You went inside?" I asked in disbelief. Huntley had specifically said that wouldn't be wise.

Rosa's curious gaze swept over everyone. "What's going on?"

"Uh, who are you?" Daphne asked.

Veronica suddenly grabbed my arm and yanked me away from the car. "They're coming!" She let go and ran toward Huntley's car.

Daphne, Weston, and Samson flew past me, running at an impressive speed.

Zander came out of the restaurant, looking around the parking lot. He couldn't see me. Not here. Not like this!

I knew it was rude to get take off like that, but I so wasn't waiting around. I backed away with my palms held out in an apology. "Uh, nice to meet you, Ms. Espi—" I flinched, realizing she'd probably changed her name after marrying Ron. "Uh, Rosa." I spun around quickly, only to smack right into a light pole.

Gasping, I stumbled back and pressed my hand to my left cheek, a throbbing heat taking over my face.

"Are you okay?" Concern danced in Huntley's gorgeous eyes.

"Let's go!" I yanked his arm, biting back the pain as tears welled in my eyes.

I let Huntley guide me, my hand still pressed to my cheek like it could stop the ache. I snuck a peek behind us, seeing Zander talking with Ron and Rosa, all of them looking at his car in confusion. Had Zander seen my collision with the light pole? This was a nightmare.

"Unlock the car!" Daphne hissed out.

"I have to unlock the driver's side first!" Huntley said.

As he fumbled to unlock his door, I chanced another glance in Zander's direction, only to find him looking right at me, anger burning in his eyes.

"Eep!" I ducked down, crouching next to Huntley as he opened his door.

"Get in!" Huntley tugged on my arm.

I scrambled inside, Huntley right behind me, pushing my back toward the middle seat. The others quickly piled in, all four doors slamming in unison.

"Drive, man, drive!" Daphne yelled from the back seat.

Huntley jerked the gear shift behind the steering wheel into reverse and checked over his shoulder, his hand landing around my shoulder in what I figured was instinct for him while reversing. Only, he wasn't used to someone being there, so his hand found my shoulder instead of the top of the seat.

"Sorry," he whispered, quickly moving his hand back up front to put the car in drive. He peeled out of the parking lot, only to get stopped at a red light right in front of the restaurant.

I slunk down in the seat, wanting to disappear. "Are they watching us?"

"Yep," Huntley said. "All four of them."

Four? That meant Simone had come out, too.

"Great." I put my hand over my face, completely horrified and in total pain.

"Do you think he saw *all* of us?" Daphne's voice was muffled like she was hiding as well.

"Yep," Huntley said. "So none of you need to hide. Also, your Mickey ears are visible, Daphne."

"Yeah, so not moving until we're back on the freeway," Veronica said. "I don't care how uncomfortable I am."

Samson peeked up just a little so he could look out the window. He let out a low whistle. "That Simone girl is quite the looker."

"Samson!" Daphne and Veronica shouted at the same time.

He ducked back down. "What? She is!"

A warm hand landed on my back, and I knew it had to belong to Huntley. Everyone was cowering in the smallest position possible.

"Okay, this has to be the longest light ever," Weston said.

Huntley's hand moved around in comforting circles on my back.

This was hands-down the most mortifying moment of my life.

CHAPTER TEN

*T*had about a million missed calls and texts from Zander by the time we got back to Yorba Linda.

Zander: *Answer your phone, Taylor.*

Zander: *We need to talk.*

Zander: *What's wrong with you?*

Zander: *Have you completely lost your mind?*

I stopped reading them, my stomach clenching tighter after each one.

I made Huntley go to Daphne's house instead of mine in case Zander somehow got his tire inflated and decided to come over.

As we piled out of Huntley's car, I deleted every text and voicemail message from Zander, not wanting to hear his voice.

Then my phone lit up with an incoming message. Zander had reached out to me through social media as well. Why hadn't I unfriended him?

As fast as I could, I pulled up every social media account I had, unfollowed and blocked Zander so he couldn't communicate with me that way.

The front door opened before we got to the porch. Daphne's

mom, Laura, held out her arms—something dangling in her hand—and I immediately went to her, hugging tight. Everyone scooted past us into the house.

Laura pulled back and pressed an ice pack to my cheek. "How are you doing, honey?"

I wiped some tears from my face as I held the ice pack in place. "Awful. It's just *so* embarrassing."

"Girl, I have more than my fair share of these moments, trust me." Laura walked me into the house and shut the door behind us. "And you know what always makes it better?"

The smell hit me, and I grinned. "You made cookies?"

Laura's boyfriend, Cody, strolled toward us, wearing an apron with pirate skull crossbones on it. He held up a hand covered with a matching oven mitt. "Peanut butter cookies will be done in just a couple of minutes."

"My favorite," I said.

Laura kissed the side of my head. "I know."

Cody was a lot younger than Laura. Like fourteen years younger. But their relationship seemed to be going well. He was an old soul. And a hot one at that, though Daphne freaked whenever I said so.

Laura looked over at Huntley. "Oh, I don't think we've met."

He held out his hand. "Huntley Esposito, ma'am."

"Laura Richards." She shook his hand firmly and smiled over at Daphne who had started humming "Despacito." "This explains why Daphne has been playing that song non-stop." She patted Huntley's arm. "You'll have to ignore her. She's my special, special child."

Huntley laughed. "I'm actually getting used to her."

"It's an acquired taste," Laura whispered.

"What happened?" Cody pointed to Huntley's face. "How bad does the other guy look?"

Huntley gently pressed his fingers against his cheek and

nose. "Well, the other guy was a can of soda. Don't sneak up on anyone in the Thomas household."

"Noted." Cody's intrigued eyes went to Samson before they settled on me.

I smiled sheepishly.

Laura set her hand on my arm, her shiny new diamond bracelet cool against my skin. "Dr Pepper?"

"Yes, please." I took a seat at the kitchen table and held the ice pack against my cheek. "And some ibuprofen if you have some."

Veronica and Samson had already gotten themselves drinks and sat at the table across from Weston and Daphne.

"Where did you get the bracelet?" I asked Laura.

She blushed as she opened the fridge. "Cody gave it to me for our six-month anniversary."

"Well, six months of dating in person," Cody said. He kissed Laura on the temple. "It's been a year since we started talking online."

Laura looked inside the fridge. "Taylor, how big of a Dr Pepper do you want? I have about every size imaginable."

The nice thing with Laura was that she was a fellow Dr Pepper lover like myself.

"The bigger, the better," I said.

She brought me a two-liter, a glass, and some ibuprofen. "Want ice?"

I unscrewed the top of the bottle, my body instantly relaxing at the beautiful sound of carbonation escaping. "Don't even need the cup." I chugged straight from the bottle, welcoming the cold bubbles.

Laura chuckled as she picked the cup back up. She smiled at Huntley, who had taken a seat at the head of the table opposite me. "What can I get you?"

"A can of Dr Pepper will be perfect." Huntley smirked at me. "Thanks, Ms. Richards."

The timer went off, and my stomach growled even though I wasn't all that hungry. One whiff of cookies and I had to eat them.

I held the two-liter close to my chest and sniffed.

"Well, that went horribly." Daphne squirted some cherry syrup into her Coke.

"Our problem was we were unprepared." Weston held out his can of Coke to Daphne so she could give him some cherry syrup as well. "Never go into battle unprepared. You need a plan of attack, and backup plans for when things go awry."

Samson nodded. "Agreed. This was amateur hour at its best."

Veronica's sharp gaze swept between the two guys. "You guys do this kind of stuff often?"

Weston shook his head. "Video games."

"Parents always claim they're a waste of time." Samson turned his can of Sprite in circles. "But I've learned valuable life lessons from them." He slid his can over to Daphne. "Hit me."

With a wicked grin, Daphne poured some cherry syrup into his can, then glanced around the table. "Anyone else?"

Huntley watched the whole exchange in intrigue. "Why don't you just buy Cherry Coke?"

"I prefer to mix it myself so I always get the right amount." Daphne narrowed her eyes at her mom. "And *someone* forgot to buy more bottles of Cherry Coke at the store."

Veronica put her glass of lemonade near Daphne. "Fine. I'll try it."

Daphne poured a delicate dropping of cherry into her glass. "Gotta start conservative and work your way up. This stuff is pretty strong."

Samson coughed, pounding a fist against his chest. "Yeah, you may have gone overboard on mine."

"Sorry, Six," Daphne said. "I just thought Sprite could *really* use the help."

"Ouch," Samson said through a smile.

Veronica took a sip of her lemonade. "Oh, perfect. That's good."

Huntley looked across the table at me. "Maybe you need to call off your Vow of Vengeance."

Everyone turned to him and froze. It was even chirping crickets in the kitchen where Laura and Cody were.

Huntley waited for someone to say something, but I think they were all just as shocked as I was.

Huntley sighed. "As Daphne said, that was horrible. You wouldn't want that to happen again."

"And as Weston said," Laura said, coming over and setting a plate of peanut butter cookies in the middle of the table, "it's because you were unprepared." She shook her head at Daphne. "Have I taught you nothing?"

Cody handed out napkins to everyone, pausing when he got to Huntley. "The thing you need to understand about every lady at this table is that they don't back down from a fight. They will keep raising the stakes until someone ends up in the hospital." His gaze flickered over to Daphne.

"You have to admit it's a great story to tell." Daphne touched her cheek in the place where she'd gotten stitches after her show-down with Rosalind and Sierra. The whole thing involved a sparkling-cider-spewing lion statue, escargot, and the lot of them being covered in cake and sparkling cider. "I mean, no one will forget that party. Ever."

I set my two-liter of Dr Pepper on the table and then reached across, snatching up a handful of cookies before anyone could take some.

Laura suddenly gasped, her wide eyes on Huntley. "Oh, I didn't even ask. You aren't allergic to peanuts, are you?"

"Uh, no." Huntley's eyebrows furrowed in confusion.

Laura let out an audible sigh of relief. "Good."

Daphne grabbed a cookie from the plate. "You'll need to get used to random questions if you're going to hang out with us."

Laura put her hand on her hip. "That wasn't random. I made peanut butter cookies, which involves peanuts, and if he had an allergy to them—"

"He would have mentioned it when he came into the house and smelled peanut butter cookies." Daphne's tone dripped with sarcasm.

Cody looked at Huntley. "My sister Emma is allergic, so it's always on our minds."

Huntley nodded. "Guess that makes sense. Thanks for checking."

"Too bad he would have been dead already if he were," Daphne mumbled as she munched on her cookie.

Laura smacked Daphne upside the head, making Daphne yelp. "Which is why it's important to ask!"

Daphne straightened out her Cherry Coke Mickey ears, shooting an intense glare at her mom.

I finished off my fourth cookie—I had practically devoured them in seconds—and then looked over at Laura. "So, what do you suggest?"

"What's your endgame here?" Cody leaned against the kitchen counter, facing the table.

I took a long sip from my two-liter and then picked up another cookie. "This whole thing just came out of the blue. No warning. No indications that something was wrong. Plus, he's already moved on. It's just so annoying! Why does he get to stay happy and pretend like we never happened, and I get left with this horrible sinking feeling in my stomach that I wasn't good enough for him?" I looked at my clenched fist, the cookie now in pieces. The thought hadn't crossed my mind until now.

"So, you want to do the same to him?" Laura wiped the cookie crumbs into her hand and took it over to the trash.

I lowered the ice pack. "He needs to know he can't just

break up with me like that. He blindsided me and practically cheated on me." I sniffed. "Two days before he dumped me, he'd randomly bought me a sparkly red bracelet and told me he loved me. Unless you can magically fall out of love with someone in a blink of an eye, he was lying to me." I looked over at Samson. "My brothers always taught me to stick up for myself and make the enemy pay for what they did."

"Oh, he needs to pay," Veronica growled at the same time Daphne said, "Let's destroy him."

"Amen." Samson held up his can of Sprite in a salute. "The guy needs to learn his lesson. You need to communicate in a relationship. Let the other person know how you're feeling, especially if you're starting to have feelings for someone else."

"What have you planned so far for the Vow of Vengeance?" Laura asked.

I pulled out the crumpled piece of paper from my pocket and handed it to Laura.

She opened it, disappointment settling in her green eyes when she read it. "Taylor's Vow of Vengeance. Get even." She flipped the paper over, but it was blank. She sighed. "This is it? Daphne, I really have taught you nothing, haven't I?"

Daphne threw up her hands. "It's her vow, not mine!"

"It was your idea!" I said. "You wrote that!"

Daphne slowly lowered her hands. "Good point."

A smile slowly spread on Laura's face. "Hey, Cody?"

"Yes, my wench?" Cody said.

Everyone snickered except Huntley, who looked like he might pass out in shock.

Daphne, seated to his right, reached over, and patted his arm. "Inside joke involving a pirate and wench costume the first time they ever met in person. He doesn't really think that lowly of my mom. If he did, I would have killed him by now." She clenched her fist, her narrowed eyes on Cody. "A very slow, and painful death."

Huntley nodded like he was trying to process it all, rubbing the back of his neck and muttering, "Most bizarre experience ever."

I was honestly surprised he hadn't booked it out of the house already.

"Alexa," Daphne said, "play 'How Bizarre' by OMC."

"Classic," Veronica said with a smile.

Laura let out a small whimper. "How are songs from the nineties now 'classics'?"

"Uh, I think we got sidetracked." Cody looked at Laura. "You were saying something?"

"What?" Laura scrunched her face together in deep thought. Then her eyes lit up. "Oh! Right. Remember when we were talking the other night about pranks we loved to play on people when we were kids?"

Cody's eyes lit up as well. "Oh, this would be perfect."

Laura looked at me. "How big do you want to go?"

"Go big or go home," I said.

Laura moved toward the hallway. "Everyone make sure your parents know where you are. It's going to be a long night. I'll go get some supplies."

Cody tightened his apron. "Looks like we're going to need more cookies."

CHAPTER ELEVEN

aura came back out with a huge poster board and markers. We picked the best pranks that would cause maximum annoyance to Zander.

I had worried what Huntley would think, but he got just as involved as everyone else. It was pretty easy to get sucked into the Richards ladies' way of life and the flare they offered. I mean, these were the same people that went to costume parties once a month with Cody's friends.

By the time Samson, Huntley, and I walked through the doors of our home—well, mine and Samson's, not Huntley's—it was almost three in the morning.

I slipped off my booties in the dark entryway. "I'm exhausted." Too exhausted to even turn on the light. Moonlight shone through the massive windows above the door, which was more than enough to see.

"Same." Samson yawned, placing the back of his hand against his mouth and stretching his other arm into the air. Prime time for a 'sneak attack,' but I was even too tired for that.

Huntley took off his shoes, leaving them in the entryway. "I'm wired. I'm not sure if I'll be able to fall asleep."

Suddenly the front room lights went on, practically blinding me.

"Well, well, well." Ryker. At least, I thought so. My eyes were still trying to adjust to the sudden light, and it almost sounded like he had cotton in his mouth.

When I finally blinked away the spots, I saw Ryker standing in the front room with his arms folded. He was fully dressed as if it were the middle of the day, his long hair nicely combed, one cheek completely puffed up, ruining the tough vibe he was aiming for. Plus, with Spencer on his shoulder, he was hard to take seriously.

"Look who finally decided to come home."

Whoa, he really did have cotton in his mouth. Oh, the dentist. I'd forgotten.

He took a step toward us. "Where have you three been?"

"Why do you sound like that?" Samson asked. "What's in your mouth?"

"I had a tooth pulled, and I happen to be a bleeder," Ryker said. "And you can't avoid my questions."

"I'm so not dealing with this." I moved toward the stairs.

"Wait right there, young lady. We're not done. Zander came by late tonight." Ryker coughed and then pulled his bloody cotton ball out of his mouth.

"Gross, Ryker." I scrunched my face.

He touched his lips. "I hate numbing medication. It feels weird to talk." He paused, looking at my cheek. "What happened to your face?" His gaze flicked over to Huntley, almost in an accusatory way, surprising me. What was *that* about?

"A light pole," I said.

Ryker let that sink in a moment before he spoke. "Want to

tell me why Zander was pounding on our door close to midnight?"

I turned my body toward him, my hip jutting to the side. "Ryker, you're not our dad, okay? We don't owe you an explanation."

The bedroom door off to the side opened, and Quinn came strolling out half-asleep. He mumbled something incoherent.

"What?" Samson and I asked at the same time.

Quinn smacked his lips together as he tried to open his eyes all the way but failed miserably. "Loud. Quiet. Sleep. Baby. Wife."

I slowly walked over to him and turned him around so he faced the door to the room. "Go back to sleep, Quinn. Sorry, Aria. We're going to bed."

Aria's alert voice came from inside the room. "Well, now I'm awake. Will someone make me pancakes?"

"I'll do it!" Huntley rushed into the kitchen like he couldn't get away from Ryker and his obnoxious personality fast enough.

"Syrup." Quinn's head nodded back, and he stumbled where he stood, like he was seconds away from falling back asleep.

"You guys can't just ignore this." Ryker pointed his finger at the ground like it added weight to what he was saying. "You've been gone for hours, Taylor's face now matches Huntley's, and Zander was yelling at me, which I do not appreciate."

Huntley came out from the kitchen area and smiled sheepishly at us. "Uh, can someone show me where everything is in the kitchen? I forgot I don't live here."

"Give me a sec." I gently prodded Quinn. He shuffled back inside his room, half asleep. Once he was close enough to the bed, I patted his cheek. "Lie down, Quinn."

He mumbled something, climbed onto the bed, pulled the covers over himself, and was full-on snoring in seconds.

"Ugh. I need to invest in earplugs." Aria was propped up

against the white cushioned headboard, pillows surrounding her. "What happened to your face?"

"A light pole." I backed toward the door. "Do you want chocolate chips in your pancakes?"

"Yes, please," Aria said. "And peanut butter on top. No syrup. Oh, and maybe some bananas. Do we have bananas?"

"I'll check," I said. "I'll be back in a jiffy." I shut the door behind me and joined Samson and Huntley in the kitchen. Ryker was standing near the island, lecturing the guys about responsibility.

"I know we're in college, but Taylor isn't," Ryker said, completely oblivious to the fact that I walked into the kitchen. Or, he didn't care. "She can't be out this late."

Samson opened the cupboard and pulled out the griddle, setting it on the island. "Like we've already told you, we were at the Richards' house. It wasn't like we were out partying."

I went up behind Samson, gently pushing the back of his head. "Yeah, because you'd have to have friends to get invited to parties."

I ducked just in time, avoiding the wrath of the spatula I hadn't known Samson was holding.

"I have friends," Samson said, still trying to whack me, but I dodged his swing every time. "But everyone is still at the dorms, or they went home for the summer like I did." He finally connected with my skin, stinging a little. "I'm starting to regret it, though."

"But then you wouldn't be able to participate in the Vow of Vengeance," Huntley said. He looked at me. "Bowl?"

I grabbed a mixing bowl from the cupboard and brought it to him, then got the pancake mix.

"What's the Vow of Vengeance?" Ryker asked, arms back to being folded.

"None of your business." I poured some water into a measuring cup and then handed it to Huntley. "Oh!" I hurried over to the pantry and grabbed the chocolate chips. "Can't forget these."

Ryker slapped the countertop hard, making Huntley, Samson, and I jump. Spencer scurried to the top of Ryker's head, his fat tail flicking.

"I'm trying to have a conversation here!" A little bit of blood dribbled down Ryker's chin.

Aria waddled into the kitchen, taking a seat at the table. "And I'm wanting less conversation and more cooking."

I pointed to Ryker's chin. "Might want to clean up there, buddy." I poured some chocolate chips into the batter Huntley was mixing.

With a grunt of frustration, Ryker marched out of the room, Spencer still perched on his head.

"More, please." Aria raised her eyebrows in hopeful anticipation.

With a smile, I dumped the rest of the chocolate chips into the batter.

Aria bunched her hand together and kissed the tips of her fingers. "Perfection."

Samson let out a sigh of relief as he held his hand above the griddle he had turned on. "Do you think he'll come back?"

"I hope not," Huntley and I muttered at the same time. We shared a look and then laughed.

Our laughter cut off when we saw my mom standing there in an oversized tee, basketball shorts, and messy hair, her hands on her hips and a glare in her eyes that made me shrink back.

"It's three in the morning," Mom said, not moving from her position.

"Yes, it is." Samson looked at Huntley. "Griddle is ready."

With a sigh, Mom sat next to Aria at the table. She stared at my cheek. "What happened to your face?"

"A light pole," I said, almost on autopilot now.

Mom nodded her head at Aria. "I'll have what she's having."

"You sure?" I asked, unsure if Mom knew what she was getting into.

Mom ran her fingers through her hair, her fingers getting stuck in the mess. "Why the heck not?" She gave up on her hair and interlocked her fingers, setting them on the table. "Taylor, I'm not going to be able to meet with Francisco on Tuesday morning. You'll have to go for me."

Huntley finally moved, realizing Mom wasn't actually mad we were up, and handed the batter to Samson. The griddle sizzled as he poured a large, heart-shaped pancake in the middle.

I leaned my palms on the counter. "It's at seven in the morning."

Mom sighed. "I know, but work has been super busy, and I have a meeting that morning. You're the only one of my kids I trust to handle it."

"Hey!" Samson pointed the spatula at Mom. "That hurts."

Mom rolled her eyes, then softened her gaze at me. "Taylor, I really need your help and your vision. I'll let you have free rein of the entire event."

That was definitely intriguing. All the possibilities came swarming back into my head. I could picture the set-up with scoreboards, basketball hoops, and stadium seating, and I bet Francisco could take it to a whole other level.

"Let's not get ahead of ourselves," Samson said. "Taylor can't handle all that by herself. Plus, I could throw a killer party."

"Then go with her," Mom said.

Samson flipped the pancake. "No, thanks."

Mom choked back a knowing laugh. "Come on, Tay, I know you could *actually* throw your dad a killer party."

"Right here, Mom." Samson transferred the pancake to a plate and offered it to me.

I twisted the lid off the peanut butter. "Well, your offer pleases me, and I will happily accept with one condition." I held up the knife I was holding, peanut butter hanging from it. "Huntley gets to come with me. Francisco likes him."

Mom drummed her hands on the kitchen table. "Done deal. Well, if that's okay with you, Huntley."

I finished spreading the peanut butter on the pancake. Huntley had diced up a banana, and together we placed the pieces on top of the peanut butter, creating a smiley face.

Huntley brushed off his hands. "As long as nothing is chucked at me, I'm in."

I pushed him on the arm, making him laugh. Shaking my head, I brought Aria her pancake, along with a fork and knife.

Aria hugged my middle. "You're officially my favorite sibling."

"Okay." Samson threw down the spatula in fake anger. "All she did was spread some peanut butter on it. See that heart-shaped pancake underneath, Aria?" He placed a hand over his heart. "It comes straight from here."

Aria had already stuffed a piece of pancake into her mouth, her eyes crossing as she moaned her approval. When she finished off the bite, she grinned at Samson. "You're officially my second-favorite sibling. Taylor also paints my toenails for me, since I can't reach them anymore."

Samson nodded, rubbing his chin. "Second? I'll take it." He dropped his hand. "Although, it's not like I have much competition with Ryker. And you hardly know our other brothers."

Aria licked some peanut butter off her finger. "You're sliding into third—"

"I'll take second!" Samson grinned wildly. "I think this is the closest I've come to first place in anything in my entire life."

I wiped a fake tear from my cheek. "Oh, look at our Samson, all grown-up and going places."

Mom cleared her throat. "Uh, Samson?"

"Yeah?" he asked, still smiling.

"Pancake?"

His smile faltered. "Oh. Yeah. On it."

I glanced over at Huntley to see him smiling wide, enjoying our weird family interaction. I took a mental picture of the whole scene in my mind, wanting to remember fun family time before everyone else showed up and our world exploded in chaos.

CHAPTER TWELVE

*A*fter Zander had the audacity to show up at my house in the middle of the night, pounding on the door and dragging Ryker into the situation, I woke up ready and raring to go.

The first step in the newly perfected Vow of Vengeance required reaching out to one of Daphne's buddies, Dax. The guy had helped when Daphne made that questionable bet with Sierra and some unfavorable photos of Daphne got out. The guy knew his way around technology.

Daphne and I went to see Dax at his work. We got in the line at Subway, waiting for our turn so we could talk to Dax. It was at the tail end of the lunch rush, but there was still a pretty decent line.

"He'll help, right?" I asked.

"For sure." She adjusted her Cherry Coke Mickey ears. "Most likely."

I gently pushed her arm. "Most likely? I need more than that."

Daphne stood on her tiptoes, trying to see over the line.

"Dax lives for this kind of stuff. He'll be excited at the prospect of potentially ruining someone's life."

I reached into the pocket of my romper and pulled out my phone. "I hardly doubt we're going to ruin Zander's life by doing this."

Daphne leaned toward me, her voice in a conspiratorial whisper. "But Dax doesn't need to know that. Gotta amp up the fallout."

We took a step forward in line, but I still couldn't see Dax from where I stood.

"So, Huntley, am I right?" Daphne wiggled her eyebrows.

"What's that supposed to mean?" I asked.

She grinned. "Veronica's right about him being your type."

"She told you that?"

Daphne tilted her head to the side, giving me a *duh* expression. "Of course she did." She bumped my arm. "And she's right."

"Daphne, he's old and would no way ever think of me like that."

Her green eyes sparkled in a knowing way. "But you want him to think of you like that."

I put a hand on my hip. "I want to teach Zander a lesson and flush him out of my system for good."

"So you can flush Huntley in." Daphne did a little dance. "Oh, yeah."

I paused, staring at her. We moved forward in line again.

"What does that even mean?" I asked.

Daphne stopped her dance. "I have absolutely no idea. But you're right. We need to focus on Zander." Her lips twisted into a mischievous smile, but she didn't say anything.

"You can't make that face and not tell me what you're thinking."

Daphne patted my shoulder. "When the timing is right, you'll know, my young grasshopper."

I swatted her hand away, making her laugh.

We finally reached the front of the line.

Dax Powers had his hair bleached, which was a terrible look for his pale skin. He grinned at us.

"Daphne!" Dax held his hand over the counter to fist-bump her. "How's it going?"

"Great!" She adjusted her bag strapped around her body. "How long have you been working here?"

"Just since summer started." Dax drummed his fingers on the counter. "What can I get you?"

"Six-inch roast beef on white, please and thank you," Daphne said.

"Got it." Dax turned around, grabbed a fresh footlong from the oven, and cut it in half.

"So, Dax." Daphne's voice dropped. "We have a favor to ask."

He glanced over at the lady working the register, who was probably his supervisor. "I can't get you free subs. Sorry."

"This has nothing to do with food," Daphne said.

"Cheese?" Dax asked.

Daphne twisted her lips to the side in thought. "Let's go with provolone. No! Swiss. Wait. Provolone. Uh. I think?"

Dax put a slice of each on the bread before he piled on the roast beef.

"Genius," Daphne said. "Why have I never thought of that? Anyway, we have a new target for you."

Dax's eyes lit up. "Like the Sierra job?"

Daphne nodded. "Exactly. Only this time it's a dude, and you won't be erasing pictures, you'll be adding them and maybe updating some statuses."

Dax looked at me. "What are you having?"

"Oh, hey, I'm here too," I said, smiling at Daphne.

Daphne slapped her forehead with her palm. "Sorry. Dax, this is Taylor. Taylor, this is Dax."

Dax nodded his head. "Bread?"

"I'll take the other half of the bread you cut," I said. "Club sandwich with American cheese."

Dax quickly made mine and then scooted our sandwiches down the line. "Veggies?"

Daphne glanced at all the options. "Uh, lettuce, tomatoes, and since I won't be making out with Weston in the next couple of hours, let's throw in some onions and peppers."

Dax chuckled as he put the vegetables on the sandwich.

"I'll have the same, but change the peppers for pickles," I said.

"Peppers for pickles," Daphne repeated. "That's fun."

"Who's the target?" Dax asked.

Daphne pointed her thumb at me. "Her ex as of a few days ago, *and* the dude has already moved on."

Dax sucked in a sharp breath. "Low blow, man."

"You're telling me," I mumbled, pulling out some cash and a piece of paper from between my cell and its protective cover. "His name is Zander Morris." I handed Dax the paper. "Everything you need to know is on there."

Dax tucked the paper into his pocket and then picked up the mayo and mustard. Both Daphne and I nodded, so he squirted some on our sandwiches.

"I get off soon," Dax said, wrapping our sandwiches and honestly doing a bang-up job. "I'll get on it right away."

"How much?" I asked.

"Jill will ring you up." Dax handed the lady our sandwiches.

I leaned toward him. "No, I meant for the other thing."

Dax waved a hand. "Don't worry about it. I love doing this kind of stuff. It helps pad my resume. Plus, I can't charge a friend of Daphne's." He placed a hand over his heart. "I wouldn't feel right about it."

The irony that he couldn't take my money but could hack into someone's phone without batting an eye made me chuckle.

"Thanks, Dax," I said.

"No problem." He moved toward the other end so he could help another customer. "You'll know when it's done. You ladies have a great day."

Daphne and I paid for our sandwiches and then left.

"Did you give him specific instructions?" Daphne asked as we walked out to her car.

I shook my head. "Just a basic outline. Told him he could have creative rein."

Daphne's eyes went wide. "Oh, I can't wait to see what he does. So glad I failed P.E. in Utah and had to retake it here. Never would have met the guy otherwise."

"See, failing a class can have its perks." I slid into the passenger seat and shut the door.

"We're such good role models." Daphne started her car.

"The best."

We shared a look and then busted out laughing.

CHAPTER THIRTEEN

hen Daphne dropped me off at home and I went inside, it was eerily quiet. I set my sandwich down on the kitchen table and walked over to the bottom of the stairs.

"Hello?" I yelled as loud as I could, wanting to be heard in every nook and cranny in our home.

Silence.

"Hello?"

More silence.

I rubbed my hands together. "Well, this is a rare treat. Home alone."

I ran upstairs and quickly changed into lounging shorts and a tee, wanting to be comfortable. Then I went outside and ate my sandwich by the pool, dipping my feet in the warm water. I took a bite and then put my head back, soaking in the rays from the sun. I wanted to bask in the moment forever.

Soon, way too soon, my whole family would be here, and I would never have a moment alone.

Although, the longer time dragged on, the lonelier I got.

Always having someone around kept me busy. Now I was alone with my thoughts, which strayed to Zander.

How do you go from being in a happily committed relationship to getting over the person and dating someone else?

Maybe Daphne was right about me truly not knowing Zander. I never thought him capable of something like this. It wasn't like I thought we'd be together forever, or even get married, but I guess I was expecting us to start fighting or wanting to spend less time together until the point we were done.

Not just be making out one night, and then, when we finished having him be like, "thanks for all the good times, but I'm out."

I balled up my sandwich wrapper and chucked it toward the trashcan near the table. It went in.

My eyes wandered over to the basketball court. With no one home, I could play.

I lifted my feet out of the water and jogged over to the court, picking a basketball up from the bin off to the side.

I was the only person in my family who never played basketball. Well, not competitively. I shot hoops now and then with my brothers growing up, but it never really interested me.

Okay, that wasn't the truth. I just hated that playing basketball was *expected* of me. I mean, both my parents played college basketball. Dad even played in the NBA for a bit. So did my oldest brother, Neo. Everyone else played in high school. Ryker and Samson were the first two not to play college ball. Ryker lacked the talent, and Samson lacked the drive.

I dribbled the ball, getting reacquainted with the movement. I did try out for volleyball my freshman year, but I wasn't all that interested.

There were moments where I wondered how I would have done if I'd applied myself. I had to have *some* talent in me. It was in my blood.

I shot the ball and watched it ricochet off the hoop, bounce onto the ground, and roll out of sight.

"Wow, that was absolutely terrible."

I spun around to find Huntley standing there, holding the basketball in his hands.

"Yeah, well, I wasn't actually trying very hard," I said.

He tossed me the ball, which I caught against my chest. "Well, let's see what you got when you try."

I turned back to the hoop, dribbled toward it, and did a layup, easily making it.

"Not completely awful." Huntley snatched the ball from the ground and threw it through the hoop with ease.

One thing that I did love about basketball? That *swoosh* when a ball went through the hoop and connected with the net. There was something oddly satisfying about it.

"Let's see you try from farther away, though," Huntley said.

Bending down, I scooped up the ball and dribbled over to the three-point line and set my feet. Aim for the basket. That was all I needed to do.

I let out a breath of relief when I made it.

"Ryker said you don't play." Huntley rebounded the ball. He dribbled the ball between his legs, and how could someone make that look so hot?

I fanned my face, though it did little good.

"Ryker talks about me?" I asked.

Huntley nodded. "All the time. He talks about the whole family." He grinned. "I feel like I've known you guys forever."

I arched an eyebrow, my weight going to my left foot. "And you still wanted to stay here for the summer? Ryker's warnings didn't scare you away?"

Huntley tossed me the ball. "Warnings? Aside from once saying you could be annoying—something about spoiling Christmas for him—he talks about you guys with such admiration."

"I thought he told you it was total chaos in our house." I dribbled the ball, thinking over his words. Admiration?

Huntley chuckled. "In a good way. Says he wouldn't have it any other way."

I frowned, thinking about all the crap I gave Ryker. "Man, I'm pretty mean, aren't I?"

Huntley threw up his hands. "All I know is what Ryker told me, and how I've seen you and Samson treat him since I got here."

I stopped dribbling, resting the ball against my hip. "Which is like crap." I squirmed. "Now I feel bad."

"Maybe you should apologize."

"Maybe."

Ryker was always so serious around the family. He critiqued everything we did, which I always chalked up to him hating us, but maybe that was just Ryker. He just liked to add the cynical side of things, though it was coming from a genuine place.

"Maybe Samson and I will hug-attack him later." I took aim and shot the ball, watching it swish through the hoop, making me smile.

Huntley scooped up the ball. "Hug attack?"

Samson had been walking toward us but paused when he heard me say, "hug attack." He winked at me, and I gave the briefest of nods.

"Yeah." I moved toward Huntley. "Something like this."

At the same moment, Samson and I both threw our arms around Huntley and squeezed tight, swaying him side to side.

"Oh, the hug attack." Quinn stepped out in the backyard.

Samson and I released Huntley, only to find him smiling like crazy.

"Hug attack." Huntley rubbed the back of his neck. "Exactly what it sounds like."

"Like what sounds like?" Ryker asked, coming out onto the patio, Spencer perched on his shoulder.

Samson and I shared a brief look before we ran over to Ryker and attacked him with our hugs.

"Oh, come on," Ryker said, though there was a little bit of laughter through the frustration. He squirmed, trying to get loose, which caused us to squeeze tighter. Spencer crawled onto the top of my head, his little claws digging into my scalp.

"Uncle!" Ryker screamed, and Samson and I let him go. The tiniest of smiles pulled at his lips, but Ryker just grunted and shook his arms out like he was shaking off our cooties.

I bent down, letting Spencer crawl back onto Ryker's shoulder.

Quinn grabbed one of the basketballs from the box near the court. "Anyone up for some hoops?"

Ryker folded his arms. "Why does it always have to be basketball? Or wrestling? Or something physical?"

Out of the corner of my eye, I saw Samson move toward Quinn. Samson threw his shoulder into Quinn's stomach, wrapped his arms around him, picked him up, and threw him to the ground, a loud grunt escaping Quinn's mouth as the basketball fell out of his hand and rolled away.

"Yeah, baby!" Samson yelled as he flexed. "Payback, Quinn."

Ryker sighed.

I gently squeezed his arm. "Why don't we play Risk?"

Ryker turned to me, surprised. "Don't toy with my emotions, Tay. I can't handle it right now."

I smiled. "I'm being serious." I pointed a finger at him. "But you can't get mad at me if I make a move you deem stupid."

He stared at me long and hard. Then Ryker smiled. A full-on smile I hadn't seen on him in forever. "Deal. I'll go set-up!" He ran into the house with a lightness in his steps.

Quinn stood, grabbed the basketball, and tossed it in the box. "Tay, you *hate* Risk."

I groaned. "I know. Don't remind me. But Ryker loves it, and we never play."

"So?" Samson's incredulous look made me roll my eyes.

"We can do something nice for the guy every now and then." I moved toward the house. "And you don't have to play, Samson."

Samson rubbed the scar next to his eye and sighed. "I'll play. But I don't have to like it."

Quinn looked up at the sky and then looked back at us. "Okay. Fine. I'll play too." He looked at Huntley. "You in?"

"Well, with all these rave reviews," Huntley said in a deadpan voice, "how could I say no?"

Samson and I pulled out every single treat we could find in the house. It would be the one thing that would get us through the long night. Risk could go on for hours.

It wasn't until a little after midnight that we finally finished, with, thankfully, Ryker winning. Those were hours of my life I'd never get back, but Ryker's grin made it worth it. As much as Ryker drove me crazy, I still loved the guy.

I stood, stretching my arms above my head. "I'm ready for bed." My watch buzzed, letting me know of an incoming text from a number I didn't recognize. The message scrolled across the screen of my watch. *It's done.*

Samson peered over my shoulder. "What's done?"

I pressed my palm onto his forehead and shoved him away. "I don't know."

Then it hit me.

"Let me see your phone," I held out my hands.

My phone was in my room, plus, I'd blocked every single social media profile Zander had.

Samson rubbed his forehead. "After that? No."

"Samson!" I yelled.

Huntley held out his phone, so I snatched it and brought up the main account Zander had.

His profile picture had been updated to him hugging an adorable sloth.

"Aww, look at that little guy," Samson said.

I frowned, thinking it really wasn't what I had in mind for a prank. I mean, everyone loved sloths.

But then I dove more into his account.

His relationship status had been updated once again, only this time—

"He's dating the sloth?" Samson asked.

I pressed a hand to my mouth as I kept digging deeper. Dax had gone all out. He'd created a profile for the sloth, who he named Barry. There were tons of photos of Zander and Barry together doing all sorts of activities. The two of them out for a ride on a tandem bicycle. Sharing a soda together at Disney-land, matching Mickey ears and all. Walking hand-in-hand on the beach. Zander giving Barry a piggyback ride.

"These look legit," Huntley said.

He'd crowded in with me and Samson, and I tried to ignore his body pressed against mine. It was no big deal. I mean, Samson was doing the same thing. Yet, that side radiated noth-ing. Huntley's side radiated a heat that made it difficult to breathe.

"They aren't?" Samson said. "They look real."

They really did. Dax was a wizard.

He'd gone back months and created different statuses for both Zander and Barry, and their undying love for each other. In one post, Zander raved about how happy he was to finally have found someone to go his pace in a relationship—super slow.

My favorite was a picture "Zander" had posted of him and Barry sharing an Eskimo kiss with the caption, "this ship will never sink."

I shoved Huntley's phone into his chest and ran upstairs, seeking out my phone. I quickly texted Dax.

Me: *This was the greatest thing ever. Seriously, Dax.*

Dax: *It was a lot of fun, too.*

Me: *I bet. So creative. I owe you big time.*

Dax: *The best part is I changed his password so he can't log in and take everything down. If he tries a password reset, my program I installed will override it for the next week.*

Me: *Wait, you actually got on* his *phone?*

Dax: *Uh, yeah, that's what I do. Grabbed it from his locker at his work. I changed his wallpaper to a pic of him and Barry. Also, his lock screen.*

Zander was going to be so mad.

Score one for me.

CHAPTER FOURTEEN

The second part of the Vow of Vengeance involved getting Zander's younger sister involved. Good thing was that Zoie was at the ripe grumpy age of fourteen and absolutely hated her older brother. She hated me as well until Zander and I broke up. Then she was suddenly #TeamTaylor, a hashtag she used frequently on social media.

Zoie let me know Zander's work schedule, which was going to help a lot. Samson, Huntley, and I picked a day when Zander wouldn't be home, and went over to the Morris' household. There was this part of me that wondered why Huntley would want to hang out with us teens, but then I remembered his other option was Ryker, and it totally made sense. The two of them had nothing in common, aside from sharing a dorm at the same college.

Before we even stepped out of the car, Zoie opened the front door to the house and began shouting. "I've already disabled the doorbell camera, so no one will know it's you."

I hopped onto the curb and headed down the walkway. "Smart thinking." I paused when I got to the entryway. "Is anyone else home?"

Zoie shook her head. Her light blue eyes reminded me of Zander, and I had to shut down the anger that wanted to flare inside me. I would not break down in front of his sister. I needed her to see that I was strong and doing just fine on my own.

Zoie peeked over my shoulder. "Which brother is that?"

"Samson." He hopped onto the porch next to me. "The cool one."

Zoie looked him up and down. "I highly doubt that, but whatever." She held the door open. "Come on in."

After we slipped inside, Zoie was about to shut the door when she saw Huntley's car. "Whose car is that? And who's in there?"

"My lookout." I shut the door for her. "Any more questions?"

Huntley was to text me if he spotted anyone else coming into the Morris household.

Zoie shrugged, already over her curiosity, and waved her arm for us to follow her. "His bathroom is down the hall."

I held back a laugh. "I know."

I'd been over to their house about a zillion times over the past year. My throat constricted, and I blinked back the hot tears forming in my eyes as we passed Zander's bedroom. My hands clenched into fists, and I had to stop myself from punching the wall. I may have been ticked at Zander, but I didn't need to ruin his parents' home, no matter how tempting it was.

Zoie paused outside the bathroom door and folded her arms. "I'll only let you enter on one condition."

"Okay..." I said.

"Please tell me it was you that hacked Zander's phone and made him date a sloth." Zoie's eyes held so much hope.

"I wasn't the one who did it," I said, "but it happened because of me."

Zoie grinned. "That makes me so happy, you don't even know. I think he cried himself to sleep last night." She nodded toward the bathroom. "What exactly are you doing?"

I pulled a few packets of cherry Kool-Aid out of the pocket of my shorts and shook them at Zoie. "We're putting these in the shower head. Please tell me your family hasn't pulled this prank before."

The Morris family *loved* pulling pranks on each other, which is why I figured his parents wouldn't mind me doing this.

Zoie's grin magnified to the point I thought it might burst. "The closest is when Dad filled the bath water with grape flavor back when I was a toddler. I don't remember it, but according to Mom, Dad was expecting me to freak out, but once I saw the purple water, I wanted to get in immediately. Backfire on his part."

I chuckled. "That sounds about right."

Zoie lifted a shoulder in a shrug. "What can I say? I like an adventure."

The end of "Dream On" by Aerosmith, the part where Steven Tyler gets crazy-high, sang out from my phone. Daphne was calling. She, Weston, and Veronica were staked outside Zander's work.

I quickly answered the call. "What?"

"He's leaving work," Daphne spewed.

"What!" I looked over at Samson. "Why is Zander leaving?"

"Weston ran in and asked his supervisor," Daphne said. "Apparently, he's not feeling well."

"Okay, thanks." I hung up the phone, hurried into the bathroom, drew back the shower curtain, and climbed into the tub. "We only have a few minutes. Zander's work isn't far."

Samson joined me in the bathroom, putting one foot inside the tub and twisting off the shower head while I opened the packages of Kool-Aid. I poured the first one in, crumpled the package and stuffed it in my pocket, moving on to the next packet. On the third one, Samson teetered a little. He reached out to steady himself, his hand smacking mine. The packet fell to the tub, a bunch of Kool-Aid powder spilling.

"Crap." I looked over at the door to see Zoie watching us. "Can you go get a cup of water? We need to wash away any evidence."

She nodded curtly. "On it." She dashed off and out of sight.

I bent down, picked up the packet, and poured what was left into the shower head.

"Sorry," Samson mumbled.

"Don't worry about it. We just need to rinse the extra powder down the drain."

I watched as Samson twisted the shower head back into place and stepped out of the tub. I looked down, surveying the damage. Red powder was smeared on the bottom of the tub, but not too much.

Zoie came huffing into the bathroom and tossed me a water bottle. I practically ripped off the lid and got down on my knees, pouring water on the powder and trying to guide the river of red into the drain with my hand.

"I'm going to need a towel." My hand had turned red. I think I made it worse with the water.

"Maybe we should have done that from the beginning," Samson said.

I frantically tried to wipe everything down, only to smear red all over the front of the tub.

A towel landed on my head, and I closed my eyes, biting off the swear words that wanted to fly. "Thanks, Zoie." My voice was tight with irritation.

I yanked the towel off my head, tossed Samson the empty water bottle, and wiped down the tub.

"Don't Talk To Strangers" by Rick Springfield rang out from my phone. It was my ringtone for unknown numbers.

"Aren't you going to answer that?" Samson asked.

I wiped my stained-red hands on the towel. "It's probably a telemarketer."

"Or Huntley…" Samson said.

I gasped. Of course. I'd given him my number but hadn't programmed him into my phone. I fumbled to get my phone out of my pocket right as the front door opened. I answered. "Hello?"

"Zander is home!" Huntley yelled.

Footsteps pounded down the hall.

"He's in a rush!" Huntley said.

I ended the phone call, silenced my phone, and hoped Huntley understood my abrupt hang-up.

"Hey, Zander," Zoie said out in the hall. "Why are you home early?"

With wide, panicked eyes, Samson quietly climbed into the tub with me, and together we closed the shower curtain, trying not to make a sound.

"Out of my—" Zander cut off, and a weird sound came from the doorway.

In mere seconds, the toilet lid was thrown up. Someone thumped to the floor and began vomiting.

Both Samson and I grimaced, pressing our arms to our noses to block out the stench. Samson dry-heaved next to me.

I inhaled the musky perfume on my shirt, but still being able to hear someone throw up was enough to make me want to. I closed my eyes like that would help, but of course, it did nothing.

Samson reached his free arm out, steadying himself with the wall as he continued to dry heave. He wasn't too loud, and Zander was so freaking loud, I highly doubted he could hear Samson.

I angled the arm pressed against my nose so that my shoulder jammed into my ear, then used my other hand to block my other ear.

We stood there for what seemed like hours, though it was probably only minutes.

I heard muffled talking, so I lowered my hand to hear.

"I need a shower," Zander mumbled.

Samson and I turned to each other. Crap. Zander couldn't find us in here. I scrunched my face in disgust. How weird would it be for Zander to find me and my *brother* in his shower?

I shook the thought from my mind. So gross.

"Maybe you should lie down and get some rest," Zoie said. "You look like crap."

"I feel like crap." Zander's voice echoed like his head was still over the toilet.

"Then go rest, idiot," Zoie said. "Make sure your stomach is good and settled before you try to stand up in the shower." She chuckled. "Though I do love the idea of you falling in the shower, getting a concussion, and maybe turning into a normal person. Want me to get the water started for you?"

Samson looked at me in terror, but I shook my head as I smiled. Zoie was handling this perfectly. I had underestimated her. She knew exactly what to say to make Zander *not* want to take a shower.

"I hate you," Zander mumbled.

"Aww," Zoie said. "I hate you more, bro."

The toilet shook like Zander was using it to help himself stand up. There was a pause, and then his feet slowly shuffled out of the bathroom. A few seconds later, the door to his bedroom closed.

I let out a breath of relief.

The shower curtain slid open, and Zoie smiled at us. "You're welcome."

Both Samson and I quickly got out of the tub.

"Thanks, Zoie," I said. "I owe you."

She leaned against the bathroom counter. "Just hearing his reaction will be plenty of payment. I'll try to get a recording of the aftermath. I'd place a camera in the bathroom, but I don't want to see more of my brother than I have to." Her eyes lit up. "Oh, I have the greatest idea. I can finally get him back for putting Icy Hot on the toilet seat last week." She grimaced. "Weirdest feeling ever."

"What do you have in mind?" Samson asked.

She mimed zipping her lips. "I don't want to spoil it. Takes the shock value out of it."

Samson tapped my arm. "We should probably go. We've been here too long."

"Right." I smiled at Zoie. "Thanks again, Zo. We truly appreciate it."

"Trust me," she said. "The pleasure is all mine." She pointed to the doorway. "Now, get out of our house before you go and ruin everything."

Samson and I quickly—and quietly—slipped out of the bathroom and down the hall, and hurried to Huntley's car.

As soon as we climbed in, Samson and I let out a huge breath.

"What happened?" Huntley asked, eagerness in his eyes.

I fastened my seatbelt. "Get far away from this house, and I'll tell you."

I reached back, giving Samson knuckles. Second item on the Vow of Vengeance would hopefully be checked off by the end of the night.

CHAPTER FIFTEEN

aphne, Veronica, and I were each in a tube, floating in my pool. We'd created a little triangle, each of us linking one of our arms with the tube on the left of us.

"I really wish I could be there to hear his reaction," Veronica said.

I was happy to see her get into a bathing suit and join us in the pool. It was a little snug on her, but not as bad as she had made it seem. I had no idea why she had been so weird about it the other day.

"Same," Daphne said. "Hopefully, Zoie can at least get that on a recording."

I twisted the leather bracelet on my wrist. "That's the one crappy thing about this prank. We can't be there to see it all unfold."

Daphne recoiled a little. "I do *not* want to be there to see *anything.*"

Veronica and I both laughed.

"Oh!" A chorus of shouts came from the basketball court near the pool.

I looked over to find Dad and Samson smirking at Quinn

and Huntley. They were playing two-on-two basketball, and from their faces, Dad and Samson were winning.

Mom, Ryker (and Spencer), and Aria sat around a table in the shade, chatting away. A few more days, and brother number three, Porter, his wife Emory, plus their two kids, would be here for an extended vacation. Emory was pregnant with kid number three, and they wanted to spend some time with our family before the baby came and things exploded into chaos in their home.

That meant four more people in the house.

Dad really needed to finish The Hideout. I glanced over at the big tree in the middle of the backyard. Dad had put caution tape all around—like that would actually stop anyone—telling me I couldn't go inside until he had everything finished.

The one nice thing about my siblings showing up at different times was that at least it gave me time to adjust between each arrival.

I loved my family, but sometimes I would go on overload when everyone was over.

"Can I stay with you while my family is in town?" I asked Daphne. Why hadn't I thought of that before?

"Don't you want to hang out with them?" Daphne asked.

"Yes, but not every second." I slowly moved my legs forward and backward in the water, loving the feel of resistance on my skin. "There's no way I'll be able to sleep. Especially with the kids."

Veronica smirked. "Let's be honest. Your six brothers back together will be worse than the kids combined."

I chuckled. "True."

Daphne's eyes lit up. "Does this mean Wrestle-Mania is coming back?"

My brothers used to hold it four times a year when they lived here. Once my oldest brother, Neo, moved out, I talked the others into letting me be the sixth person. But then Ollie left, followed by Porter and then Quinn, leaving Samson and boring Ryker. Samson and I would do random battles, but they were short and not as exciting as having everyone there.

"They're planning on it," I said.

"Are they going to let you play?" Veronica asked.

I switched to my snooty-Ryker tone. "That would make things uneven."

Daphne let out a low growl. "I can even things out."

Veronica and I looked at each other and then broke out laughing. No way Daphne would survive wrestling against my brothers. She couldn't handle a pillow fight.

I scooped up some water and threw it toward Daphne. "You'd be out within a second."

She wiped the water off her face. "True. But I'd still be the eighth man. Someone has to go out first."

"So, you're the sacrificial lamb," Veronica said.

Daphne reached over and grabbed my hand. "You know I'd sacrifice myself for you, right?"

I squeezed her hand. "Yeah." I smiled sheepishly. "But Veronica would be the better alternative."

Daphne's jaw dropped, then she slowly lifted it, accepting the truth, and she sighed. "Can I at least be the referee?"

"Do you know the rules of wrestling?" I asked.

"Announcer," Daphne said. "I can be the announcer."

I arched my eyebrows, picturing Daphne in the role. "That's actually a pretty good idea. It would add some flare that Wrestle-Mania definitely needs."

Daphne pumped her arm. "Heck, yes."

I looked over at Veronica, who had grown quiet. She tugged on her ponytail.

"You okay?" I asked.

Her uneasy gaze swept back and forth between Daphne and me. She opened her mouth to say something, but then snapped it shut.

Daphne reached forward and slapped her palm on the water. "Don't make me come over there, Veronica."

"To my tube?" Veronica scoffed. "I'd like to see you try."

Daphne moved toward Veronica, a fierce warrior look on her face, so I quickly moved my tube between the two and sighed at Veronica. "You know you can't say something like that to Daphne. She'll actually do it."

Veronica laughed. "I know."

Daphne folded her arms on top of her tube and rested her chin on them. "Veronica, something's up. You've been acting differently. You haven't been yourself."

Veronica looked over her shoulder where the guys were still playing basketball and then came toward us, grabbing both our tubes and yanking us closer. "This stays between us?"

"Of course," I said.

Daphne, however, remained quiet. Both Veronica and I glared at her.

She sighed in defeat. "Fine. I won't tell anyone."

"Which means Weston, too," Veronica said. "None of this, 'we're one' crap."

Daphne blew out a long breath, a war battling in her eyes. She finally hissed—yes, hissed—and then sagged her head in defeat. "I won't tell Weston or anyone else. Promise."

Veronica stared at Daphne for a few beats before she finally spoke. "When Dad moved back home a few months ago, Mom started cooking dinner again. She was able to quit her second job and had more time to do so."

"Love your mom's cooking." My stomach growled just thinking about her tamales and empanadas.

"So do I," Veronica said. "But things have still been a little tense at home. I think Dad is trying to overcompensate for the time he was gone. He's just always hovering around." She swirled the pool water around with her hands. "Anyway, this led to stress eating, which has led to me gaining some weight."

Daphne shrugged. "So what? You look hot."

Veronica's voice dropped. "DeShawn doesn't seem to think so."

My hands balled into fists. "Has he said something?"

She paused, and it took me a moment to realize she was fighting back tears. She ran a hand down her face, covering it with pool water, maybe to mask any real tears that escaped.

"He comments on my clothing, saying they're too tight," she whispered. "Not in a good way. He keeps saying I need to lose weight. He'll make snide remarks when I'm eating." She tugged on her ponytail. "He likes my hair this way because he says it makes me look skinnier, having it pulled back tight."

Anger burned inside me. "I swear, the next time I see him, I'm going to kill him."

Veronica's eyes went wide. "I don't want either of you saying anything to him. It will just make him mad, which will exacerbate the problem."

"Exacerbate," Daphne repeated. "Exacerbate. Such a weird word."

I took long, deep breaths, trying to calm myself. I tended to overreact when angry. I needed to think through this logically. "Okay, here's what you're going to do."

Veronica looked at me, hopeful.

"You're going to dump his sorry butt—" I started.

"Yeah, you are!" Daphne said.

"—you're going to stay exactly the way you are—"

"Yeppers," Daphne said.

"—and Daphne is going to make you some clothes you feel comfortable in," I finished.

Daphne's eyes lit up. "Girl, you rock the curves. Forget DeShawn. I mean, we already established years ago that he was a loser. You saw right through his façade all the way back in second grade, for crying out loud!" Her smile grew. "I have so many ideas on what to make you. Let's go shopping for fabric tomorrow."

Veronica didn't look as excited as I thought she would be. She picked at the skin on her lips with her teeth.

"You don't have to go with me if you don't want to." Daphne rubbed Veronica's arm. "I have excellent taste in fabric, and I know your style. This will be Wonder Woman Extraordinaire."

At the mention of Wonder Woman, I realized Veronica hadn't worn any of her regular Wonder Woman gear. She wasn't religious with her like Daphne was with Captain America, but I know she looked up to her.

"It's not that." Veronica sighed. "I don't know if I can break up with him."

Daphne waved a hand. "Oh, that part is easy. Just call him and be like, 'Hey, DeShawn, you're an idiot and I don't date idiots, so we're through.' Easy peasy."

"DeShawn has a bad history with his exes," Veronica said. "He makes their lives miserable. I hadn't really noticed until recently, but that's probably because I've been paying closer attention to his words and actions instead of his ripped body."

It was weird seeing Veronica so defeated. So down on herself. She'd been such a strong, independent girl for as long as I could remember.

And it ticked me off that DeShawn had stripped that from her.

"Want me to do it?" I motioned to the guys playing basketball. "I can even show up with my posse."

Veronica shook her head. "I think that will make things worse. Let me handle this. I just need to figure out the best way to approach the subject."

"Taylor!" Aria screamed my name from where she sat at the table. "Hurry over here. Now!"

Veronica, Daphne, and I shared a look before we paddled

over to the stairs in the pool, shimmied out of our tubes, and ran over, not bothering to grab our towels.

Aria held out her phone. "You *have* to see this."

I snatched the phone from her and looked at the screen. Zoie had uploaded a video to social media with the hashtags: #grannyZander #TeamTaylor #serveshimright.

"Press play!" Daphne screamed into my ear.

The video started in an empty hallway with the focus on the bathroom door. A few seconds in, high-pitched screaming came from inside the bathroom, screeching that sounded like a little girl in terror. A barrage of thumping followed, along with what sounded like the shower curtain hooks unlatching, and then the rod clanging onto the tile floor like the whole thing had been ripped off.

"Oh. My. Gosh," Veronica said.

The shrieking in the bathroom intensified before Zander shouted, "Where's my towel?"

"Uh, he better not come out in his birthday suit," Daphne said from my other side.

"Zoie wouldn't upload *that*." I paused. "Would she?"

There was a groan, some more thumping, and then the door flew open, and Zander ran into the hallway, arms flailing. He stopped when he saw Zoie, which is where she ended the feed. The best part, though? The last image was red water dripping from his hair down his face and soaking into a pink floral granny nightgown.

"Why is he wearing that?" Veronica asked through her fits of laughter.

"I have to watch that again," Daphne whispered in awe.

"You have a couple of texts on your phone, Taylor." Mom held my phone out to me.

I handed Daphne Aria's phone so she and Veronica could watch the video again. By then, all the guys had come over, so they huddled around the girls to watch.

I checked my texts. They were from Zoie.

Zoie: *Did you see the video?*

Zoie: *Right when he started the shower, I jimmied the lock, ran in, took his towel, and replaced it with my grandma's nightgown she accidentally left at our house.*

Zoie: *Mom wanted to mail the nightgown back to her, but I had this inkling it would come in handy one day, and it sure did.*

Zoie: *Also, my parents came home and saw the mess in the shower and on the wood floor in the hallway.*

My heart dropped. I hadn't thought about how messy the aftermath would be. Maybe I needed to go over and clean it up.

Zoie: *My parents thought this was the most hilarious thing, ever.*

Oh, good.

Zoie: *Mom said you win for best prank of the year. And don't worry. They're making Zander clean it all up.*

"This is better than I could have ever imagined," Samson said through his laughter.

Huntley grinned at me. "Looks like you won round two."

With a wicked grin, I ran over to them, and we watched the video again. And again. And again.

CHAPTER SIXTEEN

For the first night since Zander had dumped me, I fell asleep quickly. The image of Zander dripping in red and flailing in a granny robe brought me the comfort I needed.

My family had all played Ticket to Ride after dinner, really capping my night off with much needed laughter.

So, when the sounds of thumping woke me up a little after one in the morning, I was still smiling.

Stretching my arms and legs, I blinked awake, trying to pinpoint the noise. It sounded like something was hitting the window.

With a reluctant sigh—it was seriously so nice being snuggled under the covers—I climbed out of bed and shuffled my way over to the window.

Something splatted against the window right in front of my face. My eyes went cross, trying to focus on the object. I stepped back as something else hit the window.

Yellow yolk dripped down the glass, white pieces of the shell mixed in. I went to open my window, but then stopped myself. I hadn't put the screen back on since I threw all of

Zander's things out the window, and I *so* didn't want to get hit with an egg.

I moved so I could look out a spotless part of the window. Zander stood on the lawn, holding a carton of eggs. He flipped me off and then threw another egg, the crunch of shell on glass causing my blood to boil.

With a growl, I stormed out of my room and ran down the stairs. I was about to open the front door when I decided to run into the kitchen and grab some eggs for myself. I couldn't go into battle without a weapon of my own.

I smiled when I saw two eighteen packs. Freshly bought, so none were missing. I suddenly loved my large family.

Tucking the cartons against my chest, I slammed the fridge door closed with the heel of my foot and ran toward the front door. Quinn's voice stopped me before I got there.

"What's going on?" He stood near his bedroom door, rubbing his eye with his fist. "Why does everyone keep waking us up?"

"Go back to bed, Quinn." I stepped toward the entryway. "This doesn't concern you."

"Yeah, okay." He turned around and slipped back into his room.

I loved half-asleep Quinn. No logic whatsoever.

"Where are you going?"

I jumped, almost dropping the cartons of eggs.

Huntley was suddenly in front of me, helping me wrangle the cartons. The guy was shirtless. Again.

I was losing focus and had already wasted too much time. Couldn't he sleep with a shirt on? Was that too much to ask? I pushed one of the cartons into Huntley's gorgeous chest. "Zander's throwing eggs at my windows."

Huntley placed his hand on my back and shoved me toward the door. Guess that was all he needed to spring into action.

Zander was opening the driver's side door to his car. He paused when he saw Huntley and me rushing toward him.

"You," Zander growled, moving toward me, splotches of red dye on his face from the Kool-Aid. "I can't beli—"

Huntley chucked an egg, connecting with the back window of the car. This time, the crunch of the shell was so very satisfying.

Zander's eyes went wide in panic. I threw one of my eggs, hitting him in the chest. As he hurried to get in his car, I threw another, hitting the back of his head.

Huntley and I went into warrior mode, throwing as many eggs as we could, running after Zander's car after he took off down the street. The backside of his car was covered in yellow by the time he turned the corner and zoomed off.

Huntley and I paused in the middle of the street, panting. Huntley's carton was almost empty. I still had seven eggs.

"Whew!" Huntley placed a hand on the top of his head, the muscles in his bicep twitching. "What a rush."

I stared at his arms, licking my lips. "A definite rush."

He lowered his arm, resting a hand on his hip. "Why did you have so many eggs?"

I peeled my gaze away from his toned body and forced myself to look into his eyes. "Always assume there's a lot of everything in the Thomas household."

Huntley chuckled. "Guess that makes sense."

"Thanks for helping." I walked back toward the house. The asphalt was warm against my bare feet.

Huntley walked next to me, almost like we were out for a summer stroll. In the middle of the night. Carrying almost empty cartons of eggs. And he wasn't wearing a shirt.

"Guess Zander didn't appreciate the Kool-Aid prank," Huntley said with a laugh. He tapped my arm. "I feel like you won this one, too."

I held up a hand. "Wait until we've seen the damage he's done to the house."

We stopped on our lawn, right below my window. At least a dozen eggs were smashed all over the window and the stucco around it.

"We should probably get this off," Huntley said. "Eggs can ruin paint."

I yawned, the weight of the night kicking in. "Can't it wait until morning?"

Huntley glanced around the yard. "Where's the hose? I can take care of it."

I sighed. "This is my fault. I should be the one to clean it." I handed him my carton of eggs and trudged over to the hose.

I knew Zander would be mad, but I hadn't really considered retaliation. Of course he wouldn't just let it go. I wouldn't.

I turned on the water, changed the nozzle on the hose to jet, and lugged the hose toward my window.

Squeezing the handle, I held up the nozzle, aiming for my window. It was surprisingly therapeutic to wash off the egg, really blasting my window with water. I pictured Zander's face on the glass. With a snarl, I whipped the hose back and forth, thinking of how he'd hurt me, blindsided me, and quickly moved on.

My eyes narrowed as I pictured Simone's stupidly gorgeous face. I moved onto the stucco, really drilling the water into the cracks. How could she do that to another girl? Take her man without blinking an eye?

I paused, lowering the hose. Did she know about me? Maybe she hadn't. I mean, she had to know about me now, thanks to the Newport incident, but maybe he'd been seeing her and hadn't mentioned me. Maybe we'd both been played.

My fist tightened around the handle of the nozzle. She had to have known about my existence. It wasn't like Zander and I were subtle about our relationship online. We posted stuff all over social media, tagging each other in photos. One search of his profile, and she'd know he was in a relationship.

A warm hand wrapped around my clenched fist. "Easy there, Taylor." Huntley gently took the nozzle from me and turned off the water.

I glanced at the flowerbed before me, noticing a group of flattened flowers. I hadn't realized I'd been directly hitting them with the jet spray.

"Maybe we should go inside and grab something to drink," Huntley said. "Cool down."

I slowly nodded and trudged across the lawn and back into the house, the weight of everything really sinking in. I hated this place I was in. The whole situation sucked, and I wished it would all go away.

Aria shuffled around the corner, pausing when she saw Huntley and me in the entryway. In one hand she had a jar of peanut butter, the other holding a stick of leafy celery. She sucked some peanut butter off the celery, her wide eyes going from my pajamas to a shirtless Huntley holding two cartons of eggs.

Using the celery stick, she motioned between Huntley and me. "Do I want to know?"

I sighed. "Zander."

Nodding, Aria scooped a bunch of peanut butter onto the celery. "Who won?"

My sigh intensified. "Simone."

Aria's confused eyes swept over to Huntley. "Simone was here, too?"

"No." I closed my eyes and rubbed them with my palms. "I'm going to bed." I clumped up the stairs, leaving Huntley to explain everything to a bewildered Aria.

CHAPTER SEVENTEEN

*T*uesday morning, Huntley and I headed over to the venue to meet Francisco. I thought it would be way too early for me—I mean, who was up by seven during the summer?—but I was super excited about planning the party for Dad.

Dad had done so much for our family. He'd worked hard to make sure we had a good upbringing and were well taken care of. He deserved a grand celebration, especially while he was still young enough to enjoy it.

We'd tried to do something big for his fiftieth birthday, but Neo was teaching in Japan; Ollie's wife, Charlie, was giving birth to their first child; Porter had just graduated high school and was spending the summer in France before he started college; and Ryker had broken his arm, which, according to him, was the travesty of the century.

This time around, everyone was in the country, and I was finally old enough that I'd remember it. Aria promised Dad that she wouldn't go into labor before the party—like she had much say in the matter. Charlie was yet again pregnant (baby number four!) but only six months along, and Emory,

Porter's wife, was three months pregnant (baby number three!).

Honestly, Veronica had been pretty spot-on about needing a chart to keep track of everyone in our family.

"Have you heard from Zander?" Huntley asked, breaking me from my reverie.

I looked over at him in the driver's seat. "He's sent some vulgar messages via friends, but I've deleted them fairly quickly and done my best to ignore them."

"I keep thinking about that video." Huntley chuckled. "We ended up watching it, what, fifty times since the other night?"

I laughed with him. "Try a hundred. The fact that Zoie switched out his towel for the nightgown was priceless."

"I'm still surprised his parents were cool with it. My mom would have been freaking out over the mess. And Ron—" He sucked in a sharp breath.

I waited a few moments before I spoke. "What's the deal with him, anyway? He seems like a..."

"Jerk?" Huntley finished for me. "He is. I don't know what my mom was thinking when she married him. She was just so lonely when my dad died—"

"Your dad died?" I frowned, thinking how awful it would be to lose my dad. "How old were you?"

Huntley's hand tightened around the steering wheel. "Seven. Died in Iraq."

I shifted in the passenger seat so I could face him. "That's awful. I'm so sorry."

He half-heartedly shrugged. "Kind of likely to happen when you join the military in the midst of a war." He glanced over at me before his eyes went back to the road. "I'm proud of my dad. He died doing what he loved and protecting a country he loved." He ran a hand over his close-cropped hair. "Mom took it hard. Ron was the first person to pay attention to her. He bought her the restaurant."

"Wait, your family *owns* that restaurant?" I placed a hand against my cheek. "Why didn't you say anything?"

The smallest of smiles appeared on his lips. "Would that have stopped you?"

I opened my mouth to say, "of course," but realized it probably wouldn't have stopped me. I was on a mission.

"So your mom stays with him because of the restaurant?" I asked.

Huntley pulled into a parking spot at the events center. "That restaurant is her pride and joy. When she realized how awful Ron was, she turned her focus solely to the restaurant. It's the one thing that makes her happy."

I frowned. "*One* thing."

Huntley turned off the car, his eyes unfocused on the dashboard. "I look too much like him."

I wanted to reach across and hug him. I could. The bench seat up front meant there was no center console stopping me. But I couldn't force myself to move. His words were still sinking in.

Huntley got out of the car and bent to look at me. "You coming? Or do I have to handle Francisco all by myself?"

I finally moved. I got out of the car, ran around the front of it, and threw my arms around a surprised Huntley. He let out an "oof" as we collided. I hugged him hard, wishing I could help in some way but knowing I couldn't.

No wonder he was sensitive about his parents. I would be, too.

Huntley held me close, almost like he hadn't been hugged in the longest time. What if he hadn't? Oh, that made me squeeze tighter.

"Taylor," Huntley rasped.

"Yeah?" I still held him fiercely.

"I gotta breathe."

I finally released him. "Thanks for sharing that with me. I'm sure it isn't easy to talk about."

"Thanks for listening." He rubbed the back of his neck. "You're the first person to show an interest in my life."

My hands balled into fists, and I bit back a growl. "I'm so sorry you got Ryker as a roommate. If it had been Samson or Quinn, they would have friended you from day one. Heck, you probably would have been adopted into the Thomas family by now."

Huntley chuckled. "I must say, your family really is chaos, but it's a good chaos. I can tell that, even though you give Ryker so much trouble—"

"I still love the guy." I folded my arms. "I wouldn't tease him so much if I didn't care."

"Exactly," Huntley said. "And, honestly, Ryker has been a good listener; he just never knows what to say. Usually just starts spewing out facts about geckos."

"You're late," a crisp voice said.

I spun around to see Francisco standing at the entrance to the events center, tapping his foot in annoyance.

"I have a meeting at eight, so we need to move," Francisco said.

Huntley and I hurried up the stairs and followed Francisco to the Cascade Ballroom.

There was an incredibly nervous petite lady standing in the middle of the room, clutching a tablet to her chest like it was armor. She wore a black pinned-striped suit and had her brown hair in a neat bun. Her expectant gaze never wavered from Francisco.

He motioned to her. "This is my assistant, Seiko. She'll be taking all the notes, but only address me." He looked at Hunt-ley. "So, what did you have in mind?"

I straightened my blue leather jacket. I normally didn't wear it during the summer, but I felt the occasion called for it. "My mom already mentioned the basketball theme."

Francisco let out an annoyed sigh. "Yes, unfortunately. This is such an elegant space. We could do so many grand themes—"

Oh, I'd had enough of this man.

"Listen, buddy." I strode toward him. "This party is to honor an amazing man, and we're paying for it, so you're going to do exactly what we want, okay?"

The smallest of smiles landed on Francisco's lips as he finally looked me in the eyes. "Tell me your vision."

I stood tall. "My dad played forward for the BYU Cougars. I was thinking stadium seats like you'd find in the Marriott Center on the west side of the room." I walked to the middle of the room near the assistant, who was typing furiously on her tablet. "Recreate the BYU basketball court, with the oval Y logo in the middle, the words Brigham Young on each end." I motioned to both the north and south. "Basketball hoops on either end—shot clocks and everything—and a four-sided scoreboard hanging in the middle of the room." I looked over my shoulder at Francisco. "Obviously, it can't be as ginormous as the one in the Marriott Center since this room isn't *that* big, but a mini replica will suffice. We can have slideshows with pictures of my dad's life running on the screens." I moved toward the east. "Along this wall will be tables for all the food and presents—"

"Let me interject just a second," Francisco said, a worried look on his face. "If you suggest hot dogs and popcorn—"

"For the food, I'd like everything you'd find in the Marriott Center." I ignored the curses from Francisco. "I'm talking popcorn, nachos, pretzels, candy, Coke products with BYU souvenir cups, ice cream from the BYU Creamery, Café Rio, and you *will* have Cougar Tails and Cougar Crunch, even if you have to fly them in from Utah."

Francisco mouthed *Cougar Tails?* and grimaced.

"What's a Cougar Tail?" Huntley asked.

I smiled at him. "A really long maple donut. They're delicious. And the Cougar Crunch is caramel popcorn. Also delicious." A thought crossed my mind. "Also, contact the owners of J. Dawgs. See if they'd like an all-expenses-paid trip down here to grill us some hot dogs." I batted my eyelashes at Francisco. "Extremely delicious as well." I glanced at Seiko. "You need me to slow down?"

She smirked at me. "No, ma'am. Bring it."

I returned her smirk, loving this woman. "Okay, next, for the games I want to have a slam dunk contest. Seiko, while you're contacting people in Utah for us, let's get Cosmo the Cougar down here. Greatest mascot in the world, and I'm sure he would love to get in on the dunk contest."

"Miss Thomas," Francisco said, "I'm not sure if—"

I held up a hand. "Are you about to tell me you can't get this done for our family? You said you were the best, did you not?"

"But the prices—" Francisco started.

"I may not be dressed in designer clothes," I said, putting my hands firmly on my hips, "but my family can afford this. We choose where we spend our money and where we save our money." I motioned to the room. "We've been saving for this event for the past ten years. I assure you, money will not be a problem."

Francisco straightened the lapel of his expensive-looking blazer. "We will get on this right away."

"Great." I turned to Huntley, who was covering his mouth, but I could see the laughter in his eyes. "I've worked up an appetite. Want to grab some pancakes?"

He lowered his hand, revealing a bright smile. "I'd love to."

"Wonderful." I turned back to Seiko. "Contact us if you have any questions. We'll be happy to help in any way possible."

She stood tall, a confidence on her that made me giddy. "Will do, Miss Thomas."

I wiggled my fingers in a wave at Francisco and sauntered out of the room.

CHAPTER EIGHTEEN

"That was the greatest thing I've witnessed in my life," Huntley said over our breakfast at a local IHOP.

I poured some maple syrup on my stack of pancakes, soaking them through. "Francisco's face, though. I thought he was going to pass out."

Huntley put some salt and pepper on his scrambled eggs and hash browns. "I'm assuming your family does actually have the money to pay for this, right?"

I cut off a piece of my pancakes. "Yeah. I know we don't live in a mansion—"

Huntley pointed his fork at me. "But it is a really nice house."

"I know," I said. "Mom and Dad always spent money where they thought it was needed, like creating family memories. We don't need fancy clothes or cars."

"Your parents are awesome," Huntley said.

I smiled at him. "I think so, too. I got lucky."

I took a large bite of my pancakes, stuffing my cheeks full.

"Hold still." Huntley lifted his phone. "I gotta capture this."

I closed my eyes and did the best smile that I could with chipmunk cheeks, along with pancake and syrup stuck to my teeth.

Huntley chuckled. "You won't kill me for uploading this, will you?"

Shaking my head, I finished off the bite in my mouth. "I wouldn't have let you take the picture if it bothered me."

Huntley finished his post and then went back to his breakfast. "Are you ready for the next phase of the Vow of Vengeance?"

"I have six older brothers. I'm always ready for vengeance."

"Probably explains why you have tough skin as well," Huntley said.

"You think?"

He nodded. "You seem to handle yourself just fine." He pushed an empty plate aside and switched over to his stack of pancakes. "Although, I know to never cross you."

I took a long swig of my Dr Pepper. "It's usually people's worst and last mistake."

Huntley laughed. "I don't doubt that for a second."

I worked on my pancakes some more before I asked my next question. I wasn't sure if I should pry, but it felt like the right thing to do in the moment.

I licked the syrup off my fork and set it on my plate. "Tell me about your dad. Do you remember much about him?"

Huntley had just stuffed a bite of pancakes in his mouth, so he chewed slowly, his eyes telling me he was trying to think it through. He swallowed, took a sip of his Dr Pepper, and then sat back on the bench. "I remember bits and pieces. The older I get, the fuzzier the memories get."

"Have you written any of them down?"

He shook his head. "No."

"You should," I said. "That way, you can at least always remember what you can now."

"That's actually a really good idea," he said.

"Don't sound so surprised."

He smiled. "I'm not." He folded his arms. "I remember my dad playing the guitar for me every night. He'd sing songs he wrote and try to teach them to me."

I sat forward, totally invested. "Is this why you play the guitar?"

He nodded.

"Do you remember any of the songs? Like the melodies or the words?"

Huntley stared at his plate of half-eaten pancakes. "Just bits and pieces. There are moments when I'm on the verge of sleep and they'll flow through me."

"Huntley." I waited until he looked at me. "You *need* to write down everything you remember. In those moments when you're falling asleep, you need to somehow wake yourself up and write them down. Or at least play the melody so it sticks in your mind."

A small smile tugged at his lips, drawing my attention there. For the briefest of moments, I wondered what it would be like to kiss him and, whoa! Where had that come from?

He was older, and I was freshly out of a relationship. I did not need another guy in my life.

"Taylor?"

"Hmm?"

"You okay?"

I blinked, trying to regain my focus. I'd totally slipped off into la-la land. Under the table, I pinched my arm. No more thinking about Huntley as anything other than my brother's college roommate.

"Yeah, sorry." I grabbed my drink and noticed it was empty. "Just a lot on my mind."

The waitress came up. "Refill?"

"Yes, please." I slid the glass over to her.

"Will this be separate checks?" she asked.

I was about to say, "yes," but Huntley spoke first. "One check is fine. Thanks."

As she walked away, I arched an eyebrow at him. "I know I paid for lunch the other day—well, my mom did—but I'm not buying your breakfast, too."

Huntley leaned forward, his focus back on his pancakes. "I'm buying. Think of it as a thank you for listening to me. I haven't talked about my dad for a long time."

I pushed my finished plates off to the side. "Well, I still only know two facts about him: he plays guitar and was in the military. What else?"

"Camping." He cut into his pancakes. "He loved anything outdoors." Huntley slipped into his memories easily, recalling stories from his childhood and how adventurous his dad was.

There was a moment where Huntley busted out laughing, remembering this time his dad had accidentally peed himself when they were on a ride at Disneyland, but he didn't want to leave the park so he bought the first thing he found, which were some pink Minnie Mouse shorts that were too small for him.

But in that moment, Huntley looked so carefree and happy. So much like that was the true and honest version of him. I snapped a picture, wanting to remember it, but also to show Huntley how happy he was when he talked about his dad.

We were about to get up to leave when suddenly Zander was there, pushing me back into the bench and taking a seat next to me.

"What are you doing?" How'd he even known I was here?

"You blocked my phone number and everything on social media," Zander said, an anger in his eyes I'd never seen before. He was always so laid back and chill. "So I had to track you down so we can talk."

"Zander, that's totally weird." I looked at the table still

covered in our dirty dishes and thought about climbing over them and away from Zander.

Huntley leaned toward us from across the table. "Maybe we should talk outside."

Zander threw a sharp look at him, but Huntley didn't even flinch. Zander clenched his jaw. "Stay out of this."

"Zander—" I started.

His heated gaze landed back on me. "This needs to stop."

"What needs to stop?" I clutched the edge of the table to keep myself from punching Zander.

"You following me, hacking my phone, showing up at my house," he said, breathing deep. "Do you know how much of a mess you caused? And I'm not just talking about the shower and my car. My personal life, well…"

"Let me guess." I sat tall. "It's an uncontrollable disaster that has left you confused and angry?"

He blinked, taking in my words. He wet his lips. "Uh, yeah, exactly."

I shoved a finger into his chest. "Which is exactly how I felt when you dumped me out of the blue!"

Zander rolled his eyes. "It was not out of the blue. We'd totally fizzled out."

I held up a fist, wanting to grab his shirt and shake him, but I restrained myself. "You call making out in the car to the point the windows steamed up, *fizzling out*?"

I bit back the growl that had risen up my throat. I needed to remember we were still sitting in IHOP with an elderly couple watching from the bench across from us. I awkwardly held up a hand in an apology.

"Taylor, grow up," Zander said, snapping my attention back to him. "We're done, so get over it."

"Says the guy who found me here," I said. "How did you even know I was here?"

He pointed at Huntley, but his angry eyes were on me. "He posted a disgusting picture of you, tagging you here."

"Disgusting?" Huntley sounded shocked. "I thought it was cute."

"I said, stay out of this," Zander said, a little too loud for our current situation.

I shoved Zander. "Outside. Now."

His nostrils flared as he stared at me, like he was debating what to do. He finally got up and stormed out of IHOP.

I pulled some cash out of my purse and set it on the table where the elderly couple were sitting. "I'm so sorry about this. Let me buy your breakfast. I hope you two have a great rest of your day."

"Thank you, dear," the lady said.

Huntley and I left, meeting a fuming Zander outside. He paced the sidewalk, running his fingers through his normally perfectly gelled hair.

"You say *I* need to grow up?" I placed my hands on my hips. "Look at you! You're throwing a tantrum in public."

Zander tried to tower over me, but I held my ground.

"You followed me to a restaurant," Zander said, "you vandalized my car—"

I rolled my eyes. "I let out the air. Big whoop."

"You sabotaged my phone, and you came to my house and ruined our shower!" He pointed a finger at me. "You're the one throwing the tantrum."

I slapped his hand out of my face. "I did not ruin the shower. Zoie would have told me if I did. I just made you have to clean it for once."

"Do you know how many messages I've received from her video?" Zander squeaked. "Since everything about Barry?"

"I hope a lot," I said. "And honestly, Zoie's the one who made the video and left the nightgown as your only option. Go home and yell at her."

Huntley came up, placed a hand on each of our shoulders, and forced us apart. I hadn't realized how close we'd gotten. Our noses were almost touching.

"I think it's safe to say you're both mad at each other," Huntley said. "Maybe you should go home and cool off, Zander."

Zander shoved Huntley in the chest. "I said, stay out of this, pretty boy."

Huntley grinned. "Aww, he thinks I'm pretty."

"Is there a problem here?" a gruff voice said.

I whipped around to see two police officers standing there.

"No, sir," I said. I placed my hand on Huntley's arm. "We were just leaving."

Zander stepped up so quickly that none of us could react. His mouth was right up against my ear. "This isn't over, Taylor. If you want a war, we can have a war." He took off to his car.

I pressed a shaking hand against my forehead, trying to process everything.

"You okay, miss?" one of the officers asked.

I slowly lowered my hand and turned to him. "Yes, thank you. Just an angry ex."

The officer nodded. "Looks like it's a good thing you're no longer together."

I snorted a laugh. "I'm starting to realize that."

"Well, you kids have a good day," the officer said before he and his partner went inside the restaurant.

I looked over at Huntley, who was watching Zander pull out of the parking lot. What must he think of me? This was so embarrassing. I couldn't believe Zander showed up here.

Then I remembered I'd done the same thing. Maybe I really did need to grow up.

CHAPTER NINETEEN

*H*untley was quiet on the ride back to the house. He'd turned up the music when we'd gotten in the car, and the classic rock soothed my soul. I leaned back in the passenger seat, wondering if Zander was serious about starting a war. And if he was, what did that entail? Would it be worse than throwing eggs at my window? I hadn't thought about the fallout when I started the Vow of Vengeance.

But there was no going back now. I would not lose this war.

Huntley reached over and turned down the music a little. "How you feeling?"

I opened and closed my fists repeatedly, wishing I had stress balls in my hand. "I can't believe he showed up at IHOP."

"You did the same to him," Huntley said.

I sighed. "I know. But I didn't go in there and interrupt his dinner date. He wasn't even supposed to see me."

"Uh, was this a date?" Huntley asked.

I gasped. "No! Of course not! But he didn't know that. It could have been. Not that it was!"

Oh my goodness, what was wrong with me? I was rambling like Daphne.

Huntley chuckled. "Taylor, it's fine. But can you blame him?"

No, I couldn't. I would be demanding blood if I were in his shoes.

"You're not going to stop the vow, are you?" Huntley asked.

"Not until I win," I mumbled. Zander would *not* come out on top. It wasn't over until he felt all the pain I did.

We'd barely pulled in front of my house when my phone rang. I answered, seeing it was a call from my mom.

"Hey, Mom."

"Porter's flight was delayed," she said. "I have a meeting I need to get to that I can't miss. Is there any way you can pick him up from the airport?"

I glanced at the empty driveway. "Where's *the shuttle?*"

There was a honk, and I looked in the road to see Mom speeding down the street. She screeched into the driveway, probably leaving skid marks.

I quickly got out of Huntley's car and hurried over to Mom, who was already out of the van and tossing me the keys. I barely caught them against my chest.

"Let's go!" Mom opened the passenger side door of the van. "You need to drop me off at work." She got into the van and slammed the door.

"Okay, then." I spun around, facing Huntley, who was standing on the curb. "I guess I'm leaving. Maybe you should do some writing. Or play some songs." Then I realized I'd never seen him with an actual guitar. "Do you have a guitar?"

Huntley's jaw clenched. "I did." The heat in his eyes told me it was a painful topic.

Mom blared the horn of the van.

"You up for getting a new one?" I asked, backing toward *the shuttle.*

Huntley arched an eyebrow. "Maybe. Why?"

I smiled. "Hop in. We're going to get you a new guitar."

The horn blasted again.

I ran around the van and jumped in before Mom got out and dragged me there herself.

Huntley hopped into the back, his face a mixture of wariness and excitement. Maybe he wasn't ready for a new guitar. We could at least peruse them, get the thought of a new one floating through his mind.

"How are you doing, Huntley?" Mom looked over her shoulder. "Looks like the swelling has gone down a bit."

Huntley rested his arm on the back of the bench seat. "Much better, thank you."

"I'm surprised you still want to be around Taylor," Mom said.

I wanted to reach over and slap her, but I liked to keep both hands on the wheel when driving *the shuttle*. Which she knew. From the smirk on her face, I was dead on.

"Still think I'm a better choice over Ryker," I said. "I mean, unless you like boring games like Risk and talking about geckos."

Mom chuckled. "I'm not sure how that kid turned out so serious."

I flipped on my blinker, coming to a stop at the end of our block. "Are you kidding? He's so like Grandpa Carlson, it's not even funny."

Mom's laugh grew. "He really is like my father, isn't he?" She reached over and gently pushed my arm. "How are *you* doing?"

She was talking about Zander.

I gripped the wheel tightly. "He showed up at breakfast like a freaking stalker and basically declared war." I grunted. "I'm so done with guys. They're the worst." I looked in the rearview mirror. "No offense, Huntley."

"None taken," he said with an amused smile.

Mom was quiet for a few moments before she busted out

laughing. I glanced over to see her leaning forward and clapping her hands before my attention went back to the road.

"Okay, I really don't know what's so funny," I said.

Her laughter grew until it went into high-pitched squeaks, coming out in quick bursts. She waved her hand in front of her face like that could calm the laughter.

It didn't.

With a sigh, I reached over and turned up the radio, waiting for Mom to get it out of her system.

Mom had a habit of breaking out into an uncontrollable laughter, usually starting with something minorly funny, and then growing like she didn't know how to stop. I could see her out of the corner of my eye wiping tears from her cheeks.

A smile found its way to my face. It had been a while since I'd heard Mom laugh this hard. She'd been so stressed with Dad's birthday coming up and all the kids coming to stay at the house. She wanted everything to go smoothly and for everyone to have fun, even if that meant sacrificing her own happiness.

We were almost to her office when she finally calmed to a reasonable level.

"Feel better?" I asked.

Mom nodded. "So much. And now my stomach muscles hurt." She reached over and played with some of my hair. "Honey, I know you better than any of my other children. You'll never be done with guys."

"*That's* why you were laughing so hard?"

Mom wiped at her cheek again. "You're just so stubborn and so passionate. You always make promises that you can't follow through with."

My hands tightened around the steering wheel. I was going to prove her wrong. I could follow through with this one.

I stopped outside her office building, my eyes fixed ahead.

Mom unbuckled her seatbelt and reached across to kiss me on my temple. "You know I love every single one of those traits, right? I love your dedication and drive." She opened the van door. "I love you, Taylor. I'm so glad we have you."

I softened a little, but still looked straight ahead. "Love you, too."

"Porter and the fam land in an hour. Don't be late. See you later, Huntley." She shut the door and left me to stew in my thoughts.

I was totally going to prove her wrong.

CHAPTER TWENTY

*I*f I'd had time, I would have made a sign for my brother and his family. Instead, it was just me waiting past security, trying to spot masses of curly hair. Huntley stayed in the van. We'd worked out a plan to scare my brother, so I wanted to keep his presence under wraps.

My sister-in-law, Emory, had massive curly brown hair that she passed on to their two daughters, Fiona and Genevieve. Porter had once tried to grow his hair out to see if he had any curl, but it was just a straight, scraggly mess that Emory made him shave off.

"Aunt Tay-Tay!" The two girl's voices meshed into one as I strained to see them. Their bright faces suddenly appeared behind some fellow travelers.

I dropped to my knees and held my arms open. Both six-year-old Fiona and three-year-old Genevieve flew into me. I hugged them tight, then went back and forth between the two, covering their cheeks in kisses, making them laugh.

"I'm expecting the same greeting," Porter said in a deadpan voice.

I released the girls and sought out Emory, getting on my tiptoes to hug her. She was six-one, which was still way shorter than Porter's six-seven frame. She was three months pregnant, but she wasn't showing yet. Her hair covered my face as we hugged, and I so didn't care.

"Look at you!" Emory released me from the embrace. "My goodness, Taylor, when did you get so hot?"

I laughed. "Still working on it, I assure you."

She waved a hand. "Please. You're gorgeous." She placed a hand on my shoulder. "Zander is an idiot."

"I'm starting to realize that," I said through my smile. "It's seriously so good to see you. It's been too long."

The last time I'd seen their family was when Mom and I went to visit them in Seattle after Genevieve was born. We tried to video call with them every Sunday, like we did all my brothers, so at least the girls would know who we were.

Porter cleared his throat. "Tay, really?"

"What?" I asked. "I'm so happy to see the girls."

"And?" He held out his arms.

With my scrunched smile I saved only for Porter, I threw my arms around his waist. "Hey, Porter."

"Oh, hey, Taylor. Good to see you." He picked me up from off the ground and spun me around like he always did when I was a little girl.

I squirmed. "Seriously, Porter?"

He set me down. "You love it."

I tilted my head to the side. "I really don't." I held out my hands toward the girls, and they quickly snatched them. "Let's go get your bags."

As we waited for their suitcases to come out from the baggage carousel, I bent down and pulled the girls close to me, keeping my voice low.

"I have a friend waiting in the van," I said. "He's going to scare your mom and dad, so don't let them know."

I'd thought about not telling any of them, but then I thought a strange guy in the van might terrify the two girls to the point it wasn't funny.

They both grinned and nodded their heads.

Porter was the one brother always playing pranks growing up, so payback was in definite order.

As soon as we wrangled everything together, we headed toward *the shuttle*. When we neared, I looked over at Porter. "On a scale of one to ten, how tired are you?"

"Wide awake, sis."

"Good." I let go of Fiona's hand so I could pull the keys out of my jacket pocket and tossed them to him. "You're it."

Porter caught the keys and jingled them. "This brings back so many memories." He wiggled his eyebrows at Emory. "We had some hot times in the back."

"And the middle," she said with a wicked grin.

"Oh, gross, you two," I said through laughter. "Although, honestly, the real question would be which of the Thomas children has *not* had a make-out sess in *the shuttle*."

Porter's smile dropped. "You."

I winked at him. "Riiight." I paused. "Wait. Ryker probably hasn't." Not only did he not have a license, he wasn't really into dating.

"What's a make-out?" Genevieve asked, her bright blue eyes staring up at me.

I squeezed her hand. "When you snuggle with someone."

"I like to make-out," Genevieve said. "It's my favorite."

Emory covered her laugh with her hand.

Porter narrowed his eyes at me. "Thanks, sis."

I grinned. "You're welcome."

We loaded up *the shuttle* and then climbed in. I helped Genevieve into her booster seat, buckled her in, and took a seat between the two girls.

Porter settled into the driver's seat and pulled out his phone. "Hey, Google, where's the nearest In-N-Out?"

Emory looked over her shoulder at me. "He's been talking about Double-Doubles since he found out we were coming here."

I glanced at him in surprise. "Double-Double? Getting old there, bro? What happened to the Triple-Triple?"

He patted his stomach. "Can't eat the way I used to."

Emory turned up the A/C. "Not if you want to live to see your daughters get married."

"We're getting married?" Genevieve asked.

Fiona shook her head at her sister. "Not yet, silly. At least another ten years."

Porter adjusted the rearview mirror so he could see his girls. "Thirty."

"Fifteen!" Fiona countered.

Porter sighed. "Twenty and that's my final offer."

Fiona folded her arms and pouted. "Fine. Twenty years."

Emory grinned at me. "Happy we're here?"

I returned her smile. "Ecstatic."

Genevieve patted my arm. "Aunt Tay-Tay, can we have a slumber party?"

I poked her nose. "Of course." Then I poked her toes on her sandaled feet. "And we're painting these pretties."

She raised her little arms in the air. "Woot woot!"

"Let me guess." I leaned forward. "You taught her that, Porter?"

He repeated her action. "You know it. Now, let's go get me that Double-Double."

Huntley, who had been lying down on the floor in the back, suddenly jumped up and settled into his seat. "A Double-Double does sound good right about now."

Emory jumped as she screamed. If she hadn't already been buckled in, she probably would have flown from her seat.

Porter also yelled, his palm slamming against the horn of the van, the blaring sound echoing around the covered parking lot.

Fiona, Genevieve, and I busted out laughing.

Huntley switched to the row right behind us, smiling at the girls. "Hey, I'm Huntley."

They both waved at him.

"Hi, Huntley!" Fiona said.

"What happened to your face?" Genevieve asked with a frown. "Does it hurt?"

"Who are you?" Emory asked, her eyes still wide in shock as she stared at Huntley.

Huntley grinned. "I'm Ryker's roommate." He softly touched his cheek. "And this is thanks to Taylor." He looked at my nieces. "Never sneak up on her, okay? She might throw a can of Dr Pepper at you."

Fiona rolled her eyes. "Tay, you're supposed to drink it, not throw it."

Porter and Emory were still staring at Huntley, both of them trying to catch their breath.

"Why didn't I record this?" I asked.

Emory finally relaxed, settling back into her seat. "Be prepared for payback, Tay."

"Looking forward to it," I said. "Huntley and I want to go to the Orange County Market Place. Do you want to come with, or should we drop you at home?"

Emory looked at Porter. "I want to go. I haven't been in forever."

Porter finally peeled his eyes away from Huntley and looked at his wife. "Uh, yeah, we can go." He put the van in reverse. "But first, I need that Triple-Triple."

Emory smirked at him. "Can you handle that?"

Porter let out a long breath. "I need it now."

I held up my arm, turning my palm to Huntley, who high-fived me.

Maybe having all the brothers back home wouldn't be such a bad thing after all.

CHAPTER TWENTY-ONE

After getting Porter his Triple-Triple, we headed toward the Market Place, which was basically an outdoor swap meet. We paid the admission fees and then split up, Porter and his family going in one direction, while Huntley and I went in the other.

It was a warm day, so I'd left my leather jacket in *the shuttle*, leaving me in a tank and shorts. Thankfully, I'd put my long hair in two buns on top my head, letting my neck breathe. It had been a brutal summer.

Huntley and I slowly walked down one aisle, checking out each vendor.

"So, you don't have to answer this if you don't want." I stopped at a booth with a display of leather and beaded bracelets.

"Always a great way to start a conversation," Huntley said with a smirk.

I picked up a bracelet with four black leather strips woven together, the style singing to me. "What happened to your guitar?"

Huntley reached for a bracelet with large golden-brown

beads. I tried not to think about how it matched the gold flecks in his gorgeous eyes.

"Ron." Huntley wrapped the bracelet around his wrist.

I waited for him to go on, not wanting to poke the topic too hard if he wasn't ready to talk about it. On the table, there was a woven bracelet with red, black, and white, similar to a poncho style. "This is totally Samson."

Huntley brushed behind me, and I did my best to hold in the shiver that wanted to erupt inside. "I'd been acting up, and Ron thought it was a fair punishment to destroy my guitar."

I had just picked up a bracelet with light and dark brown twine twisted together, reminding me of my oldest brother, Neo. I had to stop my jaw from falling to the ground. "Ron destroyed your guitar?"

Huntley sighed. "Right in front of me. It belonged to my dad."

I shook the bracelets in my hand at him. "I swear, the next time I see that man, I'm going to strangle him."

Huntley eyed the bracelets in my hand. "You're going to need something longer than that."

"I could tie them all together." I spotted a brown leather bracelet with a silver tree medallion on it, thinking of my mom.

He grabbed a bracelet, the multi-shaded brown beads reminiscent of a lizard. "This is Ryker."

I took the bracelet from him. "Yeah, it is." I looked at him. "What did your mom have to say about it?"

"Absolutely nothing," Huntley said with an edge to his voice.

"It's a good thing I wasn't there."

"Why?" he asked.

On the display rack, there was a wooden cylinder beaded bracelet calling Quinn's name. "I would have taken a piece of the broken guitar and jammed it through his massive gut."

The owner of the booth looked at me with wide eyes as she took a tentative step back.

I smiled at her. "Totally kidding."

Her skeptical expression told me she didn't believe me, but, hey, I didn't believe myself, either. I hated bullies.

Huntley came to my side, his presence unbelievably close, making my heart pound. "Are you going to get all of those?"

I did everything in my power to focus on the bracelets and not turn to look into his eyes like I desperately wanted to do. "Well, I have one for six out of the nine members of my family. Just need to find three more." I picked up a braided black leather one. "Ollie."

"Who does that leave?" Huntley asked, still at my side, making it unbelievably difficult to concentrate.

Did he have the slightest idea that him being so close was driving me wild?

Why was it driving me wild? He was old, and I was done with boys.

I swallowed, trying to work moisture back into my mouth. "Dad and Porter." I spotted a mahogany beaded bracelet. "Dad."

"What are you thinking for Porter?"

"Nothing beaded." I looked over the wide variety of bracelets. "And no leather."

Huntley picked up a bracelet made up of beige, silver, and black twine. "What about this?"

I took it from him, looking it over. "This is actually perfect. What made you choose it?"

Huntley chuckled. "Guess I saw the three different pieces of rope and thought one for each child and the noose he would put around someone if they ever did something to his kid."

The booth owner's eyes went wide again.

I pulled some cash out of my wallet. "I assure you, ma'am, that we will never actually murder someone."

"Unless they deserve it." Huntley took out some of his own cash.

I handed my money to the owner. "For the nine bracelets."

Huntley held out his cash. "And for mine."

The owner snatched our money and nodded, like she was excited to have our money but couldn't wait for us to leave.

Huntley and I shared a laughing look before we continued down the aisle of the market. I had Huntley hold my bracelets as I put them on one by one, starting with mine and going in order of age until I ended with Dad. It took up a large portion of my forearm, but I absolutely loved it.

After we'd turned onto another aisle, Huntley froze. I followed his gaze to a navy-blue acoustic guitar under the canopy of a booth.

"Looks like someone found their other half." I moved toward it.

Huntley hurried past me, rushing to the guitar. "You don't understand, Taylor. This looks *exactly* like my dad's."

My jaw dropped as I went to his side. "Uh, you have to get it, then. Fate brought you together."

His gorgeous eyes found mine, and I put my hand on a table to steady myself. A whimper tried to crawl up my throat, but I shoved it back down. No one should be allowed to be that hot. No one.

"I just can't believe it." His gaze went back to the guitar that was now in his hands.

I looked at the man who owned the booth. "How much?"

His gaze traveled between Huntley and me. "Five hundred."

Huntley's head snapped up. "Are you serious?"

The owner folded his massive arms. "Are you serious about playing?"

"Sir, with all due respect, this guitar is just like the one his father had," I said.

"So, it's worth more." The owner tapped his chin.

"His *dead* father," I said.

The owner softened a hair. "Four fifty."

I stood tall. "His horrible excuse of a step-father ruined the guitar."

The owner sighed. "Four twenty-five."

"Right in front of him," I said. "He had to watch as the man destroyed the only part of his father he had left."

The man loosened his stance. "Four hundred."

Huntley just stood there, watching our interaction.

"Did I mention his dad died serving this very country?" I said. "He fought in Iraq so we could have the freedom to walk around this very market with peace in our hearts."

"Three fifty, but that's as low as I'm going," the man said. "That's a really good guitar."

I looked over at Huntley, seeing what he wanted to do. I honestly had no idea whether it was a good guitar or not.

Huntley stared at the guitar with a longing in his eyes that made me want to just buy it myself as a gift for him.

He closed his eyes, held the guitar close to him, and then set it back down. "I can't right now. Not while I'm paying for college."

"You're paying for your college?" the man asked.

Huntley nodded. "My mom can't afford it. I got a small scholarship that's helping, but as much as I want this guitar, it's just not feasible right now. I promised my dad that I would make my education my top priority." He turned away as tears welled in his eyes. "Thank you for your time, sir."

I blew air out of my mouth, trying to stop myself from crying.

Huntley only made it a few feet before the owner called out. "Wait, son."

Huntley slowly turned back around, wiping a tear that had fallen down his cheek.

The man held out the guitar. "Take it."

Huntley's good eye went wide as he shook his head. "Sir, I can't do that."

The man came out from around the table. "I insist."

Huntley's hands shook as he took the guitar from the man. "I...I don't know what to say."

The man clamped his hand on Huntley's shoulder. "Promise me you'll finish college and make your dad proud."

"I will, sir," Huntley said. "I promise."

The two guys embraced. I wiped away my tears as I watched the interaction. There were still so many good people in the world.

I offered the owner a soft smile as Huntley and I left. Huntley held the guitar close to his chest.

"I still can't believe we found this," he said with a smile. He wrapped an arm around my back and side-hugged me. "Thanks for bringing me here, Taylor. I didn't realize how much I needed this."

Warmth spread inside me. Huntley had this small piece of his life back. He deserved it after everything he'd been through. He deserved it for just being a great guy to begin with.

Why, oh, why, did he have to be old? In normal circumstances, twenty-one really wouldn't be old. But when that twenty-one-year-old was dating a seventeen-year-old, that was weird. I guess in a few years, when I was in my twenties, it wouldn't be so odd. But there was no way Huntley would stay single that long. He was just that awesome.

We met Emory, Fiona, and Genevieve near the entrance of the market.

"Where's Porter?" I asked.

"He found a place that has Sacramento Kings flags." Emory eyed Huntley's guitar. "He wants a big one to fly from the flagpole in front of our house."

I sucked in a sharp breath. "Oh, Dad is going to be *mad*."

Dad was a hardcore Lakers fan, which didn't quite drift

down to all his children. Most of my brothers ended up being Kings fans. Ollie was now a Houston Rockets fan, since he lived there. Ryker was the only remaining Lakers fan, but it was mostly because he knew that was what Dad wanted. Ryker himself didn't care about sports all that much.

Emory motioned to Huntley's guitar. "Do you mind?"

He reluctantly held it out to her.

She took it gently into her hands. "This is beautiful." She took a few large steps away from us, making me wonder what she was doing.

Suddenly an arm wrapped around my middle and I was thrown to the ground, along with Huntley.

The air knocked out of me as I lay there on the ground, staring up at the sunny sky.

"Sneak attack!" Porter said. He let out a growl like he was in a wrestling ring. He bent down so we could see his face. "Payback."

With a smile, he offered Huntley and me his hands, helping us to our feet. Porter grinned at his daughters. "And that, sweethearts, is how it's done."

Fiona and Genevieve clapped their hands.

"Again, Daddy!" Genevieve exclaimed.

Emory handed a groaning Huntley back his guitar. She looked at me. "Still excited to have us home?"

I rubbed my sore back. "Not so much."

"Let's go home and swim it off." Emory wrapped an arm around me.

"Yay!" Fiona and Genevieve yelled.

Porter snatched his girls up off the ground, holding them both level with his hips. They took off toward *the shuttle*, the girls holding their arms out like they were flying.

"That's why you wanted to see Huntley's guitar," I said.

Emory nodded. "Didn't want it to get ruined."

"Which I truly appreciate," Huntley said.

Emory smiled at him. "Of course."

We were about to walk out of the market when someone called out Huntley's name. The three of us spun around to see a middle-aged man jogging over to us, a gruff smile on his face.

"Officer Mike?" Huntley held out his guitar for me to take so he could embrace the man now before him.

Officer Mike slapped Huntley on the back as they hugged. "Kid, it's good to see you." He released him. "How've you been?"

Huntley stuffed his hands in his pockets. "Good. Got the first year of college under my belt, which is nice."

First year? Maybe he'd had a late start. Not everyone jumped into college right after high school, especially with all the crap he'd gone through.

"Any more trouble?" Officer Mike asked with an arch of his eyebrow.

Huntley shook his head. "No, sir."

"I'm proud of you, kid," Officer Mike said. "It was so good to see you. Take care."

"You, too!" Huntley said.

As Officer Mike walked away, Huntley took his guitar back from me.

"Who was that?" I asked.

Huntley smiled at his guitar. "Oh, uh, my parole officer."

Parole officer?

Oh, no.

CHAPTER TWENTY-TWO

hy would Huntley have a parole officer? What had he done? It couldn't have been *too* bad, right? Otherwise, by-the-book Ryker wouldn't allow him into our home.

By the time we finally rolled into the driveway, everyone was home, waiting for us.

"Mamas! Papas!" Genevieve yelled when she saw them come out of the house. I unbuckled her, and she flew out of her seat, climbing past me and stepping on my feet in the process, until she got to Fiona, who was opening the van door.

"Hurry, Fi, hurry!" Genevieve whined as she bounced on her feet.

"I'm trying!" Fiona said. "Chill already." She finally got the door open, and the two of them scrambled out of the van, running straight for my parents and into their arms.

Once we got everyone and all the luggage into the house, Dad pulled some steaks from the fridge.

Huntley had disappeared upstairs with his guitar.

"Got the grill going." Dad smiled wide. "Got us some porterhouse steaks in honor of Porter."

Porter's smile faltered, but only for a blip. "Sounds great, Dad."

Dad went out onto the patio, eager to get going.

Mom sighed, a total mom-glare being thrown at Porter. "Let me guess. In-N-Out?"

Porter threw up his hands. "I had to."

"Did you?" I asked.

Porter rushed over and wrestled me to the ground.

I let out a grunt. "Seriously, how much weight have you gained?"

Porter put his hands on my arm and used my body as a support to stand. "Gotta get the dad-bod going."

Emory tilted her head to the side. "Do you?"

With a wicked grin, Porter ran at her and tackled her onto the couch. Genevieve and Fiona quickly ran over, jumping on top of them and squealing.

Samson helped me to my feet and wrapped his arm around my shoulder. "We got four whole weeks of this."

"And I still don't know if I'm happy or sad about it," I said, watching my nieces pummel their parents.

Ryker joined us, rubbing his hands together, for once without Spencer on his shoulder. "Are you kidding? This is awesome!" He ran over, grabbed Genevieve from the couch, and held her high above his head, making her "fly" around the room. Genevieve giggled in excitement.

"I really don't understand him," Samson muttered. "Like, at all."

"You and me both," I said.

Ryker *loved* our nieces and nephews. Like, he *lived* for them. When it came to kids, he had an abundance of patience. For anyone over the age of sixteen, though, the guy had a zero-tolerance policy.

Fiona climbed down from on top of her parents and ran up to Samson and me. "Can we go swimming?"

"Do you know where your swimsuit is?" I asked.

She pointed to her pink suitcase. "In there."

"Last one in the pool is a rotten egg!" Samson took off upstairs to change.

Fiona and I shared a wild-eyed look, then took off ourselves, hurrying to get in our bathing suits.

As I passed Ryker's bedroom, I heard a guitar playing from within. Creeping to a stop, I pressed an ear to the door, listening to Huntley play. He sounded rusty, like he hadn't played in a while, which he probably hadn't. Kind of difficult to play when you didn't have a guitar.

I smiled. He'd found the perfect guitar. My smile grew. That man had just *given* it to Huntley.

"What are you doing?" Ryker asked.

I spun around to find him standing in the hall, staring at me. Taking him by the arm, I steered him down the hall and away from his room.

"Where's Spencer?" I asked.

"In my room, napping," Ryker said. "I was going to get him so the girls could see him."

I really needed to cut to the chase. "Do you know much about Huntley's past?"

Ryker nodded. "I know all of it. Why?"

"We ran into his parole officer at the market," I glanced over my shoulder to make sure the door to the room was still closed.

"Well, when you live a life of crime, that's bound to happen." Ryker used his snooty, authoritative voice that drove me mad.

"Life of crime?"

Ryker sighed, shaking his head like my parents did when I disappointed them. "I know he seems like a stand-up guy, and he is now, but his past is pretty rough. He made some really stupid choices, getting him thrown into a juvenile detention center."

My throat constricted. He'd been in juvie?

"Those decisions are going to haunt him for the rest of his life," Ryker said, a faraway look in his eyes.

Yeesh. What had Huntley done?

"What kind of choices are we talking about?" I asked.

Ryker set a hand on my shoulder. "Best not to think about that."

Too late for that.

"I don't want anyone treating him differently," Ryker continued. "I thought spending a summer with our family might keep him on the straight and narrow."

I held in a laugh. "If anything, it might lead him to become an alcoholic."

"That's not funny," Ryker said with a frown.

Oh, had drinking been one of his downfalls? But if he was twenty-one like Ryker, then he was legally allowed to drink now.

For some reason, the thought of dating someone who was old enough to casually drink everywhere they went seemed odd. Like I wasn't ready for that level of maturity in a relationship.

What was I talking about? I wasn't ready for a relationship at all. Why did the thought keep creeping into my mind? I needed to find a way to shut it down.

"I have been wanting to thank you and Samson," Ryker said, bringing me back to reality.

"Why?"

"You guys have been great with Huntley," he said. "I don't think I've ever seen the guy this happy." He scolded me with his eyes. "But you shouldn't be keeping him out late like you did the other night. Nothing good happens after midnight."

I rolled my eyes. "Thanks, Dad. And we were at the

Richards', like I said. Laura and Cody were there. The hardest thing we had to drink was Dr Pepper."

"Just focus on being a good influence on the guy," Ryker said. "And do me one more favor?"

"Yes, great and powerful leader?"

"Don't fall for the guy." He brushed past me, going into his room and shutting the door behind him.

Heat flared in my cheeks. Why had Ryker felt the need to say that?

I was so not falling for Huntley Esposito.

I wasn't.

CHAPTER TWENTY-THREE

While I was excited to have my family in town, it was still my summer vacation. The last one of high school. I wanted to create memories with my friends.

Samson and Huntley helped me load up *the shuttle* with beach gear and snacks. I'd reluctantly invited Ryker—Mom's orders—but, thankfully, he said no. He wanted to spend as much time as he could with Porter.

Porter was the one sibling everyone got along with. He had what I liked to call a bendable personality. He could shape his words and actions to whatever was deemed necessary depending on the people he was with at the time. He handled Ryker well.

We picked up Veronica, Daphne, Weston, Sierra, and Bentley, and headed to Huntington Beach. I desperately wanted to ask Veronica about DeShawn, but I had to wait for a time when everyone wasn't around.

When we were grabbing stuff from the back of *the shuttle*, there was a moment when only Daphne and Veronica were with me. The rest had started walking to the beach to find a space for us.

Daphne put on a gigantic red floppy hat, so big that she had to lift her head to be able to see out from under it.

Veronica grabbed the towel bag and gave it to Daphne, who wrapped her arms around it in an awkward hold.

"Have you talked with DeShawn?" I picked up a bag of snacks plus a bag with portable speakers. Music was a must, according to Daphne. And I totally agreed.

Veronica shook her head as she took the last cooler out of the back of the van and shut the doors. "I haven't had the chance."

We moved toward the beach, going slow so we had more time to talk.

"The longer you wait, the worse it's going to be," Daphne said.

"I know," Veronica said, "but I haven't drummed up the courage."

Daphne stopped walking. "Who are you and what have you done with my friend?"

"What are you talking about?" Veronica shifted the cooler from one hand to the other.

Daphne scoffed. "I wasn't aware you were capable of *not* having courage. You're usually drowning in it."

Veronica groaned and walked toward the others. Daphne and I hurried to catch up.

"Can we just *not* talk about this today?" Veronica asked. "I'll break up with him, I promise. Just, not today."

Daphne and I shared a glance, but we dropped the topic.

When we got to the others, we set-up a couple of shade umbrellas and laid out our towels.

Bentley pulled a volleyball out of one of the bags and tossed it in the air. He'd already pulled off his shirt, showing off his tan and toned abs. His black hair was in a wild mess instead of his normal slicked-back style.

"Uh, what's that?" Daphne asked.

Bentley grinned. "It's called a volleyball, Daph. And we're going to play."

Daphne huffed. "No, we're not."

Weston stepped up next to Daphne, wearing a long-sleeved beach shirt and shorts. "Yeah, so not playing."

Sierra took off her black sundress, revealing a black bathing suit that matched her hair. She sat down on her towel and pulled some sunscreen out of her bag. "What do you two have against volleyball?"

"Everything," Weston and Daphne said at the same time.

Daphne held out a finger. "It's a sport."

Weston held out one of his fingers. "Athleticism."

"Coordination," Daphne said, another finger extended.

"Exercise," Weston said, adding to the count.

"Sun exposure," Daphne said.

Weston nodded, pointing at Daphne. "Let's double-down on that one."

Bentley chuckled. "Come on. It'll be fun. No one cares if you suck."

Veronica held up a hand. "I do. I'll be on a team with Samson, Bentley, and Sierra." She grinned at me. "Good luck."

Bentley, Sierra, Samson, and Veronica took off toward the volleyball net near us.

Huntley looked over at me. "Why do I have a feeling we're going to get creamed?"

"Because we are," Daphne said.

"So creamed," Weston said.

"By the end, they'll be able to take our creamy mess and plop it on some ice cream," Daphne said.

Weston licked his lips. "Ice cream sounds so good right now. Maybe we should go get some."

Daphne nodded. "Good idea."

I huddled the four of us together. "Let's just go out there and have some fun. Don't take it seriously." I pointed my thumb behind me, where the other four had started stretching. "Let them drain the fun out of it. We're going to put it in."

"I like the sound of that," Daphne said. She ran to the bag and pulled out the portable speakers. "We'll get some music going and have a volleyball dance party."

I waited for Weston's response.

He glanced at the others, who were now running in circles to warm-up. He turned back to me. "So, we can dance?"

I nodded. "Yep. You can leap to the ball if you want."

His eyes lit up. "Sweet."

Daphne moved toward the net, but I stopped her, motioning to her ginormous floppy hat. "That has to go, though. You won't be able to see."

Daphne huffed. "I was hoping you wouldn't notice."

"How can I miss it?" I asked.

Daphne tossed it on her towel. Somehow, she had a pair of Mickey ears on underneath, each ear the shape of two cherries. She looked at Huntley. "Don't worry, I haven't forgotten about your guitar ears. It's going to take some time, but luckily, we've got all summer."

"As long as I get them before I head back to school." Huntley then proceeded to take off his shirt, tossing it down with all the others.

I wanted to look away. I wanted to stare at anything and everything except his chiseled chest and abs, but I couldn't. My eyes were sucked in, and I was so glad I was wearing sunglasses.

I couldn't be attracted to this guy. It was completely and utterly out of the question.

Plus, the whole checkered-past thing. Mom and Dad would never allow us to date.

"Let's play, losers!" Sierra shouted near the volleyball net.

Daphne sighed. "Why did I become friends with her again?"

Laughing, I took Daphne by the arm and led her over to the

others. She set the speakers down and synced her phone up to it. "Levitating" by Dua Lipa began to play.

Veronica cupped her hands over her mouth. "Louder." She wore a crocheted dress over her bathing suit, looking exceptionally hot. I really didn't understand her fuss over her weight. We needed to get her mind off it.

Bentley tossed the ball over the net. "We'll let you serve first."

I caught the ball and backed toward the rope that lined the sand to create a court. "So kind of you."

Sierra clapped her hands and got into position. Veronica, Samson, and Bentley fell into place without having to communicate, like they were some sort of professional team.

I glanced over at Huntley, who stood near the net, and then Daphne and Weston, who were dancing in the middle on our side of the court.

"Weston!" I yelled, pointing to the right side of the net. "Please stop dancing and go there." I pointed to my left and behind Huntley. "Daphne, shimmy your way over there."

Daphne moon-walked to her spot. Well, the best she could in sand.

Huntley and I shared a knowing look. We were definitely going to lose. Then we shared a smile. Win or lose, we most certainly could have fun.

Clearing my throat, I sang out loud along with Dua Lipa and tossed the ball into the air, serving it overhand.

The ball went straight to Veronica, who calmly hit it to Samson. He set the ball, and Bentley jumped to spike it.

During the transition, I'd twirled my way to the right. Bentley's ball came soaring down. I dove, my arms extended, and connected with the ball.

"Jazz fingers, Daph!" I yelled as I scrambled back to my feet, brushing the sand off me in the process.

Daphne held up her arms, wiggling her fingers, and

headed for the ball. It was a sloppy set at best, but she'd set the ball for Huntley to swoop in and do an acrobatic spike that was more of a flop thanks to the angle of Daphne's set. It went over the net at least, and our spectacle distracted the others long enough that the ball fell to the ground on their side.

"We did it!" Daphne jumped into the air a couple of times before she ran at Weston, throwing her arms around him.

Huntley and I watched on as they cheered, so excited to receive a point. They danced and kissed like they'd just won the Olympics. And Weston hadn't even actually done anything.

Huntley leaned toward me, speaking loud enough to be heard over the music. "Are we going to tell them there are still twenty-four points to go?"

"Nah." I waved my hand. "Let them bask in the moment. This might be a once-in-a-lifetime chance for them."

We chuckled for the briefest of seconds before I heard Sierra say, "0 serving 1." It wasn't even their turn to serve. Right?

The next thing I knew, the ball was headed right for Daphne and Weston.

"You get the ball!" Huntley yelled as he sprinted toward Daphne and Weston. He pushed them out of the way in the nick of time, giving me room to hit the ball back over the net.

Samson easily blocked my return, and the ball sailed once again toward Daphne and Weston (and now Huntley) on the ground. The ball connected with Daphne's butt and shot back into the air. I spun to my right, clasped my hands, and hit the ball to the left.

Huntley stood at that exact moment, and the ball smacked right into his face.

I threw my hands over my mouth in total shock. Huntley bent over, holding his hand over his already bruised and swollen nose.

I blinked a couple of times before I realized I had to do

something, not just stand there like an idiot. So I went to him, cupping his face in my hands.

"Are you okay?" I asked.

Huntley groaned and lowered his hands. "Am I bleeding?"

"Surprisingly, no." His nose was a little red, but other than that, there was no additional damage to his face.

He placed his hands over mine that were still cupped on his face. "Maybe I just need to steer clear of you when you have objects in your hands." He grinned and then grimaced.

"I'm so sorry, Huntley," I said. "Do you need some ice? I can grab some from the cooler."

"That might be a good idea," he said.

We paused, staring at each other. It was then I realized how close we were standing, my hands on his face, his hands on top of mine, and everyone else staring at us.

I quickly dropped my hands and ran over to the cooler to grab some ice.

"Get some for my butt, too," Daphne said with a groan, immediately easing the tension that had built.

Sierra, Bentley, Veronica, and Samson came around to our side of the net.

Veronica put her hands on her hips. "I'm thinking maybe sports is a bad idea for these four."

"Oh, thank goodness." Weston let out a huge breath of relief before going to the cooler to grab some ice for Daphne.

He hurried back over to her and was about to press the ice to her butt but stopped himself short. "Uh, have we reached this stage of our relationship?"

Daphne threw up her hands. "I don't know. Where is the butt-touching level? Six-month mark? Year?"

"We need to take into consideration the unusual medical situation we're in." Weston stared at the ice in his hands. "And it's melting. Soon it will just be water."

Daphne rushed over to her towel, lay down on her stomach, and motioned to her butt. "Just pile them on."

As Weston went to work, Huntley broke out in laughter, pressing a hand to his face through the pain.

I rounded on Sierra. "Why did you serve? We got the point, which means it was our serve."

Sierra threw up her hands. "I didn't know. I play basketball, not volleyball." She smiled sheepishly at Huntley. "Sorry."

Huntley calmed his laughter. "Just a day in the life with Taylor."

Heat consumed my cheeks in embarrassment as the ice in my hands melted, water dripping between my fingers and onto the sand. I turned my attention to the cooler sitting off to the side, tempted to just stick my whole head in there and disappear forever.

CHAPTER TWENTY-FOUR

*V*eronica and Samson teamed up against Bentley and Sierra, and the four of them started their own game of volleyball.

Huntley came over to the cooler, took a couple of cubes from inside, and pressed them to his nose. The ones I had grabbed had completely melted.

I wiped my hands on my swimming suit, letting it soak up the water. "Why do all these accidents keep happening?" I'd never felt so … off before. Had Zander messed me up that badly? Not being in control had thrown me out of whack, and I didn't like it one bit.

Huntley shrugged. "Wish I knew. The weird part is, I still want to hang around you. I should be running for the hills to save my life."

I slapped his arm, making him laugh. "I'm not usually this accident-prone."

He held the ice cubes against his nose, water dripping over his lips and onto his chin. "Technically, I'm the one getting in all the accidents. You're just causing them."

"I need a drink." I bent down and retrieved a can of Dr

Pepper from the cooler. I looked up at Huntley. "Want one?"

"Yes, please." He held out a hand. I handed him the can as gently and slowly as I could.

Daphne giggled from under one of the umbrellas. "That's cold."

The ice cubes kept sliding off her butt. Weston would catch them and toss them back on, moving swiftly like they were in some sort of relay.

"How did those two find each other?" Huntley asked.

"Divine intervention," I said through my smile. "Those two were made for each other."

"I've honestly never seen anything like it." Huntley shook out his wet hands. The ice cubes had melted. He squinted his eyes up at the sun. "I think I need some shade."

We sat down on our towels, scooting them next to Daphne and Weston.

"They're all melted," Weston frowned at Daphne's butt.

She rolled onto her side. "It was bound to happen. It's ice." She smiled at me. "Now do you understand why Weston and I were adamantly opposed to playing?"

I nodded. "I just keep thinking if you continue to try, maybe one day you won't horribly suck."

"Oh, sweet, naïve, Tay-Tay." Daphne shook her head. "Sports aren't for everyone, and that's okay."

"I'm totally fine with sucking at sports," Weston said.

Daphne wiggled her eyebrows at him. "Unless kissing was a sport. You'd win the gold."

"Technically, *we'd* win." Weston lay down on his towel so he was parallel to her.

Huntley leaned back, putting his weight on his hands. "Honestly, with how many things they're throwing into the Olympics now, I wouldn't be surprised to see kissing added."

"Summer or winter?" I asked.

He twisted his lips to the side in thought. "There are arguments for both, really."

"Either way," Daphne said, "Weston and I are taking home the gold."

"Oh, yeah." Weston held up his hand, which she happily high-fived.

Daphne lay back down on her stomach, placing her chin in her hands. "Hey, Huntley?"

"Yeah?"

"Does it bother you when I bring up Despacito?"

Huntley looked a little taken aback. "Uh, no, not really."

She nodded. "Good. I totally don't want to offend you. It's just, Despacito and Esposito rhyme, and I pretty much tie everything in my life to music, but only to people I really like. Well, also to people I hate. And to people I have adequate feelings for. But for you, I think you're cool, and I'd never want to insult you."

Huntley cracked a smile. "No harm done, Daphne. And the feeling is mutual."

Daphne turned to the side so she could pump her fist. "Heck yes." She reached back and rubbed her butt. "Man, I can't believe how much it stings to get hit with a volleyball. How are you coping with this so well, Huntley? I mean, you got hit *in the face.*"

He chuckled and touched a hand to his swollen nose. "Well, compared to getting hit in the face with a can of soda, a volleyball is a piece of cake."

"Yum," Weston said. "Cake sounds delicious."

"With ice cream." Daphne rolled onto her back and patted her stomach. "And now I'm hungry. Can we make s'mores?"

"I thought we'd do that when the sun goes down," I said. "And after some hot dogs."

"Ugh. Fine." Daphne clasped her hands behind her head.

"Maybe I'll take a little nap then. Playing volleyball really wore me out."

I picked up a handful of sand and tossed it at her. "You played for less than five minutes."

She wiped the sand off her face. "Yeah, I know. So exhausted."

Smiling, I lay down on my stomach, resting my head on my arms. A nap did sound kind of nice. It was a warm day with the slightest breeze in the air. Perfect nap weather.

I'd just about drifted off to sleep when something smashed against my back, cool and gooey. I reached behind me, wiped my back, and then looked at my fingers. It was brown and creamy. I nervously rubbed it between my fingers, not knowing what it was, and then reluctantly sniffed it.

"Is this *pudding*?" I asked.

Out of the corner of my eye, I saw something flying toward me. I turned just in time to see a balloon headed toward my face. It splattered against my skin, spraying pudding everywhere. I gasped, inhaling some of the pudding and coughing right as another balloon hit my arm.

"We're under attack!" Weston yelled.

I wiped at my face, trying to get pudding out of my eyes, but it just smeared everywhere, along with the sand on my hands.

Screaming echoed around me and the next thing I knew, someone was on top of me, holding the umbrella in front of us. I finally cleared my vision enough to see Weston and Daphne stacked next to me, both covered in pudding. Huntley was half on me, half to my side, holding the umbrella in place.

I stared at the pudding on my hands. "What is happening?"

A shrieking Sierra and Veronica dove behind us, with Bentley and Samson right at their heels. They snatched the other umbrella as a barrage of pudding-filled balloons smacked against our umbrella shield.

"It's Zander!" Veronica crawled between Daphne and me.

Pudding stained her hair and neck. "He's out there with his friends."

Splatter after splatter hit the umbrella, causing us to scoot back toward the ocean.

"We gotta get out of here," Samson shouted over the ruckus.

"Or fight back!" Sierra roared, so much venom in her tone. "I swear, I'm going to *kill* Zander." I turned to see her covered in pudding as well. We all were.

Mixed with the sand, it was an uncomfortable mess.

"Okay." Huntley moved to a crouched position. "On the count of three, we're all going to stand and make our way to the van." He grunted as another round of balloons hit the umbrella.

"Wait!" Samson said. "Taylor, make sure you have the keys!"

I shimmied out from underneath Huntley, army-crawled to my bag, and fished out my keys. "Got them!"

"One, two, three!" Huntley yelled.

We all sprang to our feet, keeping in a tight formation, both Huntley and Samson holding out an umbrella to protect us.

A balloon exploded on my foot, covering it in pudding. Sand piled on, sticking to the pudding.

Daphne and Sierra both screamed.

"We're being hit from behind!" Bentley said.

Another balloon found my head, and pudding layered my hair.

My jaw clenched as anger boiled inside. Zander was so dead.

I put my hand on Huntley's shoulder and pulled him to a stop. "We gotta do *something*. We're just sitting ducks."

Huntley turned to face me, still holding the umbrella out in front of us. "I agree. I say we charge them."

Veronica crowded next to us, wiping some pudding off her face. "Let's do it."

I glanced around at everyone else, and they all gave nods of approval.

Daphne narrowed her eyes. "It's go time, baby."

"I get Zander," I growled.

Samson and Huntley dropped the umbrellas, and with warrior cries, the eight of us ran out, forming a circle as we headed for Zander and his friends.

A balloon hit my stomach, then the side of my face, and then my leg, but I so didn't care. I went straight for Zander, hating that the sand slowed me down. It was like a slow-motion battle rush, and instead of grenades going off all around me, it was balloons exploding on contact, sending pudding and sand everywhere.

Zander's eyes got wide as I neared him, fear growing inside them. He turned toward his friends. "Retreat!"

He spun around on his heels, trying to get away from me. As I passed a bucket of pudding-filled balloons, I snatched a balloon for each hand and sprinted toward Zander, jumping when I was almost on him.

The balloons in my hands smashed against his head as we fell to the ground, the hot sand softening our fall. I quickly gathered up handfuls of sand and smeared them in with the pudding on his hair, really digging deep.

A weird siren sounded nearby. I paused and looked up, only to see a bunch of beach security vehicles surrounding our war zone.

A guard opened his door and stood, using the hood of his car and the door to hold himself up high. He spoke into a radio that was connected to the speakers on top of his car. "Everyone, freeze!"

The battle cries and screams around me silenced as everyone stopped their attack and turned to the security guard.

"Drop the balloons," he commanded. "And get on your knees."

With a sigh, I did as told, cursing Zander the entire time.

CHAPTER TWENTY-FIVE

I stood there in my swimsuit, covered in sticky chocolate pudding and sand, recounting the whole event to one of the police officers that showed up. The officer was holding back a laugh as I told my side of the story, so I knew we couldn't be in too much trouble.

In the end, Zander, his friends, and I had all been fined. My group protested my fine, saying we were the victims. The authorities just saw a pudding-covered beach that needed to be cleaned. We were all to blame in their eyes. Which, honestly, we were.

I had at least talked the officer into only fining me instead of any of my friends. I didn't want that added to Huntley's record, and the whole thing had been because of me anyway. They did say they'd all chip in to help pay for it, which was nice of them.

We took turns rinsing off in the public wash areas, getting as much sand and pudding off us as we could. I had this horrible sinking feeling that just like sand, I'd be finding pudding in all sorts of crevices in my body for days to come.

When Samson, Huntley, and I returned home, Mom, Dad, and Ryker were waiting on the front porch. Spencer was passed out on Ryker's shoulder. Not surprisingly, only Ryker looked upset.

They joined us at the back of the van, retrieving all our beach stuff.

"I can't wait to hear this story." Dad peeked in one of the coolers, pulled out a can of Coke, and popped it open.

"Let's wait until a little later." Mom inspected the umbrellas, which we'd cleaned off at the beach. They were both damaged, the wires bent funny from all the blows. "Porter and Emory went to visit some old friends. They'll want to hear it, too."

I tried to run my fingers through my hair, but it was still thinly coated in dried pudding. "That will give us time to take proper showers."

Mom gave me her infamous I-raised-you-better-than-this look. "Maybe you should lay off the whole vow for bit, Tay. Seems like both parties need time to calm down."

I put my hand on my hip. "Who told you about the vow?"

Samson raised his hand. "That would be me."

I went to punch his arm, but he maneuvered out of the way and took off toward the house.

Two arms wrapped around my legs. "Tay! You're home early!" Fiona smiled up at me. Water dripped down her hair and bathing suit. "Want to swim with us?"

I ran a hand down her hair. "Who was watching you in the pool?" Everyone else was either on the driveway or not home.

Fiona's grin grew. "Uncle Neo is here!"

I snapped my head toward my mom. "Neo is here? I thought he wasn't coming for a couple of weeks."

She leaned toward me, her voice in a whisper. "He just lost his job and his girlfriend. He's going to need all the support he can right now."

Neo was the oldest, most independent, and perpetually

single child in the family. He wasn't the type to settle down. He'd moved more times than I could count.

Fiona tugged on my arm. "Come on, Tay. Neo and Genevieve are waiting in the pool."

I grabbed my bag from the back of the van and escorted Fiona into the house. "Let me go rinse off, and then I'll be back down, okay?"

Fiona scrunched her eyebrows in confusion. "Can't you rinse off in the pool? It's water."

Mom came up behind us. "Not with pudding hair. I don't want that stuff in our pool."

"Pudding hair?" Fiona looked beyond confused now.

I chuckled. "Oh, I have quite the story to tell you." I tucked her hair behind her ear. "I'll be out in a few."

Fiona pumped her fist and then ran toward the back door.

Getting the pudding out of my hair took longer than I thought. So much had been smeared in, I bet my scalp was now brown.

I slipped into a clean swimsuit—one without pudding stains—and joined the others outside.

Samson and Ryker were in the pool, Samson with Genevieve on his shoulders and Ryker with Fiona on his. The girls were wrestling each other, trying to push the other into the pool. Aria and Mom were on lounge chairs on the Baja shelf in the pool, a large umbrella providing them shade.

Dad and Quinn were playing one-on-one basketball, the screeches from their shoes on the concrete providing the background noise.

"I was starting to think you weren't coming back out." Huntley appeared at my side, all smiles. And shirtless. Why did he feel the need to torture me so? It was totally unfair that he was so attractive.

Old. He was old. And a criminal. And I'd promised Mom I

was done with boys for the unforeseeable future, one promise I needed to stick to.

I just needed to repeat those mantras over and over until they really sunk in. Old guy. Criminal. No boys.

I ran my hand over my damp hair. "The pudding was clinging on for dear life."

Huntley nodded. "I've heard pudding can be a clinger. That's why I have a no pudding rule. I hate being smothered."

Two large arms wrapped around my middle, and suddenly I was being lifted into the air and carried over to the pool. I had no time to react as the person jumped into the pool, taking me with them, warm water enveloping me as we sunk to the bottom.

I squirmed underwater, trying to get out of their grasp.

There was only one person who loved doing this to me. Neo. I pinched his arm, really digging in my nails, until he finally let go, letting me surface.

I gasped for air, kicking like crazy, landing some solid blows against Neo's chest and legs.

"Everything okay there, Tay?" Neo asked.

With a glare, I splashed his face with water over and over again. Then I swam over and threw my arms around him.

"Hey, bro," I said, squeezing tight.

"Hey, sis." Neo hugged me back.

He released me, and I finally got a good look at his face. He'd grown a full-on beard. I'd noticed it in some of his pictures online, but it was so much more extravagant in person. It was thick and curly, the dark brown almost black.

"Oh my gosh, Neo," I said. "You look like a mountain man."

He grinned, his light blue eyes humored. "Just the look I was going for." He curled the ends of his mustache. "Have it like this when it's not wet."

I reached over and grabbed a water noodle that I could rest

my arms on, keeping me afloat. "I heard your life sucks right now."

He threw back his head. "When it rains, it pours." He ran his hand over his beard. "The job I saw coming. The girl? Totally out of the blue."

"What was her name?" I asked. Neo went through girls quick and often, so it was hard to keep them all pegged down.

"Sunshine," he said.

I laughed until I saw he wasn't laughing with me. "Wait, her name was seriously Sunshine? Like, that's what's on her birth certificate?"

He nodded. "Well, Sunshine is actually her middle name. Rainbow is her first name."

"Last name?"

"Goodfellow."

"I can't believe you didn't bring her home for us to meet," I said through my giggles. "Samson and Quinn would have had a field day with it. Rainbow Sunshine Goodfellow."

Neo arched a bushy eyebrow. "Exactly why I kept her a secret."

I reached out and patted his shoulders. "There, there, Neo. Not all relationships can be sunshine and rainbows."

He pushed a large wave of water at me, making me laugh.

"Speaking of sunshine and rainbows," Neo said, his tone turning serious. "Heard you got blindsided as well. Zander is a total idiot for dumping you."

I shrugged, trying to push down the sadness that wanted to creep out at the mention of his name. The guy had ruined my beach day and so much more. He didn't deserve my sorrow or heartache. Yet, I really, really missed him. As much as I hated to admit it, we'd had so many good memories.

What was wrong with me? I needed to remain mad, not get sad.

I wiped at a tear that had escaped down my cheek.

"I heard you've been getting even." A softness in his eyes reminded me how much I loved talking to my oldest brother. He always spoke to me with so much honesty and genuine interest, even back when I was little.

"Gotta let him know what happens when someone dumps a Thomas," I said.

"Maybe I need to pull some of your stunts on Sunshine."

"I'm happy to help."

"I'm sure you are." He looked over at Huntley, who was currently sitting on the edge of the pool being the ref for Fiona and Genevieve's wrestling matches on Samson and Ryker's shoulders. "What's the deal with him?"

I watched Huntley, smiling at how easily he blended in with my family. "He's Ryker's roommate."

Neo swam up next to me, taking some of the noodle I was using to rest his arms on. "I meant between you and him."

I looked at Neo, my jaw dropping in shock. It took me a second to compose myself. "What are you talking about?"

Neo smirked. "Mom said you've been spending a lot of time with him lately."

My gaze wandered over to my mom, who was chatting away with Aria. "She told you that?"

Did anything remain a secret in this family?

"She likes to keep me updated," Neo said. "Especially with everything she thinks worth mentioning."

Mom thought Huntley was worth mentioning? We'd only hung out a few times, and most of the time it was in a group. Not just the two of us.

"What is with everyone?" I mumbled.

"So Mom's not the only one who has mentioned something?" Neo stroked his beard. "The plot thickens."

"There's no plot!" I growled. "Why can't everyone mind their own business?"

Neo put an arm around my shoulder. "Is it so bad to have your family and friends care about you?"

"Well, no, but there's no storyline here, okay? He's Ryker's *college* roommate, and that's it."

Neo squeezed my shoulder. "Just don't do anything rash. You tend to jump and then think about it."

Why did all my brothers feel the need to counsel me? It was so annoying. I basically had seven dads.

I pushed Neo's hand off my shoulder and backed away. "Like you should be giving out relationship advice. You can't keep a girl longer than a week."

I ignored the hurt that swept across Neo's eyes. He had no right lecturing me on something I wasn't even doing. There was nothing going on between Huntley and me. Nothing.

So many more words wanted to spew out of my mouth, so I hurried out of the pool before I could say anything else.

CHAPTER TWENTY-SIX

The next week passed in a blur. It was full of planning Dad's party, taking the girls to the beach and Knott's Berry Farm, and tons and tons of swimming.

I think my family sensed my irritation at all the grilling, because they all backed off and didn't once mention Zander or Huntley.

Huntley himself had hardly been at the house, sometimes not even sleeping here.

I shouldn't have been sad about it. It didn't matter.

Yet, every time the door opened, I wondered if it was him. My heart would speed up in a wild hope, and then when I realized it wasn't him, my heart sank into my stomach, and I found myself moping around the house like an idiot.

There were so many things wrong with me.

Old guy. Criminal. No boys, I repeated in my head.

We were having a campfire out in the backyard, roasting marshmallows for s'mores. Our fire pit had benches circling it, giving us ample room to sit our large family.

I helped Genevieve slide a marshmallow on the end of the stick, and together, we held it over the fire.

"The secret is to not get too close to the flames," I said to Genevieve. She was standing between my arms, a firm determination on her cute little face. "See your dad over there?"

Genevieve looked over at Porter, who had his marshmallow directly in the flames.

"His is going to get black and taste burnt," I said. "We just need to keep rotating ours, letting it get a nice golden brown all the way around."

Porter yanked out his marshmallow, the whole thing in flames. He quickly blew it out. Genevieve and Fiona laughed as he struggled to take it off the stick.

"Oh, it's hot!" Porter shook out his hand.

"Have you completely forgotten how to roast marshmallows?" Mom asked, amused.

Porter shook his head. "Of course not." He popped the burnt marshmallow in his mouth, his face scrunching in disgust. "This is so good."

Emory threw an unroasted marshmallow at his face. "Don't lie in front of our daughters."

"Aunt Tay-Tay, is my marshmallow ready?" Genevieve asked in her sweet little voice.

I helped her bring the stick out of the fire so we could see the marshmallow. Perfectly golden.

"Look at that beauty," I said. I looked over at my dad, who had just finished helping Aria put her s'more together. "We need a graham cracker and chocolate, stat."

Dad brought over a plate with a graham cracker and a piece of chocolate on it. I set the marshmallow on the chocolate, and Dad used the other piece of the graham cracker to help guide the marshmallow off the stick. Dad squished the s'more together.

"Let this sit for thirty seconds." Dad handed the plate to Genevieve's waiting hands. "Gotta let it cool down, but it also gives the chocolate some time to soften."

Genevieve began counting to thirty, her eyes fixed on the s'more.

Fiona came over to me. "Aunt Tay-Tay, will you help me roast a marshmallow? Dad sucks at it."

"Hey!" Porter said at the same time Emory said, "We don't say suck."

Samson snickered next to me, along with Quinn and Aria.

"I can help you," Ryker said. He'd left Spencer inside, away from the fire and smoke.

"He's actually the best roaster in the family," I said to Fiona.

Excitement lit up in her eyes as she ran over to Ryker. Granted, he'd probably bore her with the calculations behind his method, but she wouldn't mind as long as she got a s'more out of the situation.

Neo slid the backdoor open and jogged out onto the patio with Huntley right behind him, holding his guitar in his hands.

"Huntley!" I quickly stood, and then paused, realizing that my entire family was staring at me. Aside from Ryker, they were mostly amused. I really hoped my red cheeks couldn't be seen in the dark.

"Nice to see you, too, sis," Neo said. He had the ends of his mustache curled up perfectly. "I talked Huntley into playing us some songs."

Huntley took the empty seat next to me on the bench. "I should warn you guys that I'm not that good."

"You gotta practice to become good." Mom smiled at him. "Are you going to sing?"

Huntley quickly shook his head. "I'm not ready for that. But I don't mind providing the background noise."

As everyone settled back into their conversations, Huntley began to play a simple melody on his guitar.

"Where have you been, stranger?" I asked him.

Huntley smiled. "Just hanging out with some old friends."

The smile I wore faltered. Were these the friends he had

back when he was getting in trouble? What if Huntley was falling back into his old lifestyle?

"Oh, fun." With my strained tone, I didn't even sound convincing to myself.

Huntley glanced over at me. "Not really."

I looked at him. "Why?"

He shrugged. "I think we've just grown apart over the years, wanting different things out of life."

That was good, wasn't it? Maybe he had just needed to remind himself why he hated that past lifestyle. I wanted to give him the benefit of the doubt, but it was probably more of my hormones crushing on him that wanted it to be true.

"You're getting really good." I motioned to his guitar.

"When I haven't been with friends, I've been down in Newport, practicing."

Reflections from the flames danced in his gorgeous eyes, and I found myself leaning toward him. I quickly righted myself.

"Did you see your mom?" I asked.

Huntley shook his head. "No. I don't think we're quite at a good place yet."

"Hopefully one day it will happen."

"Hopefully," Huntley said quietly. "Though I'm not holding my breath. Not as long as Ron is in the picture."

I placed my hand on his arm. "I'm sure everything will work out the way it's supposed to, even if it's not exactly what you want."

Huntley paused his playing, his soft gaze turning to me. "Need and want are two entirely different things, aren't they?"

I swallowed. Very much so. I needed to have a boy-free life for the unforeseeable future. What I wanted, though? Was to kiss Huntley right there next to the fire. In front of my family.

In front of my family!

I scooted away from Huntley and closed my eyes, not

wanting to see my family's reactions. I could feel them staring, and it was suddenly blazing hot, and not because of the fire.

"Someone has it bad," Samson said into my ear.

With my eyes still closed, I pressed a hand to his forehead and shoved him away, wishing I could crawl back inside the house and under the safety of the covers of my bed.

I really, really needed a distraction. One that wasn't so hot.

"Samson, will you go get us some more marshmallows?" Mom asked, a laugh in her tone. Apparently, she found this hilarious.

Samson stood. "On it."

"Oh, and grab some waters for everyone," Dad said.

"Quinn, go help your brother," Mom said.

With a grunt, Quinn got up and left the fire.

Taking a few deep breaths, I worked up the courage to open my eyes. Thankfully, no one was looking my way.

Quinn and Samson came out of the house, carrying armloads of water and marshmallows.

A loud roar came from Neo as he rushed at my brothers, slamming them both to the ground, bottled waters and bags of marshmallows flying into the air.

"Sneak attack!" Neo banged his fists against his chest, making a gorilla noise.

Both Fiona and Genevieve busted out laughing.

Porter rushed over and picked up one of the packages of marshmallows off the ground. "Whew. They're fine. No need to fret, anyone." He stepped over a groaning Samson and Quinn, coming back to the fire.

"Samson, sweetie, can you bring me a water?" Mom's eyes were fixated on the fire pit.

"Sure," Samson said with a strained tone. He slowly got to his feet, snatched up one of the water bottles, and brought it to Mom.

"Quinn," Dad said, "quit whining like a baby and bring the rest of the waters. I'm parched."

Huntley and I shared a smile before we busted out laughing.

My watch buzzed, and I glanced down at the screen to see an incoming text from Zoie. Why was she texting me?

I pulled my phone out of my pocket and brought up the text. She'd sent a screenshot of Zander's latest online post. There were two pictures of him and Simone. In one, they were sharing a kiss, the sunset at the beach for a backdrop. The next photo was the two of them smiling so brightly it was almost blinding.

Zoie sent another text: *Want me to kill him? Say the word and I will.*

I bit my lip, holding back the tears that wanted to come. I'd never seen Zander so *happy*. He'd never shared that version of his smile with me. Had he never been happy with me?

I quickly shut off the screen on my phone and jammed it in my pocket. My gaze flitted over to see Huntley staring at me, a look of pity in his eyes.

Wiping away a tear that escaped, I stood and, as calmly as I could, walked into the house and up to my room. I didn't want or need Huntley's pity.

The thing that stung most about this was that it wasn't a prank on Zander's part. It was just him living his life, completely happy and content without me.

And here I was, crying in my bedroom and crushing on a criminal that was too old for me anyway. I mean, if Zander didn't want me, why would Huntley?

I was such a fool.

CHAPTER TWENTY-SEVEN

I wrapped my hair into two buns on top of my head, slipped into a neon pink sundress, tugged on my black booties, and applied an ample amount of lip gloss. I was getting away from everything Huntley, Zander, and family.

Veronica picked me up in her Toyota Prius, a Post Malone song welcoming me into the car. We sang along until we got to Daphne's house. She practically flew into the car.

"You ladies ready to party?" Daphne asked from the middle seat in the back. She pointed to her gold rhinestone Mickey ears. "I brought my 'let's get wild' ears today."

I looked over my shoulder at her and held out my hand, wiggling my fingers in a 'give me' motion.

Daphne stared at my fingers for a second, pretending like she had no idea what I was doing, but then she finally broke out in a huge grin. "Okay, okay, I brought some for each of you, too."

After Veronica and I slipped ours on, we headed out.

"I booked some mani-pedis for us," Veronica said.

I looked at my fingernails, the red nail polish almost entirely gone. "Sounds perfect."

Daphne sighed. "Do I have to get a pedi? Can't I just stick with the mani?"

Veronica looked at her through the rearview mirror. "You're getting a pedi. I saw your feet recently. They need it."

"But it tickles, V!" Daphne said. It was her one and only ticklish spot.

"You'll be fine," Veronica said.

Daphne huffed. "Well, it's not my fault if I kick the person in the face and then end up looking like Huntley post-Dr-Pepper attack."

Thank goodness she hadn't brought up the light pole incident. I wanted to push that from my memories forever.

Veronica looked over at me. "I swear, sometimes it feels like I have Luciana with me."

Luciana was Veronica's ten-year-old sister that she constantly had to babysit.

I reached back and pinched Daphne's cheek. "Who's my big girl?"

Daphne slapped my hand away, laughing.

Veronica took us to her favorite spot for mani-pedis. She'd brought me with her a few times. Daphne wasn't into this whole thing, so she never came, which was why Veronica probably didn't mention it until after we'd picked up Daphne.

The salon was a fancy place with crystal chandeliers hanging from the ceiling, gold walls, and a sparkly tiled floor. I always felt glamorous the second I walked in the door.

The owner, Anna May, greeted us at the front desk. She was a short, petite woman with strawberry-blonde hair, pale skin, and a rich Southern accent.

Anna May smiled wide at us. "How are you ladies doing on this fine summer day?"

Veronica pointed her thumb at me. "She needs some therapy. Stat."

Anna May's curious blue eyes swept over me. "I can't wait

to hear all about it." She pointed a pink-gelled finger at me. "Leave nothing out, you hear?" She waved her hand. "Follow me."

Anna May escorted us to some gold leather chairs. I sank into mine, and so much stress melted away from my muscles.

Anna May placed a hand on the back of my chair. "Want me to turn on the massager while we get everything set up?"

"Yes, please," I said.

It was always my favorite part of the visit. The massager took me to my happy place, and this was the best idea ever.

"I need one of these for home," Daphne said from her chair on my right. She had her eyes closed, completely soaking in the moment.

"Told you that you'd love it here," Veronica said from my left. "These chairs are *ah*-mazing."

"Would you ladies like anything to drink?" Anna May asked.

"You wouldn't happen to have Dr Pepper, would you?" I asked.

Anna May smiled. "Why, yes, we do. Betty would have my head on a platter if I didn't offer Dr Pepper."

Betty, a tall brunette, was one of the nail technicians. She'd been born and raised in Texas where Dr Pepper ran through people's veins.

Betty walked out from the back, her high heels clinking against the floor. "You know I would, honey." She went to the fridge, opened it, and pulled out a can before looking at Daphne. "I never caught your name."

"Daphne," she said.

"Well, what can I get you, Daphne?" Betty asked.

"Do you have Cherry Coke?" Daphne asked.

Betty frowned. "Sorry, dear, just Coke."

Daphne gave her a thumbs-up. "That will work just fine." She patted her bag she had slung across her body. "Got the cherry syrup right in here."

Betty's frown turned into a smile. "Oh, coming prepared, are we? A girl after my own heart." She turned to Veronica. "What about you, V? The usual?"

Veronica nodded. "Yes, please."

Betty brought us all our drinks, handing Veronica a strawberry-lemonade.

Betty winked at Daphne and me. "Homemade by yours truly. Special family recipe."

Anna May checked her watch. "You're in luck today, ladies. Angel should be here any second now if you're needing some eye candy." She arched an eyebrow at me. "You needing something delicious to look at? Or is that the wrong sort of therapy?"

I grinned. "Eye candy sounds perfect."

As if on cue, the door opened, and an incredibly hot guy walked into the store, his motorcycle helmet tucked under his arm. He shook out his long hair, running his fingers through it. His leather jacket fit him perfectly, practically sculpted against him.

He sauntered over, kissed Anna May and Betty on the cheek, and then disappeared into the back.

"Do you charge extra for him?" Daphne asked.

Anna May chuckled. "No, dear. Just a perk to coming here." She glanced at Betty. "I'll take Veronica. You can handle the newbie." She winked at me. "And you get Angel."

I held out my phone to Anna May. "Do you mind taking a picture of us?"

"Of course!" Anna May took my phone and scooted back so she could get all three of us in the picture. "Say manipedis!"

Anna May handed back the phone, so I took a moment to upload it, making sure to tag Daphne and Veronica.

Betty walked over to Daphne. Daphne leaned toward her. "Fair warning; my feet are ticklish. If you don't want to get kicked in the face from my spasming, you might want to approach with caution."

Betty leaned in as well. "Sounds like you need a firm hand, which is my specialty."

Angel glided out of the back and approached my chair with a gorgeous smile on his dimpled face. "You must be Taylor. I'm Angel."

Oh my, his voice was deep and rumbly like Vin Diesel's, adding the icing to the eye-candy cake.

He crouched to inspect my feet. "What color are you feeling today?"

"Something electric," I said. "In a pink or orange."

One of his perfectly sculpted eyebrows arched up. "I have a pink that will practically zap anyone who comes near you."

I smiled slyly at him. "I like the sound of that."

We all let Angel do most of the talking, just so we could keep hearing his voice. Even Anna May and Betty looked like they never tired of it.

He was almost done with my nails when some other customers walked in. I hadn't really paid attention to those coming and going—I could barely peel my eyes away from Angel for even a second—but Daphne gasped next to me.

"No. Freaking. Way," Daphne said in a low, guttural voice that surprised me.

I followed her gaze to see none other than Simone with a few of her friends. They were chatting and laughing, completely oblivious to us.

My hands tried to ball into a fist on instinct, but Angel held my hand in place. He glanced over at Simone and the others. "I'm taking it you know her."

"She's the whole reason we're here," Veronica hissed.

"Do you think she knows who you are?" Daphne asked.

We'd cyber-stalked Simone, but I had no idea if she'd done the same to me. There was a possibility that Zander hadn't mentioned me, but after the incident at the restaurant in Newport, there was a good chance he told her everything.

Some other workers escorted Simone and her friends to a line of chairs across from us. As they settled in, Simone spoke in a loud voice, which I had no idea was normal for her or not. "She's straight-up crazy. She followed us to dinner and slashed his tires."

Uhm, I let the air out of one tire. That was it. No slashing involved. Wait. She was talking about me. My cheeks heated in anger.

"She breaks into his house, messes with his shower, and leaves her nightgown behind." Simone laughed with her friends.

That was his grandma's nightgown. Did she honestly think I rolled around in that thing? And his sister let me in the house!

"I told Zander he'd better check for cameras in the shower and his bedroom," Simone continued. "I wouldn't put it past Taylor to do something that absurd."

Her friend leaned toward Simone, scrolling through her phone. "Can we also talk about how hideous her fashion choices are? I mean, leather jackets? So lame. No wonder he dumped her."

"You're so much hotter than her," another friend said.

"Uh, I feel like they're talking really loud on purpose," Daphne said in a low voice. "Unless they naturally yell when they talk."

"I was thinking the same thing," Veronica whispered.

I turned to her. "Do you think they know I'm here?"

"Who's the stalker now?" Daphne said.

Simone scoffed, bringing my attention back to her. "She's seriously *so* pathetic. How desperate can one girl get?"

"She must be easy or something," her self-declared fashionista friend said. "Why else would he have stayed with her so long? Especially after he met you."

My hands shook as my anger practically boiled over. Angel let go of my hands and scooted back, giving me a wide berth, probably sensing my pending explosion.

"She's super clingy," Simone said. "He wanted to dump her months ago, like right after we met, but she made things so difficult."

They'd met that long ago? Had he had feelings for her this whole time? Had they hooked up before we broke up?

Oh, I wanted to grab every fingernail polish and chuck them at her smug face.

"Should we say something?" Daphne asked.

I shook my head as I pulled out my phone so I could text my brother. "I have a better plan. She's so going to regret coming here."

Simone looked over at me then, the smirk on her face telling me she knew exactly who I was and that I'd be here.

My phone buzzed. My brother was on his way. I glanced at Simone, gracing her with my own smug smile. I got up, paid for my mani-pedi, and went outside.

CHAPTER TWENTY-EIGHT

Some simple cyber-stalking pointed me to Simone's car in the parking lot. I hoped and prayed she'd be in the salon for a while, giving my brother time to get here.

I hated that I was relying on Ryker, out of all my brothers, but he had exactly what I needed. I'd worried he'd say no, but he surprised me and said yes.

Daphne bounced next to me, watching the entrance to the parking lot. "How is he even getting here? His foot-mobile?"

Normally, I would have laughed, but she'd pointed out a major flaw in my plan. Ryker didn't have a license.

I quickly dialed his number. He picked up right away. "Just give me five more minutes, okay? I'm on my way."

"How?" I asked.

"Huntley." The call ended, so typically Ryker.

Oh. Huntley. How had he gotten Ryker so quickly? Had he been at the house when I wasn't there? Could I have been hanging out with him this whole time?

Nope. I couldn't think like that. *Old guy. Criminal. No boys.*

I hadn't realized I'd been wringing my hands until Veronica put her hand on top of mine.

"Deep breaths, Tay," she said. "I'll go in the salon and create a distraction if I have to, so we can have more time."

I took long, deep breaths, trying to steady myself. I took in Simone's nice car. One her daddy had probably bought for her. The best part were the tinted windows. She wouldn't see what was coming.

As promised, Huntley and Ryker pulled into the parking lot five minutes later. Those were the longest five minutes of my life.

Veronica put her hand on my arm. "I'll stay by the entrance to the salon so I can keep an eye on them." She took off, leaving me with Daphne.

Daphne rubbed her hands together. "This is more exciting than Christmas morning."

"*If* we can pull it off," I said.

She waggled her finger at me. "Uh-uh, Tay-Tay. Positive thinking. *When* we pull it off."

Ryker came jogging up, an actual smile on his face. "I have what you need."

I looked at his empty hands. "Where?"

He pointed his thumb behind him. "In Huntley's trunk. Wanted to wait until we needed them." He looked at Simone's Range Rover. "Is this the vehicle?"

I nodded.

Ryker rubbed his chin. "I'm assuming you don't have the keys."

My heart sank. Why were there so many flaws in my plan? Oh, because I'd come up with it last minute.

"I can help you there," Huntley said, stepping up next to me.

I looked at him. "Do you know how to break into cars?"

He smiled sheepishly. "Let's just say I don't have the best past." He cupped his hands over the window, trying to peer inside. "Huh. The security system doesn't seem armed." He looked at me. "This might be your lucky day."

"Can you get us in?" I asked.

Huntley nodded. "Just say the word."

"The word!" Daphne yelled. "THE WORD!"

"Shh!" I said, slapping her arm.

"The word!" Daphne whisper-shouted.

I sighed.

Huntley went to the front of the Range Rover and removed one of the windshield wipers.

"What are you doing?" I asked.

He peeled the wiper apart, pulling out a long, silver metal piece. "Getting you inside the car." He threw the rest of the windshield wiper under the car and then bent the metal of the piece he kept, making a hook on the end.

After glancing around to make sure no one was watching, Huntley slid the hook between the window and door and jimmied the lock. He opened the door and swept out his arm. "My lady."

With a grin, I turned to Ryker. "Go get 'em."

Ryker took off, more excited than I'd seen him in a while.

"I didn't think Ryker had this in him," Huntley said, watching Ryker open the trunk of his car.

"Neither did I," I said.

Ryker came back, holding up a clear container full of crickets. He peered inside, smiling at the things. "You guys ready for a little adventure? It's either this or be eaten by Spencer."

"What's gotten into you?" I asked. "I thought I'd have to beg you to do this."

He lowered the container, the smile on his face fading. "I saw a picture of Simone. Samson showed me." He closed his eyes, and when he opened them, they almost looked watery. "She reminds me of this girl that used to tease me in elementary and middle school." He sighed. "And high school. And it's not just her appearance. I scrolled through her social media, and she's just as conceited and belittling as my bully."

I didn't know what to say. Ryker had a bully? One that lasted for *years*? I thought I knew everything that happened in my family, but I guess there were some secrets people could keep.

Veronica ran over to us. "I think they're about done!"

I motioned to the container. "How should we go about this?"

Ryker took in the Range Rover, a smile spreading on his face. "Open the back hatch."

Going to the driver's side door, I opened it, looking around until I found a button to release the hatch, and then joined Ryker in the back.

He set the container in the middle. "Okay. I'm going to tip this on its side, remove the lid, and then shut the hatch as quickly as I can. Hopefully, that will give them a little bit of time to work their way forward when the girls are in the car."

I squeezed his shoulder. "Brilliant. Thank you, Ryker."

"Glad I could assist you on your quest," he said.

I chuckled at his choice of words.

"They're paying!" Veronica said. "We gotta go!"

"You've got this, Ryker," I said before running with Daphne and Veronica over to Veronica's car.

Huntley had put his hands on top of the hatch, keeping his eyes on Ryker.

Ryker took a deep breath, tipped the container, fumbled to get the lid off, but the second it came off, he backed out, and together, he and Huntley closed the hatch. They were walking away when Simone and her friends came out of the salon.

"Please tell me you're filming this," Daphne said. She pressed down on her phone and "bad day" by blackbear began to play.

"Oh!" I quickly pulled my phone out of my jacket pocket and hit record.

Simone used her fob to unlock the doors to the Range Rover. She and her three friends opened the doors and got into the car, shutting the doors almost at the same time.

There were a few seconds of silence.

"Why isn't anything happening?" Veronica asked.

"Ryker got live crickets, right?" Daphne asked. "There's not a bunch of dead crickets back there, are there?" She twisted her lips to the side. "I guess that reveal would be funny—"

Screams erupted from the Range Rover. All four doors flew open, and the girls came flying out, flailing their arms and legs.

Crickets jumped out of the open doors, a couple of them landing on Simone's head. She screeched as she shook out her hair, trying to get them out.

"Get them off me!" the self-declared fashionista said as she flung out her arms and legs. "They're eating me alive!"

Veronica choked on a laugh. "It doesn't even look like she has any on her."

"She probably doesn't," I said through my laughter. "It's probably just the feeling that there are."

I watched the girls continue to freak out as the workers and other patrons poured out of the salon to see what was happening.

My eyes found their way over to Ryker. Even from where I stood, I could see that his eyes were lit up like the Fourth of July. Somehow, seeing him so happy was more satisfying than watching Simone get what she deserved.

CHAPTER TWENTY-NINE

Everyone was having a full-on campout in the back yard. Dad and my brothers had pitched tents, brought out blow-up mattresses, set up an outdoor movie, and turned on the fire pit again to make s'mores.

I'd quickly seen myself out, sneaking up to the solitude of my room and sitting curled up on the floor. It didn't take long for my high from the day to stoop into an all-time low.

Zander had known Simone for months. At least, according to her. She could have been making that up to make me feel bad.

Well, it worked.

Had he really wanted to dump me for months? He'd been working like crazy the couple of months before prom, saving up money, but what if he hadn't been? What if he'd been with Simone that whole time?

Was he capable of that?

I honestly wasn't sure if I knew Zander anymore. Maybe I'd never really known him at all. The thought gripped my heart tight, squeezing the life out of me.

I was such a fool. I thought we were so happy together and

had such an amazing relationship. Everyone else thought so, too. I mean, we'd won prom queen and king.

Wiping away some tears, I blew out some shaky breaths before crawling over to my walk-in closet and searching for my sash.

When the floor proved fruitless, I used the doorframe to help me stand. It was then I remembered I'd put it, along with other things from the prom, in a box on the top shelf of my closet. I reached up, grabbed it, and sank to the floor.

Sniffling, I removed the lid.

There sat the sash. The one I'd draped around me proudly. I was so excited for the honor and to share it with Zander. The guy I thought I loved.

I set the sash off to the side and rummaged through the rest of the box. My dried-up corsage. The pictures from the photo booth. The green and black bracelet I'd bought special for the occasion. My ticket to the event. I saw the receipt from the parking garage and rolled my eyes, a strained laugh escaping my mouth. I'd wanted to keep everything from that night.

I'd thought it was special. Our one-year anniversary. One year of bliss.

Yet, it had been a year of blindness. I never saw through to the real Zander.

Or had he changed during our relationship? Had I pushed him to become this cheating jerk?

I crumpled up the receipt and let out a loud roar. Frustrated didn't even begin to describe how I felt. My emotions kept bouncing all over the place. I wanted to scream, to cry, to punch something, to kiss Zander and make everything go back to how it was.

Yeah, I was naïve and completely oblivious to what was going on around me, but I'd been happy. I'd truly been happy when we were together. We'd had so many good moments. They had to have meant *something* to Zander.

I took my phone out of my pocket and stared at the screen. Maybe I could call him and get some answers. Ask him if I ever meant anything to him, or if it was all just a game. Ask him if he cheated on me.

There was a knock on my bedroom door.

"What?" I shouted from the closet. I didn't feel like getting up.

I could hear the door open.

"Are you okay?" Huntley asked.

I threw my head back, not wanting to deal with him right now. He added a whole other layer of confusion I really didn't need.

"I'm fine," I snapped, then closed my eyes, wishing I hadn't been so rude.

The door closed.

I was such a jerk.

A figure appeared in my closet's doorway, and I jumped where I sat, my hand going to my chest.

Huntley lifted his palms. "It's just me."

"I thought you left." I wiped at the tears on my cheeks.

"Mind if I join you?" he asked softly.

I pushed the contents of my prom box off to the side to create room for him to sit.

As he took a seat, he glanced around my closet, smiling. "I love that you have a perfect blend of black clothes, and clothes made of colors you can see from a mile away."

I lightly laughed. "It pretty much sums up my personality."

"I like it." Huntley leaned back, resting his weight on his palms. "Break-ups are the worst, aren't they?"

"Understatement." I sniffed, wishing I had a tissue. "Even worse when you find out they cheated on you."

"What?" Huntley sat up tall. "Zander cheated on you?"

I shrugged. "Not positive, but it's looking like a possibility. Apparently, he's known and liked Simone for months."

"I'm sorry, Taylor," Huntley said with so much sincerity it caused a lump to form in my throat. "You don't deserve that. No one does."

My lower lip trembled, so I pressed a hand to my mouth. I hated all of this. The heartache. The pain. The betrayal. The end of what I thought had been such a perfect relationship. I wanted to put everything back how it was. I was torn between wanting to rip Zander from my life to wanting to crawl to him and beg him to take me back.

I was such an idiot. Why would I still want him? Why did I care about him?

Sobs racked my chest, and soon, I was crying uncontrollably. Huntley scooted next to me, so I lay down, setting my head in his lap. He caressed my hair as I cried, letting it all out. My fist tightened around his jeans, holding on tight, like if I just held on, everything would be okay. All my sorrow would disappear, and life would be normal once again.

But life would never be the same. It would forever be altered because of that single relationship. I learned what it meant to love. To hate. To really, truly hurt. To be betrayed. To laugh. To get lost in something so deep, that climbing back out was almost impossible.

But I had to climb, or I'd waste away at the bottom of the pit.

CHAPTER THIRTY

My eyelids were so heavy when I woke. They were puffy like they were filled with leftover tears. My head throbbed. I smacked my lips, wishing I had water. Anything to drink, really.

Crying always left me feeling like crap. Some people said it was therapeutic, but the aftermath was horrible for me.

I rolled onto my back, staring at the ceiling. Where was I? I glanced around, taking in all my clothes and shoes.

I was still in my closet.

With a groan, I rubbed my eyes with my palms, debating whether I wanted to fall back asleep. Maybe I could just sleep for days until all the pain went away.

"Aunt Tay-Tay?" Genevieve's sweet voice came from outside the closet.

I rolled onto my stomach so I could see her. She stood in the doorway in her Frozen pajamas. Her curly hair was an adorable mess, making me smile.

"Good morning, sunshine," I said.

She glared at the ground. "Why are you guys sleeping in the closet?"

Us guys? I followed her gaze, only to see Huntley passed out on the floor, folded at a weird angle, his arm draped over his face.

I scrambled to my feet. My brothers and dad would *kill* Huntley if they found him in here. I smiled as sweetly as I could at Genevieve. "How about we keep this a secret?"

"Why?" Genevieve asked, tilting her head to the side.

How did you bargain with a three-year-old? Why couldn't it have been Fiona? She was old enough to understand. I could have bribed her with something.

I had to leave the Huntley part out. "Mamas and Papas don't like when I sleep in the closet, so I don't want to upset them. Especially with it being so close to Papas' birthday." I stepped over a still-sleeping Huntley and put my hand on Genevieve's shoulder, turning her around. "Can you do that for me?"

She nodded. "Yes, Aunt Tay-Tay." She got on her tiptoes and motioned with her finger for me to bend down, so I did. Her voice came out in a loud whisper. "My mom and dad don't like me sleeping in their bed. Sometimes I sleep on the floor next to the bed so they don't see me." Her eyes went wide. "You won't tell them, will you?"

I shook my head. "Pinky promise."

We locked pinkies, and Genevieve grinned wildly.

I ruffled her mess of curls. "Go get dressed, okay?"

"Okay!" She ran out of my room.

I turned back to the closet. Huntley was still sleeping. How would I wake him up and get him out of my room with no one seeing? I glanced over at the window. That was out of the question. It was a two-story drop.

Maybe if someone saw him leaving my room, I'd just say he was borrowing something. I rolled my eyes. What on earth did I have that Huntley would want to borrow?

Oh, wait! We shared the same love of music. We were just

talking about music, and I wanted to play him some songs that were on my laptop, which I couldn't take out of my room because it was plugged in. I sighed.

Then I saw the time. Six in the morning. Maybe no one else was up.

I rushed over to the closet and shook Huntley, trying to whisper-shout the urgency. "Huntley! Wake up!"

He groaned and used his arm to try to push me away.

"Huntley!" I hissed through clenched teeth. "You need to wake up, buddy."

Buddy? Ugh, what was wrong with me?

Huntley slowly peeled his eyes open, then shot up real fast, his eyes wide. "What time is it?" He looked over at the sunlight pouring through the window.

"Six in the morning." I glanced over my shoulder at the doorway to my room to make sure we were still alone. When I turned back around, Huntley was standing, his hands clasped on top of his head. I stood up as well. "We need to get you out of here with no one seeing."

He nodded. "Ya think?" He whispered some things in Spanish I didn't understand. "I really don't feel like dying today."

Voices sounded outside my room, coming closer down the hall. Who was awake at this hour?

"Well, his car is still here," Ryker said.

I looked wide-eyed at Huntley. They were looking for him.

"Maybe he went for an early morning run," Quinn said.

"He doesn't run," Ryker said at the same time Huntley mouthed, *"I don't run!"*

I choked back a laugh before shoving him into the closet and shutting the door. I scrambled over to my bed and climbed under the covers right as Ryker approached my doorway. Quinn kept on going down the hall.

I sat up, yawned, and stretched my arms over my head, really working the I-just-woke-up look.

Ryker peered into my room. "Have you seen Huntley?"

I rubbed my eye. "In my bed? No, I haven't."

Ryker narrowed his eyes at me. "That's not funny."

I threw out a hand. "You're the one asking a completely stupid question. I just woke up." I slumped against my headboard. "Why are you looking for him anyway?"

"He disappeared last night," Ryker said. "And the top bunk doesn't look like it's been slept in."

"Maybe he went to go see some friends or something," I said. "You can't expect him to stay here every second of the summer."

"His car is outside," Ryker said.

Quinn joined Ryker in the doorway. "He's not up here."

I scoffed. "You guys, he's a big boy. You don't need to babysit him."

"That's what I said." Quinn pointed at Ryker. "But this guy won't shut up about it. Even woke me up to tell me."

"It just isn't like Huntley to disappear like this." Ryker folded his arms. "I just want to make sure he's okay."

"Did you call him?" Quinn asked.

Ryker closed his eyes and shook his head. "No. Idiot." He pulled his phone out from his back pocket.

"Why are you dressed for the day?" I asked.

Ryker moved his thumb across his phone. "It's Disneyland day. Did you forget?"

I had forgotten. I threw my fists in the air. "Disneyland day!"

"Wait," Quinn said. "Why are you dressed?"

I looked down, remembering I was still in yesterday's clothes. Well, crap.

"Did you sleep in your outfit for the day?" Quinn smiled. "I'm excited for Disneyland, too."

I sighed in relief on the inside. Thank goodness Quinn was completely oblivious and didn't realize I wore this outfit yesterday.

Ryker pressed his phone to his ear, placing his other hand in his pocket. "Huntley said he wanted to go with us."

Music played from within my closet, followed by some Spanish expletives, and some thumping.

Quinn's eyebrows shot up as he looked from the closet, to me, and back to the closet.

"You've got to be kidding me." Ryker stormed over and yanked the closet door open.

I scrambled off my bed and ran over, putting myself between Ryker and Huntley. I pressed a hand to Ryker's heaving chest.

"It's not what you think," I said.

His hard eyes were looking past me, trained on Huntley. "What are you doing in my sister's closet?"

"The top bunk is super uncomfortable?" Huntley said.

Why had he formed it in a question?

"And my sister's closet is an upgrade?" Ryker said in a low, harsh tone that made me slink back, bumping into Huntley.

Huntley placed his hand on my arm to steady me, but then dropped it when Ryker's eyes went to his hand on my arm.

Huntley cleared his throat. "I think the most amazing thing here is that my phone still has life in it. I thought it would be dead by now. The battery in this baby is amazing."

Quinn, who had stood there in complete confused silence, finally shook out of his trance. "What. In. The. He—"

"Listen." I held my palms up, one directed at each brother like I'd actually be able to stop both of them from attacking. "Huntley heard me screaming yesterday and came to check on me, finding me in the closet. I broke down like a blubbering idiot, and Huntley very kindly and *innocently* stayed with me while I cried it out. Then we fell asleep. That's it. Nothing happened between us, okay?"

Quinn and Ryker's angry eyes flashed between Huntley and me. Time ticked by, and I started thinking about my funeral. Maybe Daphne could sew me a leather jumpsuit to wear in the casket.

I glanced down at my buzzing watch to see that Daphne had texted. Whoa. Had she read my thoughts. And why was she up this early? I pulled my phone out of my pocket, happy that it still had life in it.

Daphne: *I know life has sucked lately, but it's Disneyland day, Tay! Have fun with your fam! Make memories!*

Aww, she'd woken up just to tell me that.

"Tay?" Quinn asked.

I held up a finger, keeping my eyes on my phone. "Shh! This is important."

Me, to Daphne: *I'm probably going to die in the next few minutes. Can you make me a red leather jumpsuit to wear in the casket? I know you love Mickey ears, but I'm thinking cat ears. Bright and sparkly. Oh, maybe add lights to them!*

I was going to look so good in death.

"What are you doing?" Quinn asked.

I opened my mouth to tell him, but then realized he was looking at Huntley. I turned around to find Huntley removing a belt from one of my rompers.

"Creating a noose." He folded the belt in half. "I think this is too small, though. This would be a lot easier if you weren't so skinny, Tay." He sifted through one of my shelves. "Do you have a scarf or something?"

A smile bloomed on my face. One, he'd totally gone to the same dark place I had. Two, he'd called me Tay. Totally casual like we'd reached that level of friendship.

"What's going on in here?" Dad's voice sounded outside the closet, and my smile wilted and died, just like I was going to soon.

"Not sure," Quinn said. "I'm trying to decide if I want to give Taylor the benefit of the doubt."

Dad appeared behind Quinn and Ryker, his eyebrows knitting together in confusion at Huntley and me in the closet.

"If you need to borrow some clothes," Dad said, "you might want to start with one of the boys. They'll probably have something that will actually fit you."

Huntley took one of my red dresses from the rack and held it up to himself. "I don't know. I think I could squeeze into this."

I coughed, trying to cover up my laugh.

Dad smiled. "It would be a good color on you."

Ryker turned around, an incredulous look on his face. "You find a guy in your daughter's closet, and *this* is how you react?"

Dad folded his arms, lifting his chin a little. "Is there a reason why I should be worried?"

"No!" I said. "Let's just everyone calm down."

Dad shrugged. "I'm not upset." He arched an eyebrow. "Should I be?"

"No!" I sighed. "Maybe we should all get ready for the day. I mean, it's Disneyland day!"

"Yay!" Huntley twirled my prom sash in the air, his tone dripping in sarcasm.

"He was in her closet all night!" Ryker yelled, making me cringe.

Why wouldn't he just drop it?

Because he was Ryker. That was why.

Dad lowered his arms. "Is the top bunk really that bad?"

"Dad!" Ryker said. "She was in there, too!"

Dad rolled his eyes. "I know my daughter, Ryker. Just like I know my sons. Taylor wouldn't hook up with a guy she's known for a month, let alone in her closet with practically her entire family under the same roof." He clapped a hand on

Ryker's shoulder. "Just like I know you'd blow everything out of proportion." He looked at me. "Did anything happen between you and Huntley?"

I shook my head. "Aside from me crying and him being so kind as to keep me company while I did? No."

"Well, there you have it." Dad clapped his hands. "Oh, and Tay, The Hideout is finished, so you can stay there tonight instead of the closet." He walked out of the room.

Huntley leaned toward me. "I like your dad."

"He's the only sensible male in this house," I muttered.

Quinn shook his head. "I swear you can get away with anything, Taylor." He left the room as well.

Ryker pointed at Huntley and me. "I've got my eye on you two."

I pushed past him, clapping his arm. "I know, bro. I know."

My phone rang with incoming messages, all of them making me smile.

Daphne: *On it.*

Daphne: *While we're on the topic, how do you want us to style your hair? Two buns on top?*

Daphne: *Should I make matching jumpsuits for Veronica and me as well? That way we can show our solidarity.*

Daphne: *Also, I'm making the playlist for your funeral. It's going to be freaking awesome.*

Daphne: *Wait, why are you going to die?*

"Are you going to stay in there all day?" Ryker asked Huntley.

Huntley wrapped my sash around his neck. "I'm still debating whether I should kill myself before you do."

"Can you do it somewhere else besides my closet?" I asked. "I really don't want that visual haunting me every time I walk into my closet."

Huntley slipped his arm through the sash, adjusting it

around his body so "Prom Queen" was visible. "Fine. But I'm keeping the sash until I know I'm safe."

He sauntered out of the room, and I found myself repeating, *Old guy. Criminal. No boys. Old guy. Criminal. No boys.*

But, my goodness, he was attractive.

CHAPTER THIRTY-ONE

Daphne made Mickey ears for everyone in my family. She'd even finished Huntley's, with the ears in the shape of a guitar. Mine were black leather with rhinestones bordering the edges.

As we loaded into *the shuttle*, Mom took the driver's seat and Dad shotgun. Emory, Fiona, and Genevieve took the first bench, followed by Neo, Samson, and Porter.

Quinn and Aria were taking their own car, since Aria wasn't sure how long her very pregnant self would last at Disneyland.

That left Ryker, Huntley, and me.

I climbed in, going to the far back and stuffing myself into the corner. Huntley took the middle seat until Ryker came and squeezed himself between Huntley and me, forcing Huntley to scoot over.

I glared at Ryker. "Seriously?"

Using two fingers, he pointed at his eyes, and then turned his fingers to me. Always watching. With his lizard print Mickey ears, his attempt to be serious was quite comical.

We were meeting my brother Ollie and his family there. They were coming straight from the airport. It was their middle child's seventh birthday, and he wanted to spend it at Disneyland.

Ollie was the second-oldest child. He and his wife, Charlie, had been married for eleven years, yet still acted like newly-weds, which was the style of marriage I wanted. One day.

The nice thing about my family being so tall was you could spot them easily in a crowd. Plus, when you put your four-year-old daughter on your shoulders, and that daughter is wearing a Belle costume, you could be spotted from a mile away.

My niece, Brighton, waved furiously from atop Ollie's shoulders when she saw us. Then she climbed down her dad, jumping the rest of the way when she was hanging from his shoulders, not caring that she was in a dress. She barreled into my dad, who picked her up and hugged her tight.

"Papa!" Brighton giggled when my dad tickled her sides.

As Ollie hugged Mom, I went to his wife, Charlie, wrapping her up in a tight hug. Well, as much as I could with her being six months pregnant. Though, with her being tall as well, her bulge wasn't too big. I dropped my arms and set my hands on her belly. "How are you two doing?"

Charlie smiled. "The baby is doing great. Me? Every single inch of my body has swollen. Way worse than the other three kids."

My two nephews flew out from around their mom, throwing their arms around me in a hug attack. Pierson, the eight-year-old, had grown so much since I last saw him. Nixon, the birthday boy, wasn't far behind.

"What happened?" I asked, hugging them back. "You guys shot up!"

Pierson smirked. "I'm just getting started."

I looked over at Ollie, the tallest of my siblings at six-nine. "I have no doubt."

Ollie leaned down, wrapping me up in a teddy-bear hug,

reminding me how much I missed him. He kissed the top of my head. "Hey, runt." Okay, maybe I didn't miss him *that* much.

Though I was taller than all my friends, I was the runt in our family.

"Aunt Tay-Tay?" I looked down and saw Brighton staring up at me with sparkling, hopeful eyes. "Mommy said you have my ears."

I twisted around my shoulder bag so I could open it. "I do." I reached in and grabbed the yellow silk Mickey ears that matched her Belle costume. She squealed as I put them on, then put on a fierce gaze with her hand on her hip.

"How do I look?" she asked, all business.

"Smokin'," I said.

She touched her finger to her tongue and then put her finger on hip, making a sizzling sound.

Ollie shook his head. "Look what you've done to my daughter. I always wonder why she has so much sass, and then I remember she's related to you."

"You say it like it's a bad thing," I said.

"It is," Neo, Ollie, and Porter said at the same time.

I rolled my eyes. "Welcome home, brothers. So glad to have you here."

I handed out the rest of the ears, and our large group made our way into Disneyland. We stopped in front of the Mickey Mouse on the grass in front of the train station, taking the obligatory Disneyland picture.

Everyone handed Huntley their phones so he could take the pictures. He started stuffing them in all his pockets since there were so many.

Huntley took Aria's bedazzled phone into his full hands. "Can't you just share the photo?"

Aria just arched an eyebrow at him and then joined the rest of us for the pictures.

Letting out a long, loud breath, Huntley cycled through all

the phones, taking a million pictures before handing all the phones back.

Brighton slipped her little hand into mine, smiling up at me. "I love Disneyland!"

"Me, too!" I gently squeezed her hand.

Brighton looked to my other side where Huntley had fallen into line. "Who's that?"

"This is Huntley," I said. "Ryker's friend."

"Ryker has a friend?" Brighton asked, her nose and eyebrows scrunched in confusion. "I thought he just had pets."

I pressed my hand to my mouth, covering up my laugh.

Huntley grinned at her. "Technically, I'm just a roommate. I'm probably better friends with Samson and Taylor at this point."

Brighton nodded, her face relaxing. "Okay." She skipped along as we walked. "Huntley?"

"Yeah?" he asked.

"Are you in our family now?" she asked.

He stuffed his hands in his pockets. "Nope. Just a friend."

"Mommy says friends can be family, too." Brighton sniffed. "What's that smell?"

I leaned down and placed her on my hip, even though she was getting way too big to be held. "That is the smell of magic." I inhaled, breathing in the wonderful, sweet scent Main Street had to offer.

"It is a good smell, isn't it?" Huntley said.

I nodded. "It's perfection. As soon as I smell it, I instantly relax. It's like a home away from home."

"Can we live here?" Brighton asked, her eyes full of hope.

"I wish, kiddo," I said.

Brighton held her arm out to Huntley. "Can I sit on your shoulders?"

"Uh." He looked between me and my family, not sure what to say. "Shouldn't your dad do that?"

"He's too tall," Brighton said. "Like a giant. You're a nice size."

"Uh, thanks?" He looked over at Ollie and Charlie, who were near us and watching the interaction with amused smiles. Charlie nodded.

Huntley stopped walking and crouched down. "Hop on."

I helped Brighton onto Huntley's shoulders, and then helped him stand back up, fixing Brighton's dress so it wasn't draped over his head.

"Regretting coming?" I asked in a low voice.

Huntley smiled, those gorgeous gold flecks in his eyes lighting up. "Not at all."

My stomach flipped, and I found myself repeating my new mantra. *Old guy. Criminal. No boys.*

Then I stupidly glanced over at him, noticing how nicely he fit into my family, and a small whimper escaped my throat.

I was so screwed.

CHAPTER THIRTY-TWO

*P*art of me wondered if Aria or my mom had said something to Charlie and Emory about me. All day, the four of them kept maneuvering, keeping Ryker and the rest of my brothers away from me and making it so Huntley sat next to me on rides.

It started on all the kid rides, then progressed when some had to sit out from the roller coasters with the younger kids—or those who were pregnant. In line for Space Mountain, Mom kept Ryker busy talking about geckos, dragons, and iguanas, things I knew she cared nothing about. She kept him at the front of the pack, then shared a wink with my dad, who involved my other brothers and nephews in a lively conversation about basketball, leaving Huntley and me at the rear.

If they knew about his past, would they still be doing this? Or would they shut down the fantasy before it could get anywhere near a reality? Unless they were thinking it was a nice distraction from Zander. A little harmless flirting never hurt.

"Your family is awesome," Huntley said as we slowly made

our way through the maze of a line. There was something ridiculously hot about him with his guitar-Mickey ears.

I gently bumped him with my arm. "That's funny, because I have to remind myself of that every single day."

Huntley stuffed his hands in his pockets, something he'd been doing more frequently. I mean, not that I had been keeping that close of an eye on him or anything.

"Be grateful they're all here and alive," Huntley said.

I sighed. "I know, and I am. It's just that sometimes it's *so* annoying basically having seven dads." I chuckled. "Honestly, my dad is less of a dad than my brothers. He seems to at least understand me."

We paused in line, and I jutted my hip to the side, noticing I'd bumped it into Huntley's leg. I didn't move, and neither did he, which meant absolutely nothing.

"They care about you," Huntley said, his voice unbelievably near.

I turned to him, our faces pretty dang close. Neither of us moved.

"I know." I cursed myself for sounding so breathless when I said it.

Old guy. Criminal. No boys.

I took a shaky breath. "How are the songs coming along?"

He removed one hand from his pocket, grabbed a stray hair of mine that was hanging out on the back of my shoulder, and let it fall to the ground.

Old guy. Criminal. No boys.

"Pretty good," he said, his eyes on mine. Wait, they went to my lips. No. Back to my eyes. Lips. Eyes. Lips.

Old guy. Criminal. No boys.

His hand landed on the small of my back, and my breath caught in my throat. Then I realized he was motioning me forward because the line had moved, which of course was the only reason why it was there.

Except, he didn't remove his hand when we stopped.

Which meant absolutely nothing.

At all.

"Would you mind if I played them for you some time?" he asked. "Including singing? I'd like your feedback."

I kept my eyes trained forward on my dad and brothers, trying to keep my thoughts from drifting. "Yeah, of course. I'd love to hear them."

Old guy. Criminal. No boys.

"I've never actually played the songs for anyone," Huntley said. "My mom has caught me a few times, but I always stopped."

"Why?" I watched Nixon and Pierson animatedly use their hands to tell my dad and brothers a story.

Huntley paused a moment. I wanted to turn to him, but held still, like if I moved, he wouldn't answer me.

"I guess I never thought she deserved to hear them," he whispered, so low I almost didn't hear it around all the laughter and chatter from the other Disneyland guests.

I finally gave in and looked at him, something unrecognizable squeezing my heart and throat. We locked eyes, and I couldn't help myself. I threw my arms around his neck, hugging him close.

I had no idea what it felt like to have such a closed-off relationship with my mom. Or have a dad that couldn't be around because he'd passed on.

I turned my head, my cheek pressing against Huntley's as I took in my dad, standing there laughing with my brothers and his grandsons. Then I sought out my mom, watching her pretend to be interested in whatever reptile Ryker was currently talking about.

I was so blessed to have them all here. But as Brighton had said, friends can be family.

I pulled back, only to find Huntley staring at me with such

intensity that the words that were about to come out got lodged in my throat.

A lady behind us in line started shouting at us in Spanish. I tore my gaze from Huntley to look at her, only to see her waving her hand frantically.

Huntley said something politely to her in Spanish, calming her, then took my hand and moved us forward in line.

"What was that all about?" I tried desperately to not think about his warm hand in mine. He was guiding me forward, that was it. And holding on just in case he needed to do it again.

Huntley smirked. "She said we either needed to get a room or move forward. The park isn't open all night long."

My cheeks flared as a laugh bubbled up. I pressed a hand to my mouth, my gaze seeking out Huntley's laughing eyes.

This was so wrong. He was old. He was a criminal. I was freshly out of a relationship.

Then why did I wonder what it would be like to kiss him? Why did every time Zander floated through my mind, Huntley would be there too, telling me that Zander wasn't worth my time?

I needed to talk with Daphne and Veronica. Maybe they could help me sort through this mess.

Dropping Huntley's hand—which totally did *nothing* to my heart—I pulled out my phone and texted my friends.

Me: *I have a major problem.*

I bit my lip, tapping my foot impatiently as I waited for a response.

"Is everything okay?" Huntley asked.

I way over-the-top laughed. I was such an idiot. "Everything's just peachy. Coming up roses." I was starting to sound like Daphne.

Daphne!

She'd responded. *We know.*

I rolled my eyes. *You have no idea what I'm talking about.*

Veronica: *Yes, we do, and his name is Huntley.*

They knew me way too well.

"Are you sure?" Huntley asked.

"Yeah, yeah, yeah."

"Mind if I cut in?"

Daphne?

I spun around to find her—totally adorable Funshine Bear ears—and Veronica—wait, were her ears Post Malone's face?—standing there, sporting their all-too-knowing smirks. Weston was next to Daphne, wearing his Captain America Mickey ears.

I don't know what came over me, but I threw my arms awkwardly around Veronica and Daphne, the ropes from the line smooshed between us.

"I'm so screwed," I whispered in their ears.

Daphne, Weston, and Veronica ducked under the rope, and once again, Huntley had to calmly talk to the lady behind us about cutting in line, and once again, whatever he said worked.

"What are you doing here?" I whispered, pulling Daphne and Veronica close to me.

"Thought we'd surprise you." Veronica had her hair in a loose French braid, so much better than her tight ponytail.

"And I'd say it's a good thing we did," Daphne wiggled her eyebrows and sought out Huntley.

I pinched her arm, making her turn back to me.

"Your mom said she needed backup since the pregnant trio were running out of juice," Veronica said.

"Plus, Cody can get us into the park for free," Daphne said with a roll of her eyes. "I officially hate him for making it diffi-cult to hate him."

"Ladies?" Weston motioned in front of us. The line had moved.

We shuffled forward, finally getting in the tunnel that would take us to the ride.

Huntley furrowed his eyebrows, taking in Veronica's Mickey

ears. Or Post Malone ears, I guess. They were cut-outs of his tattooed-covered face.

"Is that Post Malone?" Huntley asked.

Veronica nodded with a sigh. "Yeah."

"I may have taken that pair a little too far," Daphne said, adjusting them on Veronica's head.

"Ya think?" I asked. It was hilarious, though.

Veronica threw her arm around me and set her mouth right next to my ear. "Don't hate us, but seriously, Taylor, let Huntley help you move past Zander. For anyone else, this would be a *terrible* idea."

"*Catastrophic,*" Daphne whispered. She used her hands to mime something blowing up.

"But you need the realization that there are other guys out there besides Zander," Veronica went on. "A little harmless flirting with a college guy is no big deal. It's like every girl's dream."

Daphne leaned close. "And if you get a make-out sess, *bonus!*" She sang the last word. "How many high school girls can say they made out with a college dude?"

"There's actually probably a surprising number." Veronica pulled back from me to look at Daphne.

Daphne nodded. "Yeah, you're probably right." She motioned between the three of us. "But in this circle, you could take the cake."

They both quickly kissed my cheeks and then smooshed in front of me, making me stand back with Huntley.

"I'm kind of really confused right now," Huntley said, looking at my friends.

I blew out a loud breath. "You and me both."

CHAPTER THIRTY-THREE

After Space Mountain, Mom suggested everyone split up for a bit, which resulted in Daphne, Weston, Veronica, Samson, Huntley, and I being in our own little group.

We headed over to Big Thunder Mountain Railroad, Daphne's and my favorite ride at Disneyland.

As we waited in line, Daphne started dancing, really moving along to whatever beat was playing in her head.

"Whatcha listening to?" Veronica asked.

Daphne opened her mouth, but Weston held up a hand to stop her.

"Let me guess." Weston turned to Daphne and started singing "What A Man Gotta Do" by the Jonas Brothers, totally nailing Nick Jonas' voice.

"Okay, that's impressive," Huntley said, leaning toward me.

At the chorus, Samson and Daphne joined in, singing along with Weston as they danced. Daphne shimmied over to Veronica and me like she was on the set of Grease, getting us to dance, too.

It was a rare treat to have Daphne so outgoing in a public

place, and I needed to make sure she didn't stop and notice the people watching us.

Then I thought about Huntley, wondering what he was thinking of these high school kids singing and dancing to The Jonas Brothers in a line at Disneyland.

I turned to him, just as he came toward me singing, *"What a man gotta do?"* and, oh my, did he have a sexy voice.

Of course he did. Because the universe liked to torture me.

When the song ended, I sucked in a breath, hoping no one around us would do anything to alert Daphne they had been watching. Thank goodness, they'd all gone back to their phones.

Daphne smiled at Huntley. "What do you listen to, Huntley?"

"Mostly classic rock," he said.

Her eyes turned to me. "Hey, just like Tay-Tay." She motioned to his guitar ears. "You'll have to play for us sometime."

Samson leaned against the rail and folded his arms, his smirking eyes on me. "We could do a little campfire around our fire pit in the backyard. Roast some s'mores, and Huntley can serenade us."

My cheeks heated as I remembered how I'd embarrassed myself in front of my family.

"Yum," Daphne said. "S'mores. I'm in."

Weston wrapped his arm around Daphne's waist and pulled her close. "You know what I need s'more of?" He kissed her cheek, making her giggle.

Samson stared at them, though I knew he was speaking to Veronica and me. "You weren't kidding. It *is* adorably sickening."

"Right?" Veronica leaned on the rail next to Samson and sighed. "Yet, I totally want that. Is that weird?"

"No," I said. "Who doesn't want an ooey-gooey relationship?"

"I'm still thinking about s'mores," Samson said. He chuckled when Veronica pushed his arm. He motioned to her. "DeShawn doesn't make you all ooey-gooey?"

Veronica's eyes went to the ground. "Not like he used to. Things have definitely shifted."

"Eh, you're too hot for him anyway," Samson said before moving up the stairs toward the start of the ride.

I watched Veronica as she stared at him in shock. Samson had said it in such a nonchalant way, just stating a fact. He was one to call it as he sees it. But she looked almost embarrassed, like she couldn't believe someone thought she was hot.

I suddenly had the overwhelming need to punch DeShawn in the face. What had he been telling her?

"Bow-chicka-wow-wow," Daphne said into Veronica's ear, making Veronica laugh. "He's right, V. You're totally too good for DeShawn. Let him go back to Loserville where he belongs."

We hustled up the stairs, where Daphne proceeded to ask the park worker if we could sit in the back, and then Veronica purposely got in line to share a seat with Samson, leaving me to sit with Huntley.

"*Hang on to your hats and glasses,*" Daphne said from the back row. "*'Cuz this here's the wildest ride in the wilderness.*"

I expected Huntley to put both his hands on the safety bar in front of us, but instead, he only put one on and then put his arm on the bench behind me like we were a couple or something.

Were Daphne and Veronica right? Did I just need to let loose and have a little flirty fun with Huntley? Yeah, he was an old guy, and I'd sworn off boys, but this was Disneyland. The happiest place on earth, and I had a totally hot guy next to me.

As the ride took off, I slid over, pressing the side of my body against Huntley's.

Which I also did when we got on Pirates of the Caribbean when we climbed in the back of the boat. Weston, Daphne, Veronica, and Samson were in the row ahead of us.

"This is one of my favorite rides," Huntley said, his voice so close to my ear.

"Oh yeah?" I tried to keep my voice steady but did a terrible job.

"After walking around the park, standing in lines," Huntley said, "it's nice to be able to sit in the cool air below for a bit."

I had my hands in my lap, so I shifted a little in my seat so my arm could rest on Huntley's leg. He didn't move or push me away. Instead, his arm that had been lazily behind me scooted forward, his hand cupping my shoulder.

I swear his nose brushed my ear, but maybe I imagined it. My heart beat so loudly, I worried he could hear it, which was ridiculous. Of course he couldn't.

I tried to keep my focus forward. Daphne and Weston kept stealing kisses, while Veronica and Samson were talking and laughing.

I had no idea what to do in this situation. I'd been pretty aggressive with Zander when we first started dating. I left no doubt in his mind that I was attracted to him and wanted to be with him. I was a shameless flirt. Well, plus, I loved seeing how mad it made Samson and Neo, since they were both living at home at the time. Also, Ryker and Quinn, who came home to visit a lot.

But this was a college guy next to me. I had to be amateur hour for him. I didn't want to do something totally stupid. I also didn't want to kick my flirting into high gear like I did with Zander. I hadn't worried about him wanting more than kissing because we were both young and carefree.

Huntley, though, was probably used to dating college girls who were probably willing to do *a lot* more than kissing, which I so wasn't ready for. I didn't want to give him the wrong impression and have him try to sneak into my bedroom tonight.

Though, this was Huntley. I didn't think he'd do that. He didn't strike me as the kind who just fooled around for the fun of it.

Okay, his nose *totally* brushed against my ear. Was that some sort of signal? Was I supposed to turn my head so he could kiss me? Did I want Huntley to kiss me on the Pirates of the Caribbean with my brother sitting right in front of us?

Okay, on Pirates of the Caribbean, yes. But with the brother there? No freaking way. I wouldn't hear the end of it.

But maybe Samson wouldn't notice. He was watching all the drunk pirates sing songs and whistle at that dog.

The dog. The ride was almost over.

What did I do? I wanted to reach forward and ask Daphne and Veronica. I'd never felt so out of my element before.

I was Taylor freaking Thomas. Grade A flirt. Total pro. I could take home the gold for America.

The boat jerked, bringing me back into the moment. We were headed up to the exit. Way too bouncy for kissing. Plus, Samson had turned around, asking what ride we should go on next.

As soon as we got off the boat, I took Daphne and Veronica by the hands, yelled at the guys that we needed to use the bathroom, and hightailed it out of there and into the bathroom in New Orleans Square.

"Did you kiss?" Daphne asked, her hands clasped together almost in a plea.

"No," I said.

Daphne frowned. "Well, that sucks."

I moved out of the way of some ladies leaving the bathroom and yanked my friends close. "I think he wanted too. His nose brushed my ear and—"

"So wanted to kiss you!" Veronica shook my arm. "Why didn't you let him?"

I threw up my hands. "I got nervous! He's like this sophisticated college guy, and I'm this pathetic high schooler."

"First of all," Daphne said, holding up a finger. "You are *not* pathetic. You're Taylor freaking Thomas."

That was what I said.

"And second," Veronica said, lifting another one of Daphne's fingers for her, "he *wants* to kiss you. He doesn't care that you're in high school."

Daphne tilted her head to the side. "Wait, does this make him a perv?"

Veronica whacked her upside the head. "Remind me of the age gap between your mom and Cody?"

Daphne rubbed the back of her head. "Gross, V."

"Well, I think Taylor and Huntley are closer in age than your mom and Cody." Veronica looked at me. "How old is Huntley, anyway?"

I shrugged. "I haven't asked. But he's roommates with Ryker."

"And Ryker's twenty-one." Daphne rubbed her chin. "I still say go for it. He's hot. He's into you. He's just here for the summer, and then he'll be back to his old adult life. Maybe he wants to relive his youth, and you're robbing him of that chance."

I laughed as I slapped her repeatedly on the arm. "Not helping, Daph!"

Veronica took my hand in hers. "Here's what we're going to do. We're going to actually use the bathroom, because I seriously need to pee. And then, we're going on the Haunted Mansion."

"Oh, yeah." Daphne did a little dance. "Bow-chicka-wow-wow."

"Will you stop saying that?" Veronica asked.

Daphne mocked looking horribly offended. "No, I will not." She turned to get in the line to use the bathroom. *"Pour some sugar on me."*

"In the name of love," I finished.

Maybe that was the medicine I needed to get over Zander.

Some sugar.

CHAPTER THIRTY-FOUR

The boys were waiting outside of the bathroom, munching on powdered sugar-covered beignets. Huntley offered me one when I approached his side.

I pulled one out of the bag and bit down. Now that was some ooey-gooey goodness.

"I say Haunted Mansion," Daphne said. "It's right there."

Weston wiggled his eyebrows at her. "I second that."

They went back and forth, having a wiggling-eyebrow contest.

"Just don't say it," Veronica mumbled as she moved toward the ride.

"Bow-chicka-wow-wow," Weston said.

Daphne held up her hand. "That was Weston, not me."

Samson and Huntley chuckled.

We got in line, Daphne and Weston being all adorably snuggly. I watched Samson talk to Veronica, loving how she was being her normal, carefree self, not overly worried about her appearance or anything. Maybe it was just because he was like a brother to her, but she was eating beignets in front of him and not caring if powdered sugar got everywhere, or that she was actually eating.

Huntley motioned to Veronica and Samson. "Is something going on between them?"

I pulled back in surprise. "What? No. I mean, they're friends. Veronica and I have been friends since elementary school, and since Samson's just two years older, he was in school with us and sometimes hung out with us when he was still in high school."

Huntley stuffed his hands into his pockets. "They're just so casual with each other that I couldn't tell if it was because they've been friends for so long or because maybe they liked each other."

I watched them, really watched them, trying to read their mannerisms. "I mean, they don't seem be flirting. There's no touching or swoony eyes."

"Swoony eyes?" Huntley said, making me turn and stare into his gorgeous eyes.

"You know." I batted my eyelashes at him. "Flirting with the eyes."

He turned his body toward me. "How does one flirt with the eyes?"

I placed a hand on his chest and moved close, really gazing into his eyes, cranking up the smolder I used to use on Zander. Ugh. Why did I keep thinking about him? No Zander. He was out of my life. I didn't need to compare everyone and everything to him.

Huntley's hand landed on my hip, making my breath hitch, and all thoughts of what's-his-name fade away.

"Okay, I get it now," he said with his own smolder in his eyes. Those golden flecks called to me, inviting me to come closer.

He suddenly turned away and moved forward in line. I let out a shaky breath and then caught up to him.

Maybe he was just playing with me. Maybe it was a game to him, trying to get his roommate's little sister to obsess over him.

Not that I was obsessing. I was observing, which was totally different.

I leaned on the railing, staring up at the mansion. I'd loved this ride since I was a little girl. I practically had everything memorized, from everything they said in the elevator to the songs they sang during the ride.

Huntley pressed up against my side, his hand landing on the small of my back. His thumb and index finger began moving up and down, almost like he was playing a guitar.

I smiled up at him. "Are you using my back as your guitar?"

"I gotta practice." He started humming a song I didn't recognize.

I stood tall and turned toward him so I could hear the song better. His strumming switched to my hip.

"Is that one of your songs?" I asked. It had this edgy-soulful vibe that I really enjoyed.

"Yes," he said. "A new one I'm working on."

Being bold, I set my hand on top of his on the railing. "Will you sing it to me?"

He leaned toward me, his humming intensifying, but no words left his beautiful mouth. He finally smirked. "Not until it's ready."

"Rude." I playfully slapped his chest.

We made our way inside the mansion and into the elevator. I normally loved to talk along with the ghost, knowing every word he said, but all my focus was now on Huntley. We were smashed together in the crowd, but more so than we really needed to be. I had one hand trailing up and down his arm, my other hand on his hip. He wrapped an arm around me and placed his forehead against mine, and everything around me just froze.

I had no idea what was buzzing through my body. It was like every skin cell was alive. No one had ever caused me to feel this way. Ever. It was this whole other level that I hadn't been aware was available until this very moment.

Was this what Daphne had talked about with Weston? That total loss of focus, yet total sharp awareness that this was your person?

I sucked in a sharp breath. Why had that even crossed my mind? I'd known Huntley for like a month. That was hardly much time to get to know a person.

But we'd shared a lot of personal things with each other. It was easy with Huntley. There was never any judgment on his end, just complete support and understanding.

The elevator doors opened, and everyone shuffled out. Huntley slipped his hand over mine, threading our fingers together. I kept my other hand on his arm, and we slowly walked down the hall, not paying the slightest attention to my surroundings.

We slipped into a doom buggy and cuddled up, and he smelled *so* good. It was a musky, woodsy scent that made me move closer.

The ride continued, songs being sung by all the ghosts and ghouls, but my eyes were only on Huntley.

His hand caressed my cheek, sending a shiver through me.

He slowly leaned toward me, his eyes asking if it was okay. I wanted to shout, "yes!" but I settled with screaming it from my eyes.

He closed the distance, his full lips just a breath away from mine when the ride came to a stop.

It was normal for the ride to stop every now and then if they were letting someone on or off who was using a wheelchair or needed special assistance.

But an announcer came on as I heard the chatter around me pick up.

"Will everyone please remain inside their doom buggy." The announcer sounded completely annoyed. "All guests are to remain inside their doom buggy."

I looked around, totally confused.

Suddenly Ryker appeared in front of our doom buggy. He climbed over the safety bar, shoving his way between Huntley and me. There was hardly any room to begin with, and Ryker wasn't a small guy. He jammed his lanky self between us, kicking me in the knee and elbowing me in the face.

He settled in, his eyes straight ahead. "Always watching."

Oh. My. Gosh.

I was going to *kill* my brother.

CHAPTER THIRTY-FIVE

Security guards were waiting on the moving conveyor belt when the ride ended. They immediately flanked Ryker and escorted him outside.

When the rest of us caught up with them, they were having a heated discussion.

"You don't understand," Ryker was saying, holding his hand in front of him like he always did, like it added more weight to his words. "My teenage sister was being reckless. It was necessary for me to intervene."

One of the security guards matched Ryker's stance. "The only one being reckless, son, was you." The guard's intense eyes made me so glad I wasn't Ryker.

"It is a danger to you and all the guests to have you walking around a ride while it's operating," the other security guard said. She wasn't as much mad as she was annoyed. It almost looked like she wanted to take Ryker by the ear and drag him out of the park.

Honestly, I'd help her.

"You expect me to sit around and do nothing when a guy is trying to take advantage of my sister?" Ryker asked.

"Whoa." Huntley took a step forward. "I was *not* taking advantage of her. I would never do that."

Ryker pointed at Huntley. "Stay out of this."

There was a pause, and then Huntley turned to me. "For a second, I thought he was going to call me 'pretty boy' and then I'd have to punch him in the face."

I thought back to when Zander had called him that and choked back a laugh.

Ryker jerked his head back. "Why would I call you 'pretty boy'?"

"Well, he is pretty," Daphne said, holding Weston's hand.

Weston nodded. "I concur."

Ryker turned his attention back to Huntley. "Leave my sister alone, man. She doesn't know you like I do."

The female security guard sighed. "I see that you aren't going to cooperate, and your behavior will likely continue, so we're going to kindly ask that you leave the park."

Daphne gasped. "You're kicking us out of the most magical place on the earth?"

The guard turned to her. "No. Just him." She pointed at Ryker.

Daphne put a hand to her chest and let out a loud breath. "Oh, thank goodness." She pressed a shaky hand to her forehead. "I thought we were going to have a panic attack on our hands there for a second." She blew a raspberry with her lips. "Crisis averted."

"You're kicking me out?" Ryker asked.

"Yes," the lady said, "and if you continue to argue with me, I'll make it a permanent arrangement."

Daphne did the cutthroat motion at Ryker. "Abandon ship, Ryker. You do *not* want to be banned from Disneyland. That would be a horribly depressing life." She turned to Weston. "Can you even imagine?"

Weston shook his head. "I don't want to."

The male guard motioned with his arm for Ryker to walk. "Let's go, sir."

Ryker opened his mouth, but I stepped forward, keeping my voice low. "Let it go, Ryker. This isn't worth it. Don't do this to Mom and Dad. You can yell at me later."

His nostrils flared. "You promise?"

"Cross my heart," I said.

He glared at Huntley and then started walking, the guards at his sides.

I turned to Huntley. "I am *so* sorry."

Huntley stared at me, pressing a hand to his mouth like he wasn't sure what to do with himself.

"Your brother is officially crazy." Veronica watched the guards and Ryker disappear into the crowd.

Samson folded his arms, glaring between Huntley and me. "What were you two doing?" He briefly closed his eyes and twerked his head to the side. "Maybe I don't want to know."

I pushed his shoulder. "Relax, okay? It was nothing."

Daphne did a little dance behind Samson while mouthing, *bow-chicka-wow-wow*, making Veronica, Huntley, and I laugh.

Samson spun around, and Daphne stopped.

She nodded her chin at him. "'Sup?"

"Most bizarre experience. Ever." Huntley clasped his hands on top of his head.

My phone rang, so I pulled it out of my pocket and saw my mom calling. I reluctantly answered, thinking she knew what had happened, but how could she have heard this quickly?

"Hey, Mom," I said.

"Want to meet us on Main Street?" she asked. "We're going to get some ice cream."

I let out a sigh of relief. "Ice cream sounds perfect." I hung up, tucking my phone back in my pocket.

"They don't sell Dr Pepper here, do they?" Huntley asked.

"Unfortunately, no," I said. "It's their one downfall."

"But they got Coke." Daphne patted her bag and winked dramatically. "And I've got the stuff to make it even better."

"You brought liquor with you?" Huntley asked.

Daphne huffed and rolled her eyes. "Cherry flavoring, Huntley. Get with the program."

She, Weston, Veronica, and Samson turned toward Main Street and worked their way through the crowd.

I turned to Huntley, placing a hand on his chest. "I really am sorry. I didn't think Ryker had it in him to go this far."

He placed his hand over mine. "Don't worry about it."

I licked my lips, wondering if I should ask the next question or not. I mean, I already knew some of the answer, but I was curious to hear it from Huntley. "Is there a reason why Ryker is so adamantly against anything happening between you and me, aside from just being an overprotective brother?"

Huntley lowered his hand and stuffed it in his pocket, taking a step back, his eyes becoming distant. "Nope." He took off, catching up with the others.

I wanted to give Huntley the benefit of the doubt. We'd all made mistakes, and we all deserved second chances. But I couldn't shake the doubts that crept into my head. Ryker's over-the-top anger. Huntley's stepfather saying something about "college not fixing him." Huntley knowing how to jimmy a car lock.

Maybe his crimes were a lot bigger than I'd imagined.

I closed my eyes, cursing myself. This was my problem with guys. I was reckless and stupid, jumping first and thinking later, just like Neo had said.

When I caught up to everyone, I took Daphne and Veronica by the hands and pulled them close to me.

"The Hideout," I said. "Tonight."

Daphne wrapped her arm around me. "I love when you say those words to me."

It was something we always did as kids before Daphne had moved to Utah. Whenever one of us was having a problem, we would meet up in the treehouse in my backyard, seal ourselves off from the world, and delve into a solution.

And, boy, did I have a problem that needed solving.

CHAPTER THIRTY-SIX

I climbed the new wooden ladder leading up to The Hideout. When I got inside, I let out a small gasp. Dad had gone all out.

There were new red leather curtains hanging from the windows. He'd bordered the ceiling with white twinkle lights, and black shag carpet lined the floor. He'd created a makeshift bed in the corner, with a thick pad and bright red comforter and pillows.

Daphne crawled in and went straight for the hammock chair hanging from the ceiling, making herself comfortable, like my dad had installed that just for her. Veronica plopped down on the black leather bean bag chair, looking around the room in awe.

"I think I might move in." Veronica took off her shoes and ran her toes through the carpet.

I sat down on the bed. "Same."

Daphne pulled her phone out of her pocket. "Phones off, ladies."

Veronica and I followed her lead. Then I closed all the curtains, enclosing us in The Hideout.

Veronica looked at me intently. "What happened on the ride?"

I took one of the pillows into my arms, hugging it close. "It was this ongoing magical moment. Huntley and I were connecting on this otherworldly level." I pressed a hand to my throat. "I've never felt *anything* like it. Like, not even remotely close."

Daphne leaned forward, falling out of the hammock chair. She crawled over and sat next to me. "Did you find *your person?*"

Veronica sighed. "Daphne, that's not a thing."

Daphne shot her a dark look. "It's totally a thing. You just haven't found *your person* yet, so you're all cynical about it."

Veronica rolled her eyes, sitting back in the bean bag chair. "You're delusional."

"Well, yeah. I think that was established years ago." Daphne took my hand in hers. "Did you kiss?"

I stared at our clasped hands. "No. We were right about to when Ryker swooped in."

"Since you never ended up dying," Daphne said, "and I already started planning a funeral, let's just switch it to Ryker's, because I'm going to kill him for doing that to you."

"Not if I kill him first." I leaned my head on Daphne's shoulder. "I have some reservations about the whole thing."

Veronica scooted off the bean bag chair and came up right next to us. "Okay. Let's talk it out. What's bothering you?"

I took a deep breath. "Huntley doesn't have the shiniest past."

"Who does?" Veronica ran her fingers over her braid hanging over her shoulder.

"I'm talking felony level or something," I said.

"Why do you think that?" Daphne asked.

"His stepdad said something about college not fixing him," I said, "like he'd been hoping it would."

Daphne patted our clasped hands. "Maybe he meant educationally, like, we really thought you'd finally learn how to read."

Veronica flicked Daphne on the forehead. "Or maybe he was just getting low grades and they were hoping he'd pull them up."

"Lame," Daphne said under her breath.

"Then there's the fact that he knew how to break into Simone's car," I said.

"YouTube videos," Daphne said. "Next."

I lifted my head to look at her. "Who looks up how to do that unless you're planning on doing it?"

Veronica held out a hand. "You've seen his car. It's old. He could have locked the keys in it often or something."

"Ryker said that I didn't know him as well as he did," I said.

"They're roommates," Daphne said. "He's probably seen him in just his boxers, and he has some weird mole." She snapped her fingers. "Maybe he's a snorer. Or has a weird eating habit. I once heard a story of someone who had a roommate that would pluck off his leg hair and eat it."

Veronica stared blank-faced at Daphne. "Okay, probably not *those* things, but maybe he…" She trailed off, tapping her finger to her lips. "Yeah, okay, I have nothing."

"Maybe he has a creepy doll collection," Daphne whispered.

I pressed a hand to her mouth. "You really need to stop guessing things."

She took my hand away from her mouth. "Sorry, I just really want to give the guy the benefit of the doubt. He's really awesome and perfect for you."

I paused. This was the one thing I'd been avoiding telling them, because saying it out loud would make it real. "Huntley has a parole officer."

Veronica's eyes practically bulged out of her sockets. Daphne gasped, a hand flying to her mouth.

"I'm sorry, what?" Veronica asked.

"We ran into his old parole officer at the Orange County Market Place," I said, thinking back to the day. "He seemed really excited to see Huntley, and said he was proud of him, so maybe he really did turn his life around?"

"Have you asked Huntley about it?" Veronica asked.

"I asked him if there was something to Ryker's paranoia, and he said no, but his face told me otherwise." I leaned against the wall behind me. "We're forgetting the fact that he's old. Too old for me to date right now." I punched the pillow in my lap. "I shouldn't even be thinking about dating! Zander and I just broke up after a really long, serious relationship."

Daphne turned her body toward me. "Taylor, sometimes people come into our lives when we need them. Yeah, he's not perfect, and maybe it would make sense to wait a few years before you date the guy and it's not so creepy—"

I smacked her with the pillow.

"—but I've seen you around him," she finished. "He brings out the natural Taylor. If anything, he's been a good rebound fling, even if nothing happened between the two of you. He's helped you realize that Zander didn't define you or your whole life. He was just a piece in this big puzzle of life."

Veronica and I stared at Daphne, both at a loss for words.

She removed her Mickey ears and set them on the bed next to her. "Do you need another relationship right now? No, of course not. My suggestion is to not overthink it. If it's meant to be, it will be. Let it happen naturally. Don't force it or rush into anything. Follow your heart, Tay."

I threw my arms around her, hugging tight. "I knew I'd feel better after talking to you two."

Veronica joined in our hug, and I was so grateful for my friends.

There was a thump near one of the windows. The three of us pulled back from the hug and looked over to see what it was.

Daphne shrieked and climbed on me, like she was trying to

get off the ground. Veronica backed into the wall, her fist clenching my shirt.

A green snake slithered through the curtains, sliding onto the carpet and heading towards the bean bag chair.

"There's a snake!" Daphne wrapped her arms around my throat and cut off my air supply.

I hit her arms until she finally loosened her death grip. "I can see that."

"There's two!" Veronica yelled, pointing to the other window. It was yellow and long, and so very much a snake.

I wanted to get my phone, but Daphne was all over me. Veronica had pressed into my side, grabbing onto me like she was debating climbing on top with Daphne.

"I need my phone," I hissed. The green snake turned to me, lifting its terrifying head and sticking out its tongue.

"Why did you say it like that?" Daphne whined. "It thinks you were talking to it."

"No, it doesn't," I said.

The snake changed its direction, headed directly toward us.

"Okay, maybe he did," I whimpered.

I hated snakes. They were slimy and creepy and could easily strangle you if they wanted. Or sink their sharp fangs into you.

"Do you think it's poisonous?" Veronica asked.

"I don't know!" I snapped. "I know nothing about snakes except that they're freaky!"

The yellow one joined the green one, the two almost to us.

"No." Daphne dropped to my side, letting me go. "I will not die by snake."

"What should we do?" Veronica asked.

Daphne opened her mouth and started screaming at the top of her lungs. She picked up her Mickey ears and chucked them at one of the snakes, which only pissed it off.

"The bed!" I said. "Let's use it as a shield."

Daphne and Veronica both nodded, and the three of us

scooted back against the wall, trying to shimmy the pad out from underneath us.

Once we were off it, we tilted it up, creating a wall.

"Now what?" Daphne asked.

"Uh." I had no idea. "Charge ahead?"

"What if they slither under the pad?" Veronica asked.

Daphne shrieked. "Or climb over it!"

I looked up to see the head of the green snake peering over the pad, flicking its tongue at us, and I completely lost it.

Screaming, I shoved the mattress as hard as I could, scrambling to my feet and toward the exit. The three of us squished down the hole, practically on top of each other, all of us still yelling at the top of our lungs.

Once we were on the ground, I turned to run, but rammed into Ryker and Samson.

"What's going on?" Samson asked, his eyes wide in fear. "Are you okay?"

"Snakes!" I squealed. I pointed at the treehouse. "Two! Up there."

"Really?" Ryker's eyes lit up in excitement. "Cool." He hurried to the ladder and climbed.

"There's a good chance I might have peed myself," Daphne whispered.

Quinn appeared from the side of the house and trotted over, grinning at us. "Rough night?"

"Why were there snakes in there?" I yelled.

Quinn's grin faded. "Uh, that would be Zander. Neo caught him and his friend fleeing the scene. He and Ollie are taking care of it."

Daphne nodded, shaking out her arms like she was trying to shake out the nerves. "Okay, so I need to plan Zander's *and* his friend's funerals. This changes so many things." She smirked. "Though I'd love to see Zander wearing a red jumpsuit in the coffin."

Quinn titled his head to the side. "What?"

"Just ignore her." Veronica scrambled past Quinn and headed toward the side of the house.

Daphne and I were right behind her.

Neo, Ollie, Porter, and Dad were in the front yard, surrounding Zander and his friend.

"Simone?" My jaw dropped. *She* was the friend?

She glared at me from the other side of my dad and Porter. "Payback."

Oh, that was it. The last step in the Vow of Vengeance was officially on.

CHAPTER THIRTY-SEVEN

Things had been super awkward with Huntley ever since our trip to Disneyland. We'd been keeping our distance, practically avoiding each other. Which was awesome and terrible at the same time. Awesome, because I got a little glimpse into how I really felt about him. Terrible, because it was official. I liked Huntley Esposito. Like, a lot.

I didn't even care that he was old or a criminal.

I was super surprised that when he found out we were doing our last item on the Vow of Vengeance, he wanted to participate. I'd thought he'd stay home, thinking we were stupid and reckless teenagers. But I guess he did have a shady past. Maybe he was falling back into his old ways. Maybe he thrived on stupid and reckless.

Once again, Zoie had helped with our quest. She let me know a night when her parents were out of town, giving us the perfect opportunity to finish out the V of V. I'd thought about making sure Zander wasn't home, but I liked the thought of him waking up to the damage, not seeing it when he came home at night. And with his parents gone, he'd be forced to clean it up by himself.

Knowing I might need to do some acrobatic movements, I wore shorts instead of a skirt. With some reluctance, I took off all my leather and beaded bracelets. I wanted no interference, nor any of them to break.

We waited until late at night, making sure we had the cover of darkness. Porter promised to keep Ryker entertained—Risk! —so he wouldn't show up and ruin everything.

Samson, Daphne, Veronica, Weston, Huntley, and I loaded up *the shuttle* with all the supplies.

"Is this even legal?" Veronica asked as she tossed another bag of toilet paper into the back of the van.

"Well, not technically," I said. "But it's not something we'll get arrested for. It's pretty low on the crime list that the cops care about."

Daphne lifted one of the toilet paper bags and checked the information on front. "Wait a second. Two-ply? I'm not sure Zander is worth two-ply. One-ply, yes, but two-ply?"

Samson took the bag from her and chucked it in the back of the van. "One-ply isn't sturdy enough. It will rip easily."

Daphne placed her hands on her hips. "Don't we want that? It will make it difficult for him to clean it up."

"But it also won't cover very well," Samson said. "We need to maximize the damage."

"Then shouldn't we go with three-ply?" Weston asked.

We all stopped and turned to him. If it wasn't so dark, I bet I'd probably be able to see how red Weston's face got.

"Never, ever waste three-ply," Daphne said in horror. "My goodness, Weston, I love you, but if you want this relationship to last, you need to understand the hierarchy of toilet paper."

"Strangest experience ever," Huntley whispered in my ear, causing a shiver to crawl up my spine despite the heat.

I rubbed the back of my neck, trying to collect my breath. I would *not* let him get to me. I needed to remain focused on vengeance and not Huntley's sexy voice.

Samson shut the back doors of the van. "Let's head out. We've got a lot of ground to cover and limited time."

We parked a block away from Zander's house. Zoie had verified that Zander was in bed, asleep, and that she'd turned off the doorbell camera so her family wouldn't be alerted to our presence.

We all gathered the supplies and crept over to the house, keeping in the shadows.

"I feel so dangerous," Daphne said. "Look at me, living the criminal life."

I choked back a laugh.

"I don't think toilet papering someone's house really qualifies as the criminal life," Veronica set her bags of toilet paper on the grass.

Daphne narrowed her eyes at Veronica. "Don't ruin this for me."

I gathered everyone in a circle, keeping my voice low. "Okay, we need to be as quiet as possible." I pointed over my shoulder at a window on the right side of the house. "That's Zander's room, so our main focus will be there." I motioned to the guys. "Samson, Huntley, and Weston, you three focus on the trees. I want them white by the time you're done, like a snowstorm hit their lawn." I turned to Veronica. "You're on bush duty. Frost those babies like a cake. I don't want to see any green when you're done." Then I looked at Daphne. "You're with me."

She tapped her fingers together, her laugh maniacal. "I'm ridiculously excited about this."

"I have no doubt." I smirked at her. "Let's get started."

Daphne and I went over to Zander's window, our steps light.

There weren't many nice things about Zander, but there were two I could think of at the moment. One, the guy needed total darkness to sleep, so he had blackout curtains, giving us a strong advantage. Second, he slept with a fan on, providing him with background noise and another advantage for us.

Bending down, I opened my bag full of supplies. When Zander woke up in the morning, I wanted him to have a little surprise when he pulled back the curtains.

I grabbed the red window paint and stood, shaking the pen in my hand. I turned toward the window and saw the head of a troll doll dangling from a string, the eyes gouged out. Slapping my hand over my mouth to cover my scream, I leaped into the air, dropping the paint pen onto the ground.

Daphne's smiling face appeared next to the troll head. "Isn't she perfect?"

I slowly lowered my hand, placing it right over my rapidly beating heart. "Where did you get that?"

Daphne lowered the troll, stroking its blood-red hair with her hand. "Mom had a weird obsession with troll dolls when she was a kid. I found them all in a box in the attic and thought they'd be perfect for scaring Zander. By your reaction, I was right."

I fished out another troll head from her bag. She'd put a patch over one of its eyes and painted blood dripping from its mouth. Some of the tall hair had been ripped from its head.

"Daphne, this is totally disturbing," I said.

"I know, right?" Daphne said, the smile apparent in her voice.

A grin broke out on my face. "These are *perfect*."

We pulled the rest out of the bag, then taped the strings right above the window so the heads dangled down. She had ten total, all in various degrees of destruction.

"I'd pee my pants if I opened my window to this," Daphne said in a giddy whisper.

With the paint pens, we wrote on his window, doing it backwards so he'd be able to read it, which made it difficult.

Not only did we have to spell it backwards, we had to invert the letters as well.

I'd written things like, *loser, you're pathetic,* and *I hope she cheats on you.* Then I looked over to see what Daphne had written. In big, red letters—with paint dripping down to add a nice touch—it said, *SEE YOU IN HELL.*

Daphne grinned at me, the smile fading when she saw my expression. She put the cap back on the paint pen. "Too much?"

"Well, it's perfectly Daphne," I said, trying to choke back a laugh.

Her smile came back. "Got the inspiration from a recent horror novel I read."

Veronica tip-toed over to us. "You two done? I could use some help." She looked at the trolls and then the words on the window. "Well, that's entirely creepy."

Daphne pumped her fist. "Nailed it."

The three of us finished off all the bushes in front of the house, making sure they were coated in toilet paper. Then we shook the paint pens until the paint splattered on the toilet paper, adding a nice touch.

We walked over to the sidewalk, surveying our work. The guys were still working on the trees, but what they had done was awesome. Toilet paper rained down, making the trees look like white weeping willows.

"My mom would be *so* proud." Daphne snapped a picture with her phone. The toilet papering had been her mom's idea, something that she used to do with her friends way back in the day.

Samson jogged over to us. "We just need to add some finishing touches to that massive tree in the corner. We missed a couple of spots."

I clasped my hands together. "Can I try?"

Samson tossed me his roll of toilet paper. "Go ahead."

I hurried over to the tree and walked around it, trying to find a bare spot, but there wasn't much. They'd done a pretty amazing job.

A warm presence drifted up next to me, and a hand landed on the small of my back. "Right there," Huntley said in a low voice.

I followed his line of sight, trying to push down the rush of blood flowing through me. *Old guy. Criminal. No boys.* I needed to stay focused.

Swallowing back my hormones, I tossed the roll at the tree, only to have it hit a branch and come sailing back to me. Flashbacks flooded through me, reminding me of when I tried to throw all of Zander's things out the window. It felt like eons ago. Weird that not much time had passed, but I felt like a completely different person.

"Do you need help with that?" Samson asked, his tone and eyes so very much amused.

I snatched the toilet paper from the ground, growled at Samson—who very smartly took a large step back—and chucked the roll up and over the tree. The roll left a gorgeous trail of toilet paper in its wake.

"Pretty sure Taylor can take care of herself." Huntley looked up at my coverage with awe.

Folding my arms, I turned to Samson. "You missed a spot."

Samson opened his mouth, his very far from humored eyes ready to tell me off, when the front door opened, and Zander stormed out, tugging a shirt on over his head.

"What are you doing?" Zander roared. He snatched up an almost empty roll of toilet paper and shook it at me. "You've completely lost your mind!"

Before I could respond, bright lights lit up the night. Turning around, I threw up my arm, trying to shield my face from the blinding lights.

"Everybody freeze." A male voice came over an intercom, somehow echoing like it was all around us.

"You've got to be kidding me," Huntley said through clenched teeth.

"I need everyone to slowly lower their weapons," the man said.

"It's toilet paper," Daphne said. "Hardly a weapon."

"Don't wave your arm," Weston hissed. "What if they're holding guns?"

Daphne inhaled sharply. "I didn't think about that. Is he going to kill me? Holy crap. I've been planning *my* funeral this entire time." Her tone changed, and I could hear the smile shining through. "At least I know the music will be *awesome.*" She sang the last word.

Veronica sighed and muttered something under her breath I couldn't understand.

"Ma'am, please set it on the ground," the man said.

Daphne dropped the roll, her hands shaking. Weston stared at her, a strained look in his eyes.

"Now you, too, sir," the man said.

I glanced at the guys, but none of them were holding anything. Then I saw Zander standing behind us, his eyes wide in shock, the roll now smashed in his clenched fist.

Zander licked his lips. "I live here!"

"Drop it!" the man said.

The ruined roll fell from Zander's hand.

"Now, clasp your hands behind your head and get on your knees," the man said. The lights from his car made it impossible to see him, but I did see red and blue lights flashing up and down the block.

"Uh, isn't this overkill?" Samson said as he kneeled. "We're toilet papering, not shooting up the place."

Huntley spewed every bad word in the dictionary out of his mouth, this time in English instead of his usual Spanish.

As I kneeled on the grass, my hands being cuffed behind me, I couldn't help but curse Zander's name.

CHAPTER THIRTY-EIGHT

I'd never been in the back of a police cruiser before. A lady officer had escorted Daphne, Veronica, and me to her car, set her hand on our heads, and helped us into the vehicles since we were in handcuffs.

Samson, Weston, Huntley, and Zander had been taken to another police car.

"Do you think they'll let us share a cell?" Daphne was in the middle seat, her Cherry Coke Mickey ears in her lap. "I can't be alone. I can't!"

"Quiet back there," the lady officer said from the driver's seat. The other officer in the passenger seat chuckled, his laugh borderline annoying.

Daphne leaned toward me, whispering. "If I pee my pants, do you think they'll make me change into one of those orange jumpsuits?" The male officer laughed again, causing Daphne to whimper. "He sounds like those hyenas from The Lion King. They're so freaky."

"No talking!" the lady officer said.

We rode the rest of the way in silence.

I kept thinking how ridiculous it all was. We were just toilet papering someone's house. Okay, and hanging creepy troll heads on the windows, but that wasn't a throw-you-in-jail crime. Couldn't they just fine us like they had at the beach?

I closed my eyes and sighed, wondering how I was going to explain it to my parents. I'd dragged all the others with me, which I hoped their parents understood. I was entirely to blame.

When we pulled in front of the police station, Veronica angled her head so she could see better out the window.

"Uh, shouldn't we be taken to a juvenile center?" Veronica asked. "Not like, jail, jail?"

I hadn't thought about that. We were all teenagers after all. Except for Huntley.

Oh, no. Would he get a harsher punishment because of his age? And his record?

The lady officer opened the back door on my side and helped me out of the car.

"There's a situation at the juvenile center," the lady said. I finally looked at her name tag. Officer Leavitt. "So you're getting booked here."

"I'm sorry, did you say, *booked*?" This sounded *way* more serious than I imagined.

Officer Leavitt stared at me blankly before she led Daphne and me into the station. The male officer escorted Veronica.

Once we were inside, they made us all stand in a corner while the officers talked. Samson, Weston, Huntley, and Zander were already there. Zander glared at me, his nostrils flaring impressively wide.

I tried to move my wrists, but the cuffs were on pretty tight.

Weston stared at the officers. "They must be *really* bored."

"Why?" I asked.

He turned to me. "They arrested us for toilet papering. Can they even legally do that?"

"They can arrest us for whatever they want." Huntley's eyes were tight. "Filing charges? That's another story."

Officer Leavitt approached us.

"Lawyer!" Daphne suddenly shouted, her voice quivering. "We demand a lawyer. Oh! And a phone call."

Officer Leavitt ignored her. "Follow me." She walked toward the back of the station, so the seven of us followed, the other officers at our heels.

Officer Leavitt opened a jail cell and motioned for me to turn around. She removed my cuffs, then nudged me toward the cell. Rubbing my wrists, I glanced around, taking in the small, dank area. I pressed the top of my index finger under my nose. It smelled like pee.

"Wait, you're not going to take our pictures, are you?" Daphne asked as Officer Leavitt removed her cuffs. "Like a mug shot?"

"Get in the cell, please," Officer Leavitt said.

Daphne stumbled in, her eyes pleading with the lady. "I still demand a lawyer and a phone call."

Officer Leavitt sighed. "Fine. You have one minute."

Daphne blew out a loud breath of relief. She danced where she stood, looking expectantly at Officer Leavitt.

With a roll of her big, brown eyes, Officer Leavitt motioned for Daphne to come back out of the cell. Then she shut the door, locking the rest of us in.

I sniffed, then gagged. "Seriously, what is that smell?"

"Dale peed himself," a raspy woman's voice said.

I spun around to see a scantily clad lady in the cell next to us, resting her arms through the metal slots. Her black hair was teased to the point it was a wide, puffy mess. Dried mascara stained her cheeks, her throat, and extremely ample cleavage. She was barefoot, making my toes curl just thinking how nasty the ground probably was in here.

She jerked her thumb to the side, showing off a long, curved fingernail. "Again." She looked over her shoulder at a man slunk down in the corner of their cell. "Can't use the bucket like a normal human being."

I took a step forward, narrowing my eyes at the guy. "Uh, is he alive?"

The lady rubbed her large nose. "Just passed out. The guy's drunker than my grandma at Thanksgiving." Her eyes lingered behind me, so I followed her gaze to Samson. "I'm Sapphire, by the way."

Samson scooted back, moving behind Veronica and Weston.

Huntley leaned against the cell wall, his arms folded and his jaw pulled tight. He had a mix of annoyance and terror in his eyes. Was this just another crime to add to his list?

My stomach clenched. What if I put him in real danger? I mean, the rest of us were teenagers. Yeah, Samson was nineteen, so he was technically an adult, but he didn't have a rap sheet. And the guy could charm himself out of any situation. Though, I thought Huntley could too. At the moment he looked like he wanted to punch someone in the face. His gaze flickered over to me, and I think I became that person.

Zander moved toward me and opened his mouth, more than ready to tell me off, when the cell door opened and Daphne trudged back in, her eyes red and puffy.

Veronica, Weston, and I rushed to her side.

"Are you okay?" Weston asked.

Daphne mumbled something incoherent as she sat down on the very edge of the bench, hugging herself tight.

Zander cupped my shoulder. "Taylor! You have to tell them I had nothing to do with this!"

I shoved his hand off me. "Not now, Zander!" I kneeled before Daphne, who had started breathing deeply and shakily. "It's going to be okay, Daph. Just breathe."

"Focus on the happy things." Veronica kneeled next to me and squeezed Daphne's arm. "Cherry Coke. Captain America."

Weston had sat down on the bench next to her, holding her close.

"Taylor, I shouldn't be in here!" Zander said.

"Shut up!" I yelled at him.

Daphne whimpered. I took her hand in mine. "I swear, nothing is going to happen to you. This is all some misunderstanding, okay?"

"Is your mom on her way?" Weston asked.

Daphne nodded against his shoulder and muttered something we couldn't understand.

"Taylor!" Zander roared.

I glared over my shoulder at him. "Seriously, Zander, not now. My friend needs my help."

Zander rolled his eyes. "Yeah, it's just another stupid panic attack from her freaking out over nothing. She'll live."

Oh, that was it.

Huntley and Samson both moved toward Zander, anger in their eyes, but I was on my feet in seconds, charging at Zander. I rammed my arm into his chest and threw him to the ground, knocking the wind out of him.

He laid on the ground, gasping for air.

I bent over him, took a fistful of his shirt, and yanked his face toward mine. "Don't you *dare* talk about my friends like that. Ever!" I shoved him back to the ground, kneeling on his chest. "Listen to me, you no good cheater. We are *so* done. You're a pathetic excuse for a man." I stood and straightened out my shirt.

Zander moved to get up, so I shoved my foot into his chest and pressed him down. "Stay down there for a bit and think about everything you did to me and Simone. The next time you want to leave your girlfriend for another, grow a pair and end your current relationship by letting them know you found someone else. Now, keep your face shut for the rest of the night."

"Oh!" Sapphire clapped her hands, her fake nails clinking together. "This just got gooood!"

Officer Leavitt appeared on the other side of the bars. "What's happening back here?"

Veronica jumped to her feet. "Ma'am, with all due respect, you can't just lock us up in here for toilet papering. We're minors and have no criminal history."

Huntley's eyes went to the ground.

"Toilet papering?" Sapphire chuckled. "That can't be right. They don't lock people up for toilet papering!"

"Toilet paper!" Dale suddenly shouted from the other cell before he passed out again.

"Actually." Officer Leavitt rested her hand on her hip right above her gun. "We can. Officer Call is putting the paperwork together as we speak. We have you on littering, trespassing, criminal mischief, and disorderly conduct."

"This has to be a joke." Huntley's voice was tight.

Officer Leavitt arched her eyebrows at his tone. "Don't make me add defacing private property to that list."

Daphne pressed a hand to her chest. "Okay, what? This can't... they can't..."

Weston held her close. "Just breathe, Daphne. Deep breaths. In and out."

She nodded as her breathing picked up, and she placed her other shaky hand on her forehead.

"Remember, happy things," Weston said in a soothing voice.

"Now, look what you gone and did." Sapphire scowled at Officer Leavitt. "This is an injustice, having them all locked up and charging them with those things. Look at the cuddlebug!" She motioned her hand at Daphne. "She's wearing Mickey ears! You can't arrest a girl wearing Mickey ears."

Officer Leavitt's hard demeanor faltered for a moment. She licked her lips and looked down the hall before turning back to us. "I'll be right back."

There were voices down the hall, and then suddenly, someone ran toward our cell.

Sierra bounded into view, a smug smile on her face. "What's up, losers?"

CHAPTER THIRTY-NINE

I threw back my head and groaned before glaring at Sierra. "It was you the whole time, wasn't it?"

She leaned against the bars, folding her arms, and crossing her feet at her ankles. "I was doing a ride-a-long with my dad when the call came through."

Her dad, the cop. Everything started clicking together.

"Officer Call is new to the force," Sierra went on. "Dad called Officer Leavitt on her private line and let her in on the prank. Perfect way to haze Officer Call. She said he was *so* confused on why they were arresting you guys for toilet papering."

Weston stood, his hand on Daphne's shoulder. "Wait, Officer Call didn't know it was a prank?"

"Nope," Sierra said. "So wish I could have been there, but watching the footage from the cell was worth it." She pointed at a camera in the top corner of the cell.

"So, he really could have fired on us." Weston's voice was tight. I'd never seen him so angry.

Sierra's smile faltered. "What? No. He wouldn't have shot

her. Officer Leavitt told him to draw his taser and not to use it unless she said to."

I looked over at Daphne. She was on the verge of passing out. I rushed to her side at the same time Veronica did, putting our hands on her arms to steady her.

"You weren't in any danger, I promise," Sierra said.

"She waved her arm." Weston glared at Sierra. "What if he thought her a threat and pulled the trigger?"

Sierra's concerned eyes landed on Daphne. "He wouldn't have. And it was a taser."

"Is that supposed to make it better?" Weston asked.

Sierra glanced down the hall. "Dad, open the cell!"

Her dad came into view, pulling the keys from his pocket and opening the door. Sierra rushed in and squeezed her way between Veronica and me.

"I'm so sorry, Daph." Sierra set her hand on Daphne's arm. "I thought it would be funny."

Daphne waved a hand, her voice coming out weak and shaky. "Don't worry. It was hilarious." She reached out and took Weston's hand. "He's just being protective."

Weston bent down, kissing her on the temple. "Excuse me for not wanting to watch my girlfriend get tased. Or shot."

Daphne suddenly broke out in a strained laugh. Weston loosened his tense stance. Then he smiled and ran a hand down his face.

"This is crazy," Weston muttered.

"Like I've said a million times," Huntley said, his hands placed on top of his head. "Most bizarre experience ever."

Total guilt swept over me. I hated that I'd put Huntley in this situation. I ran over, throwing my arms around him.

"Oomph."

"I'm so sorry, Huntley."

His arms wrapped around my back, but not nearly as tight

as I had mine. "It's okay. Nothing bad actually happened, so we're good."

I pulled back, my arms still around his neck. His eye was finally back to normal.

"Taylor?" Huntley whispered.

"Yeah?"

"Personal space?"

"Oh!" I dropped my arms and backed away. Usually, he smirked when he said it, but this time, his eyes were so serious, like he hadn't wanted me close.

He looked away, not making eye contact with me.

"I demand to see my daughter!" Laura's voice rang out from the front of the police station. "This is completely absurd!"

"Oh, no." Daphne hopped up and sprinted down the hall, all of us fast on her heels.

We found Laura yelling at the lady at the front desk, Cody watching on with an amused smile. He wore a vintage cream-colored three-piece suit and black and white shoes, and leaned on a black cane.

Laura had on a gold and black 1920s flapper dress. The black band around her head had a feathered flower sewn to it and beads dangling from the side. Her gold t-strap heels were adorned with beads and rhinestones.

"Ms, please." The lady clasped her hands together almost in a plea. "It's all a misunderstanding. The chief's daughter wanted to play a prank when they caught them toilet papering."

Laura's head jerked back in surprise. "Wait, they were toilet papering?"

"Yes," the lady said. "That's what I've been trying to tell you."

Laura's face went to confused to upset to amused to relieved. She placed a hand to her chest. "So, there were no drugs involved?"

"No," the lady said.

Daphne went to her mom. "Drugs?"

Laura smiled sheepishly. "You were really difficult to understand on the phone."

I couldn't stop staring at Laura's shoes. "You *have* to let me borrow those sometime."

Laura turned, her face confused. She followed my gaze to her shoes. "Oh! Of course. Any time." She reached down, adjusting the strap on top. "Fair warning, they are *super* uncomfortable. Definitely wouldn't want to wear them toilet papering."

Daphne glared at her mom.

Laura put a hand on her hip. "Too soon?" She pulled her into a tight hug. "I don't know whether to kill you or be glad you're okay. I was freaking out the whole ride over."

"That she was," Cody said.

Laura released Daphne, turning to the rest of us. "How did it go? Were you able to finish the job before the cops showed up?"

Cody sighed, putting a hand to his forehead. "I told you the toilet papering was a bad idea."

"Oh, hush." Laura waved a hand at him. "They're fine." She arched an eyebrow. "You are all fine, yes?"

We all nodded, so Laura went to each of us, giving us a hug and kiss on the cheek.

"I'm glad you're all okay." Laura released a surprised Huntley from her arms. "I could really go for a peppermint chocolate chip shake right now."

Daphne stomped her feet. "Why did you mention that? You know Chick-fil-a doesn't have them in the summer, and now I won't be able to stop thinking about them."

Cody went to Daphne and Laura, draping his arms around their shoulders. "How about I make them myself?"

"Still won't be the same," Daphne mumbled. "But if you want to try, I won't stop you."

Sierra tiptoed out from the hallway, cautiously approaching our group. "I'm sure one day we'll look back on this and laugh."

"You," Laura said, pointing a finger at Sierra, "are a chip off the old block. But you're welcome to join us for shakes." She looked at the lady at the front desk. "Are we good to go?"

"Yes." The lady's tone suggested she wanted us gone as soon as possible.

As everyone turned toward the front door, Huntley came over to me.

"Why are they dressed like that?" Huntley asked. "And why is everyone acting like it's normal?"

I stifled a laugh. "Because for them, it is normal. I'll explain in the car."

Huntley opened his mouth, his eyes a little tormented, but he just shut his mouth and walked out the door.

"Taylor."

I spun around to see Zander standing there, rubbing his chest.

"I never cheated on you," he said.

I threw up my arms. "Not physically. But you'd mentally moved on to Simone already. Total betrayal." I took a deep breath. "You crushed me, you know. We were going along just fine and then out of the blue, you said we were done. You may have had a warning on your end because you were starting to have feelings for Simone, but those warnings weren't sent to me. I had no clue what you were feeling toward her."

I clenched my fist, trying so hard not to deck Zander. "I think that was the thing that hurt the most. The fact that you moved on in a blink of an eye like we never happened. You just tossed me to the side, showing your true feelings. It wasn't like I thought we had the most perfect, most glamorous relation-ship, but I thought it at least meant *something* to you."

Zander held out a hand. "Tay..."

I smacked his hand away. "No. You don't get to call me that. Not anymore. It's for close friends and family, which you most definitely are not." I stepped up to him, holding my chin high. "You showed your true colors when you discarded me like trash. I just hope Simone doesn't suffer the same fate I did. At least have some human decency and give her a warning of some kind."

"What Simone and I have is real," Zander said. "It's difficult to explain."

My gaze went out the door, where I knew Huntley was standing. "I know what real is, Zander, and you're so far from it. You're not ready for a *real* honest-to-goodness relationship. You'll get over Simone, just like you did me, the next time some hot girl bats her eyelashes at you. Just, please, stay out of my life."

I walked out of the police station, not looking back as a huge weight lifted off my shoulders.

CHAPTER FORTY

Things were back to being awkward with Huntley, and I hated it. We'd been so comfortable around each other before Ryker ruined everything at Disneyland. The whole jail fiasco made things worse.

Huntley wouldn't make eye contact with me. He avoided me at all costs. He'd basically started acting like I didn't exist.

Everyone was out on the back patio, getting ready for Wrestle Mania. We put a wrestling mat down, with cones in the four outer corners, each linked to each other with green caution tape with the words 'BIOHAZARD' written on it.

Quinn touched the tape. "Biohazard?"

Daphne slapped his hand away. "It was left over in our Halloween decorations. It also seemed kinda fitting. Guys in a wrestling ring? Total biohazard, am I right?" She laughed at her own joke, then went back to setting things up.

"She's really taking this seriously, isn't she?" Veronica asked as Daphne went to set up the sound system.

"Would you expect anything less?" I asked.

Veronica shook her head, smiling. "Never."

Neo and Ollie brought a gigantic marker board out onto the patio, setting it up near the ring.

Porter tossed Veronica and me bright pink markers.

I turned mine around in my hand. "Let me guess. Genevieve picked the color?"

"Actually." Porter picked up our niece and tickled her stomach. "Brighton did."

Brighton pressed her palms against Porter's cheeks, squeezing his face. "It's the best color, Uncle Porter."

Porter tried to make a fishy face with his smooshed lips, and Brighton giggled. Ollie grabbed his daughter from Porter and took her into the ring, fake slamming her to the mat.

Ollie threw up his arms in victory. "And the crowd goes wild!"

Nixon and Pierson both started booing, throwing popcorn into the ring.

Ollie pointed at his sons. "You're next, boys."

"Hi-ya!" Brighton kicked Ollie's shin as hard as her little leg could.

Ollie flopped to the ground, holding his shin and screaming out in pain.

Brighton stood and brushed off her dress. "And that, Daddy, is how it's done." She sauntered out of the ring, ducking under the caution tape and giving me a wink.

Veronica smiled wide. "I really like her. She's a mini-Taylor."

We turned to the marker board.

"Okay, let's plan this out," I said.

We needed to set up the brackets, four guys on the left, four on the right. I only had six brothers, but we wanted to start with eight people so we could evenly dwindle the numbers down. Huntley and Bentley were both excited to join in.

I'd thought about participating, but I wasn't in the mood. I'd been in such a funk since jail. I was mad that I'd let the Vow of Vengeance go that far, furious that I'd put Huntley in that situation, and beyond confused about my feelings for him.

I couldn't have feelings for him. My family would never allow it with his criminal past. *I* wasn't even sure I wanted to date a criminal.

"Neo versus Porter." I wrote their names on the board on the left side bracket. "They both have the big guts going on."

Neo walked past us, pushing the back of my head. "I heard that."

"Ollie versus Ryker?" Veronica suggested for the left side opponents. "I think Ollie would be the easiest on Ryker."

I nodded. "Good call. Which puts Samson against Quinn over here on the right bracket."

"You don't want to pit your brothers against Huntley and Bentley?"

I smiled, writing their names in the last spot on the board. "Huntley and Bentley need to fight their way into this match. See who earns the right to go up against my brothers."

My mom, Charlie, Emory, and Aria lounged on pool chairs facing the ring. We'd put up large umbrellas to give them shade.

Genevieve, Fiona, and Brighton had little folding chairs with mini umbrellas attached, each chair adorned with a cup holder. The three girls had taken their seats in their swimsuits, sunglasses, and floppy hats like they were living the high life.

Daphne would be hosting.

Nixon and Pierson were the coaches, one for the left bracket, one for the right.

Dad would be the referee. He even had the white and black striped shirt to make it look official.

Which left Veronica, Sierra, and I to sit near my mom and sisters-in-law.

Weston came out from the house, an apron wrapped around

his waist. He walked up to my nieces and smiled. "Can I get you ladies anything to drink?"

They all giggled before giving him their orders.

"You're coming to us next, right?" Charlie asked as Weston turned to go back into the house.

Weston nodded. "Of course."

Daphne suddenly appeared at my side. "Nothing sexier than a man in an apron."

I turned to her. "You ready?"

"I was born ready, Tay." Daphne jogged over to a little makeshift podium we'd built, grabbing a cordless microphone from near the speaker. She hopped onto the podium. "Every-one, gather around, please!"

Once everyone was settled, Daphne went on. "Ladies and gentlemen! Welcome to Wrestle Mania!"

We all cheered.

"First up," Daphne said, "We have The Mountain Man versus The Triple Threat."

Neo and Porter stepped over the caution tape and into the ring. Pierson whispered some words to Neo as Nixon gave advice to Porter.

My brothers shook hands, and the match began.

I was doing everything in my power to keep my attention on the match, but my traitorous eyes kept seeking out a shirtless Huntley.

"I think you have some drool on your chin." Aria smirked at me. "My goodness, Tay, you really like him, don't you?"

My cheeks flared. "What are you talking about?"

"I was just thinking the same thing," Emory said. "I haven't seen that longing look since Quinn and Aria started dating."

Aria picked up a glass of lemonade. "I'll have you know, that longing look hasn't subsided in the least bit."

"No, it hasn't," Veronica said with a laugh.

Aria took a sip of her drink, then squished her face. "Okay, this needs more sugar."

Mom leaned toward us. "I put about a gallon of sugar in there already."

Aria rubbed her stomach. "This pregnancy has my taste buds all out of whack."

"It looks like The Mountain Man is bulldozing The Triple Threat out of existence!" Daphne roared.

Dad threw up an arm, ending the match. Neo had won.

Aria looked over at Charlie. "Will it always be like this? For every pregnancy?"

Charlie shrugged. "You never know until the kid's growing inside you. Pierson was easy, Nixon was a nightmare, and Brighton was a mix of the two." She patted her stomach. "So far, this kid has been a breeze. They better stay that way."

Sierra grimaced. "The thought of giving birth totally freaks me out."

"Same," Veronica said.

"Next up," Daphne said in a growling voice, "for the right bracket, we have Antman versus The Terminator!"

Quinn and Samson made their way to the ring.

Daphne turned to Quinn. "Good luck to Antman. Don't let The Terminator's short height fool you. He won State for wrestling in high school."

Samson looked incredulously at Daphne. "I'm six-three."

"Have you met your brothers?" Daphne asked.

Samson slowly nodded. After all, he was the shortest of all my brothers.

Emory leaned toward Charlie, pulling my attention away from the match. "Are you going to find out what you're having?"

Charlie shook her head. "No. The kids and Ollie all have bets going. Since I have clothes for both boys and girls, I don't feel the need to find out." She smiled mischievously. "Losers have diaper duty the first month."

"I'd be dying if I didn't know," Aria said. "This mama needs some major mental prep time."

Charlie laughed. "We'll see how you're feeling on the fourth one."

Sierra leaned toward Veronica and me, keeping her voice low. "I'm thinking about getting my tubes tied just listening to this conversation."

Aria snorted a laugh. She was laughing at Charlie, but it had been perfect timing to what Sierra had said, making Veronica and me laugh.

"Trust me," Aria said. "Quinn will be lucky if he gets more than two. I'm not going the typical Thomas route."

Mom glanced over at all her sons. "Trust me, if I didn't want a girl so bad, I probably would have stopped after Ollie. Maybe Porter. But I really wanted a girl for some reason." She swept out an arm. "But boy after boy kept coming. It was getting ridiculous. I made a vow that I wouldn't stop until I got my girl."

Sierra pulled out her phone. "Scheduling my appointment right now."

I batted my eyelashes at her. "Aren't you glad you kept going?"

"Depends on the day," Mom said.

"Oh!" Daphne yelled into the microphone. "In a victory we all saw coming, The Terminator has exterminated Antman!"

Quinn slowly got to his feet. "Who gave her permission to host this?"

Daphne went on, ignoring him. "In the last match for the left bracket in round one, welcome The Rocket and The Gecko!"

Ollie and Ryker ducked under the tape and moved to the center of the ring, shaking hands.

Ollie looked at Daphne. "I feel like these were the least creative names."

I figured Daphne had gone with Rocket since Ollie was a fan of the Houston Rockets. Ryker's was obvious.

"Maybe if you had a more interesting life," Daphne said, "I could have thought of something better."

Bentley and Samson's fists flew to their mouths. "Oh!"

Emory brought my attention back to her. "Can we get off the subject of babies and back on the subject of Taylor having the hots for Huntley?"

"And the fact that he's a million times better than Zander?" Charlie took a sip of her lemonade, then stuck out her tongue. "Aria, you're insane. That's way too much sugar."

"And it's already over!" Daphne yelled. "The Gecko had no chance against a rocket."

Ryker groaned his way out of the ring.

"You really think that?" I asked Charlie.

Charlie nodded, setting her glass on the small table. "Listen, Zander was adorable, but there was always something about him that rubbed me the wrong way."

For some reason, anger flared inside me. I had no idea why I was mad. "You were hardly around him!"

Charlie tilted her head to the side. "Tay, there are no secrets in the Thomas family. Everyone talks. Everyone has an opinion. I didn't need to be here to know the kid." She placed a hand on her cheek. "How have I gotten to the point where a seventeen-year-old is a kid? I'm not *that* old."

"For the last match for the right bracket," Daphne said, "we have two 'ntley's that need to prove themselves worthy to fight a Thomas."

"What's an 'ntley'?" Fiona asked.

Emory smiled. "It's just the last letters of their names. They are pretty similar, aren't they?"

"Please welcome Despacito and Mrs. Bennet to the ring!" Daphne declared.

CHAPTER FORTY-ONE

entley shook his head. "Really, Daphne?"

"Hey." Daphne pointed at him. "You *slayed* that role in English. Own it."

Huntley chuckled. "Well, at least your name doesn't mean 'slowly.'"

Daphne tilted her head to the side. "That's what Despacito means?"

I cupped my hands over my mouth. "Because he's going to give you a slow and painful death, Bentley!"

Huntley completely ignored my comment, I shrank into myself, completely embarrassed.

Sierra reached around Veronica and shoved my arm. "Huntley is going down. He'll be begging for mercy."

The two guys shook hands, and the match began.

Bentley and Huntley were a good match-up, similar in height and build. Huntley ended up pinning Bentley to the ground, holding him there until Dad called it.

Sierra folded her arms. "Totally rigged."

"We have two more matches to see who goes to the final

round," Daphne said. "First up, The Mountain Man versus The Terminator."

Neo and Samson hopped in the ring, shaking hands.

Veronica reached over and gripped my arm. "I don't know why, but I'm totally nervous. I'm not sure Samson stands a chance against Neo."

Neo was the strongest of all my brothers. The others tried so hard to defeat him, but they rarely could.

I couldn't focus on the match. I kept thinking about Charlie saying Huntley was a better choice than Zander. I looked at Emory. "What was your opinion about Zander?"

Emory took a sip of her lemonade before she spoke. "A little arrogant and not good enough for you."

"I honestly never thought he was cute," Aria said. "He's missing that spark."

"Which Huntley most definitely has." Charlie smiled at him.

Huntley was talking with Ryker off to the side. From the way Huntley was nodding, I think Ryker was giving him some pointers about going up against Ollie.

"See, there's that look again," Emory said.

"What look?" I folded my arms close to my chest. "I didn't have *a look*."

"You so did," Aria said at the same time Mom said, "Somebody is in denial."

Veronica let go of my arm as Daphne announced Neo as the winner. No surprise there. I was expecting Neo to take the whole thing.

"In the last match for the right bracket," Daphne said, "please welcome The Rocket and Despacito!"

I should have been watching, but all my sisters-in-law's words were bouncing around in my head. "Can we focus on the fact that I just got out of a relationship and Huntley is old? The four of you should be trying to talk me *out* of starting anything with Huntley."

Charlie chuckled. "He's not old, Tay. So what if he's a few years older than you? You're not too far from eighteen yourself."

"Do I want you to rush into anything?" Mom asked. "Of course not. Do I want you to be happy? Yes, I do. And that boy over there has made you happier than Zander ever did. We're just pointing out the obvious."

Veronica nodded. "I totally agree with your fam, Tay."

I turned to my mom and sisters-in-law. "Would you still feel that way if you knew he has a criminal past?"

I waited for them to gasp, look shocked, or something, but none of them batted an eye.

Mom waved a hand. "Honey, we've all made mistakes, and his weren't that bad."

"Wait, Ryker told you?" I asked.

Charlie moved her finger around in a circle. "No secrets."

"The important thing is that he stopped doing idiotic things." Mom smiled softly. "He focused on bringing his grades up, and then graduated early so he could start college. He's farther along than any of my boys were at his age."

I'd totally forgotten that Huntley had said he'd graduated early. So maybe he wasn't as old as Ryker. But he could still be twenty.

Then I remembered something he said to his parole officer. He'd said he had a year of college under his belt. Only one year.

Could he possibly be eighteen? That wasn't as weird, right? As Charlie had just said, I was only a few months away from eighteen.

But Huntley didn't seem as interested as he had before. Maybe he'd just thought it was fun to flirt a bit, and that was it.

No boys. That was my rule. I needed a break from them.

"In a surprising turn of events," Daphne said, "an Esposito

has worked his way into the final round of the Thomas family Wrestle Mania."

That certainly caught my attention. Huntley was going up against Neo? Oh, no.

Neo stood in the corner of the ring, stretching out his arms and cracking his neck. I looked at Huntley, who stood in the opposite corner, his shirt off, trying to torture me to death. He was toned, but he was a lot smaller than Neo.

Emory leaned toward me. "Tay, all we're saying is that it seems like you like him, and it's okay for you to like him. There's no rule that says how long you need to be broken up with one person to start liking another."

"And maybe he was just thrown in right now to help you realize that," Aria said. "We're not saying marry the guy."

Mom pointed a finger at me. "Because you're too young."

I scoffed. "Well, duh." I wanted at least a few years of college under my belt before I even started thinking about marriage.

The match began. Neo and Huntley circled each other in the ring, neither one making the first move. I found myself gripping Veronica's arm like she'd done with mine.

"Tay," Charlie said, "don't kill me, but I do want to point out that he fits in nicely with the family. He's gotten along with *all* of us, and that's a lot of people."

"No marriage!" Mom shouted, causing most of the guys to turn to us. She smiled sheepishly and shook her head.

Charlie laughed. "I'm just saying I wouldn't be surprised if Taylor had already found her person."

My person. That was what Daphne always said.

"Is that really a thing?" I asked. "Having *a person?*"

All my sisters-in-law shared a look before turning to Mom.

"Depends on who you ask," Mom said. "I think so, but not everyone will agree with me. I know the world is large, but you have to work with what you have around you. So, out of all the people in a reasonable vicinity? Yes, I think there's a person for everyone."

"Some don't find them until later in life," Charlie said.

Emory clasped her hands over her belly. "I honestly think some people don't find them in this lifetime, but they'll find them when they get to heaven. We're all meant to lead different paths."

Her gaze flitted over to my oldest brother, Neo, who had yet to settle down. He was just an adventurer, traveling the world and spreading his awesomeness everywhere he went. Maybe he'd find his person in this lifetime, maybe he wouldn't.

Neo sprang at Huntley, and within seconds, had him pinned on the mat. Huntley hadn't stood a chance. The fact that he'd made it that far in the competition was surprising.

"Sweetie," Mom said, bringing my attention back to her. "All we want you to know is that we support you and know you'll make the right decision at the right time."

Tears pricked the corner of my eyes. I was so lucky to have a family that trusted me and my instincts. I looked over at Huntley, who was being helped to his feet by a smiling Neo. Not everyone had that.

Aria choked on a sob, and I turned to find tears streaming down her cheeks. "I hate hormones!"

Charlie and Emory both chuckled as they wiped at their own cheeks.

Aria blew out a loud breath, her lips vibrating like she was blowing a raspberry. "And I found my person with your brother."

Tears streamed down Charlie's cheeks. "Same."

Emory gazed at Porter. "Same."

Mom sighed, a lovey-dovey kind. "Same with me and your father."

Once again, my eyes sought out Huntley. He was currently being congratulated by every single one of my brothers and my dad. I think they were more impressed with Huntley making it that far than by Neo winning the entire thing.

Was he my person? Could he be my person one day, just not yet? Was I totally overthinking the entire thing?

Quite possibly, yes.

CHAPTER FORTY-TWO

Francisco adjusted the lapel of his purple blazer. "This is somehow my most ghastly favorite, and most amazing party I've thrown together." He looked at the stadium seats against the wall. "Same color as the ones in the Marriott Center, I'll have you know." He pointed to the four-sided scoreboard hanging from the ceiling in the center of the room. "Yes, it's not as big as the one they have, but look at that beauty."

"Thank you, Francisco." I glanced around the venue in awe. He'd done everything I asked for, down to the basketball hoops and all the food they served at the Marriott Center where BYU played.

Neo strolled over holding one of the Cougar Tails, a really long maple donut. He was munching on a piece, and a few crumbs from the donut rested in his beard. "Sis, this is freaking amazing."

"I can't watch this," Francisco muttered to himself before walking away.

Neo wiped at the corner of his mouth. "What's his deal?"

"He doesn't particularly like Neanderthals." I brushed the

crumbs from his beard. "The donuts are for the guests when the party actually starts."

"I am a guest." Neo took another bite. "And the party has already started for me."

I grimaced at his full mouth as he talked. "Okay, maybe this is why you're single."

Neo placed a hand against his heart. "Ouch."

I held a finger to my ear. "What? I can't understand you with all the food in your mouth."

"You mean all that cougar ta—" Neo started.

"Don't even think about finishing that sentence." I walked away, my shoes squeaking against the floor Francisco had turned into a court.

I was normally all about wearing heels to a party, but this wasn't just any party. This was my dad's sixtieth birthday party, and the man lived and breathed basketball. I'd found some royal blue basketball shoes and couldn't resist. With my black dress and black leather jacket, the shoes just popped.

Daphne bounced in the room wearing an adorable royal blue romper with a white belt and white sneakers. I grinned when I saw Weston in a royal blue suit and tie, his belt and sneakers white, matching Daphne.

Veronica had a navy-blue cotton maxi dress, falling nicely against her curves, and sensible sandals. Her long hair flowed nicely around her shoulders. She came over to me. "I know BYU is royal blue, but it's also navy, and I really like this dress."

I hugged her tight. "You look gorgeous."

"Yeah, she does." Samson walked up and side-hugged her. "Weston, my man, love the suit."

Weston blushed. "Thanks. It was Daphne's idea."

"Yeah, and look how sexy you are." Daphne ran her hand down his tie, making his blush intensify.

"Breaking news." Veronica paused, pursing her lips together before she grinned widely. "I broke up with DeShawn."

"Hallelujah!" Daphne shouted.

I hugged Veronica. "You have no idea how happy this makes me."

"It was long overdue," Veronica said.

"Yeah it was." Samson rested his arm on Veronica's shoulder. "Hey, Tay, how much longer until Dad gets here? I'm starving and those J. Dawg's are calling my name."

I checked my watch. "Soon."

"Are we going to hide or something?" Veronica asked. "Jump out and say, 'Surprise!'"

I shook my head. "No, but I wanted the majority of people to be here so he could walk in and see all the people who love and care about him."

"That's sweet, sis." Samson lowered his arm from Veronica's shoulder and rubbed his hands together. "I think I'm going to sneak a Cougar Tail."

"Don't you dare," I snarled at him.

He backed toward the food tables. "Try to stop me."

I huffed but let him go. I wasn't about to get in a wrestling match with Samson while wearing a dress.

Daphne bounced on her toes. "Where's the music station?"

We'd put her in charge of the music for the event, since we knew she'd nail it. If her own clothing line didn't work out, maybe she could be a DJ.

Daphne, Veronica, Weston, and I went to the corner of the room where I'd set up a mini-DJ area for Daphne. Yeah, she was pretty much just going to link the system to her phone and play music, but I thought it would be fun to have an official spot where people could come and make requests.

Plus, Daphne worked better tucked into a corner, not having so many eyes on her.

I looked out over the crowd. A decent number of people had already shown, and the place was filling in nicely. It was fun to watch their expressions as they took in the room, noting all the similarities to the Marriott Center.

"Have you ever thought about being a party planner?" Daphne asked. "Because you'd be awesome."

"That actually sounds like a lot of fun." I'd been struggling to figure out what I wanted to study in college. I'd been leaning toward business, which would come in handy if I had my own company one day.

Veronica's eyes lit up. "Taylor Made Celebrations."

"Oh, a play on words." Daphne shimmied. "I like it."

My watch buzzed and I glanced at the screen. "Oh, Mom and Dad are here." I looked out at all the guests. "Okay, maybe we should do something. Just like a 'Happy birthday' or something."

"Do it," Daphne said.

I jogged out to the middle of the faux court and cupped my hands over my mouth. "Can I have everyone's attention?" Some of the guests nearest me quieted down, but a lot were still talking and laughing.

Francisco approached me, holding out a megaphone. "I can't believe I'm suggesting this, but maybe it would help."

"Thanks, Francisco." I took it from him, pressed the button, and spoke into the microphone. "Can I have everyone's attention?" When everyone turned to me, I went on. "Dad is on his way up. Let's just shout, 'Happy birthday' when he walks in, okay?"

"Shouldn't we hide?" my nephew Nixon asked. He was dressed head-to-toe in BYU gear, like most of my family.

Emory hustled into the room. "We don't have time. They're coming up the stairs as we speak."

We all waited in anticipation until my dad rounded the corner.

"Happy birthday!" It was loud and almost in perfect unison, like we'd practiced it.

Dad's jaw dropped in shock as he took in all the guests and the decorations. He turned to my mom, who kissed his cheek.

"Happy birthday," Mom said.

Dad threw out his arms. "This is way over-the-top, and absolutely perfect." He sniffed. "Do I smell J. Dawg's?"

"Yep," I said.

Music began to play, creating background noise for the moment. I'd told Daphne that we'd have a dance party at some point, where we could crank up the music.

Dad grinned at me. "Let me guess, you were behind most of this?"

Neo stepped into view. "With the help of your sons."

I snorted a laugh. "Yeah, they helped by staying out of it."

"Exactly," Neo said.

As the guests went back to talking, I jogged over to my dad and hugged him. "Happy birthday, Dad."

He kissed the top of my head. "Thanks, kiddo."

"Can we eat now?" my nephew Pierson asked.

When Mom nodded at him, he and Nixon took off for the J. Dawg's station, followed very quickly by all my brothers. Neo even pushed Pierson and Nixon back, taking their place at the front of the line. They punched his back, but Neo didn't even flinch as he grabbed himself a hot dog.

Dad smiled madly. "Hey! I played at BYU with that guy!" He left us, going over to say hi to an old friend.

Two hands suddenly covered my eyes. But they weren't hands. They were fuzzy, like paws.

"Cosmo?" I asked.

He dropped the paws and came in front of me, nodding his head. Cosmo the Cougar stood there with his arms folded, looking tough. Then he took off, doing a bunch of backflips across the faux court before he started break dancing.

"Show off," I muttered under my breath with a smile.

As everyone settled into the party, I went off to the side

with Veronica so I could snap some pictures. Yes, I'd hired a professional photographer, but I wanted some I could upload to social media.

I took a picture near the open doors where Brighton, in her cute little BYU cheerleader outfit, was standing on Cosmo's palm as he extended his arm in the air. She waved some pom-poms like they were doing a routine.

"Oh, my." Veronica stared at the door in shock. "Yeah, okay, I totally get it now. Tay, he's gorgeous."

I followed her gaze and found Huntley standing in the doorway to the room. He wore a black suit, black shirt, and a royal blue tie. His sneakers were royal blue, similar to mine.

"You didn't plan this, did you?" Veronica asked.

"Plan what?" I asked.

"The whole twin thing like Daphne and Weston did." She motioned between us. "It looks like you and Huntley planned your outfits."

"We didn't." I stared at him, my heart hammering against my chest.

I knew he was going to come. He'd RSVP'd.

But seeing him actually standing there, his smoky eyes finding mine, I almost forgot how to breathe.

"Despacito" began to play from the speakers, making a smirk break out on Huntley's and on my face.

Veronica gently prodded me toward him. "Girl, go get your man."

I hesitated. There was still something bothering me.

Samson came up next to me. "What's wrong? You look pained."

I frowned. "I still don't know his past. What if Huntley did something horrible?"

Samson waved a hand. "Oh, that? I wouldn't get too worked up over it. He's a good guy, sis."

I looked at him. "You know about his past?"

Samson nodded. "After his dad died and his mom remarried—"

"To a total jerk," I put in.

"He lashed out. Started getting into fights, stealing cars, vandalism, stuff like that. Even ended up in juvie for a bit." He rubbed a finger over his crescent-shaped scar next to his eye. "He turned his life around, finished high school early with off-the-charts grades, enrolled in college, and went full gear into starting his career, wanting to be able to take care of himself and not have to rely on his mom and Ron." He glanced over at Ryker, who was chasing Brighton around the room. "Ryker said he was a workaholic during the school year. He worried Huntley would work himself to death, so he forced him to come to our house for the summer and relax for a little bit."

I let everything sink in. That explained how he knew how to jimmy Simone's car. I couldn't blame him for lashing out like that. He'd gone through the loss of a dad and gained a jerk of a stepdad at such a critical age.

I think I was most surprised by Ryker, caring for Huntley's wellbeing like that. I often forgot how considerate Ryker was because he had such an odd way of showing it.

Veronica poked my side. "Now will you go get your man?"

"First, I have to see if he wants me."

With a deep breath, I moved toward Huntley.

CHAPTER FORTY-THREE

Huntley walked away, disappearing out the doors.

Veronica put her hands on her hips. "Where is he going?"

"I don't know." I moved to go after him, but my dad appeared in front of me.

He pulled me into a hug. "I'm proud of you. I was really nervous when we finally had a girl after so many boys. I wasn't sure how you'd fit in, or if I could actually raise a daughter." He pulled back so he could look at me. "But I honestly think you're tougher than all my boys combined. I just want you to know that I support you, one hundred percent."

"Um, okay." I was beyond confused. Why was he saying all of this?

"Me, too." Mom put a hand on my arm. "Trust your instincts, and maybe base your choices off the present instead of the past."

I put up a hand. "What are you two talking about?"

The music cut off.

"Hey, everyone," Daphne said. All eyes turned to her in the corner. She was speaking in a microphone attached to a stand, looking completely uncomfortable. Talking in front of a crowd was difficult for her, so I was proud of her for putting herself out there. "We want to thank you for coming out to celebrate Mr. Thomas' sixtieth birthday!" There was a short round of applause. "I think the fact that he's survived this long with seven hard-headed kids tells us how amazing he really is." Everyone chuckled, including my brothers and me.

"We have a special guest tonight," Daphne went on. "He'd like to play a couple of songs that he wrote himself." She frowned at Mr. Thomas. "He didn't write them for you, though. Sorry."

Dad laughed. "Thank goodness!"

"Ladies and gentlemen." Daphne swept out her arm. "Please welcome Huntley Esposito!"

As everyone clapped, all my attention went to Huntley. He smiled at the crowd as he took the spot in front of the microphone, his blue acoustic guitar strapped around his neck.

"Thanks, Daphne." Huntley adjusted the mic. "First, I want to start out by thanking the Thomas family. They graciously took me into their home this summer, basically treating me like one of their own."

"When you have six boys," Dad bellowed, "what's one more?"

Everyone chuckled.

Huntley's gaze locked onto me. "There was one member of the Thomas family that instantly put me at ease. She let me open up to her, unlike anyone I've ever known before." He rubbed the back of his neck. "I went through some rough times in the past and made some pretty stupid choices. I almost made one more by walking away from the best thing that ever happened to me, thinking I didn't deserve it. But after some wise counsel"—his eyes flitted over to my mom and dad—"I realized we're all given second chances. Sometimes three or four. And I wasn't going to blow mine without at least letting this girl know how I felt. This is for you, Tay."

My hands went to my mouth as Huntley took a deep breath and began his song.

Veronica and Daphne came to my sides, hugging me as he sang. I'd known he had a sexy voice, but it was beyond anything I could have imagined. He had this low, raspy tone that made goosebumps crawl along my arms and legs. The music, with a classic rock vibe, made the largest smile break out on my face.

He'd written a song for me. Lyrics, melody, something that was just for me.

I could feel everyone in my family staring at me, but I couldn't tear my eyes away from Huntley, who sang the song directly to me like no one else was in the room.

When the song ended, everyone broke out in a large applause. My brothers were all shouting and whistling, letting me know their approval of Huntley.

I really didn't *need* my family's approval, but oh, how I wanted it. They meant everything to me.

"I'll be back for some more songs but I have to take care of something first." He looked at me and nodded his head toward the main doors.

I turned to my parents. "Are you sure about this?"

They smiled at me.

"Oh, we'll be keeping a very, very close eye on you." Dad grinned. "And the fact that he'll be in college while you're completing your senior year of high school makes me incredibly happy."

"But like we've said a thousand times," Mom said. "We trust you. Be smart. Don't rush. But you deserve happiness, my baby girl."

I threw my arms around her and hugged her before I ran out of the room to catch up with Huntley.

He was waiting in the hall, leaning against the railing over-looking the area below. I stopped next to him, and words just spewed from my mouth.

"Listen, I just have to get this off my chest, okay?" I didn't give him a chance to respond. "Obviously, you know my boyfriend dumped me for another girl. I thought we'd had the perfect relationship, and I actually thought I loved the guy." I closed my eyes briefly, hating how naïve I had been. "But it was just another stupid high school relationship. Did I know it was bound to fail? Of course. Did I want it to fail? No. Because failure is not an option in my book. But so is unhappiness. I deserve happy. I deserve to find my person."

I looked out over the foyer of the events center, where a few people trickled in and out. "Everyone deserves happiness. Everyone deserves to find their person. But not everyone finds them."

Huntley slowly moved toward me. "What are you getting at?"

I turned to him, leaning on the railing. "This past month has made me open my eyes. It's made me reevaluate what I want out of life." I motioned to the open doors of my dad's party. Upbeat music and lively chatter drifted out. "I think I want to have my own party planning business. Something where I can make people's true happiness come to the surface, whatever that may be."

Huntley folded his arms. "And you'd be good at it."

"Thank you." I took a hesitant step forward. "Huntley, you're the first guy I've ever felt truly comfortable around. Like, I can be myself, no judgment. It's just easy." I looked back at the open doors. "I had no idea what Daphne was talking about until now." I turned my attention back to him. "And I know you're old and like in college and—"

Huntley held up a hand. "I wasn't aware eighteen was old."

"You're eighteen?" I'd had this hope that he was, but hearing it made me feel so much better about the situation.

He rested an arm on the railing. "Last time I checked."

But there was one other thing that had bothered me.

"You share a room with Ryker," I said. "He's twenty-one."

Huntley reached over and brushed his finger over my nose. "Eyelash." He let it fall to the floor. "I graduated high school when I had just turned seventeen, then went on to college. They had a mentor program where students who are juniors or older can room with a freshman to help them navigate their first year of college." He chuckled. "It's more like a babysitting program for kids with troubled pasts. Ryker made sure I never stepped out of line and took my studies seriously."

Ryker did that? How come he never told anyone in the family?

One thing I had been noticing lately about Ryker was that he wasn't the flashy type. He just did good things without being asked and without flaunting them.

"I think one of the main reasons Ryker was so adamant about breaking up our kiss was that he didn't want me to lose focus." Huntley slipped his hand into his pocket, resting it casually. "He wants me to keep my studies my top priority."

I thought back to what Ryker had said at Disneyland. "I think he's also worried about your past."

"He's worried about me slipping up again," Huntley said. "About me resorting back to the life of crime. But that me is long gone. I actually kind of hate past-me. Everything I do is to prove him wrong."

"That's pretty good motivation," I said.

"It is." Huntley sighed. "I really don't need a relationship right now."

I took a step closer to him. "Neither do I."

He smirked, his gaze falling to my lips. "I don't need any

distractions, Tay, and believe me when I say, you're a big distraction."

"You haven't even given me a try." I was now just a breath away from him. "I could be just as motivating as Ryker."

"How about you not say his name when you're this close to me?" Huntley's smirk faded. Those golden flecks in his eyes called to me, and I leaned toward him.

"Uh, Tay?" he said, almost as breathless as I felt having him so close.

"Yeah?"

He swallowed. "Personal space?"

Instead of scooting back, I slowly lifted my hand, resting it on his chest. "Then tell me to move."

"You know I can't," he whispered.

I leaned in, our noses brushing against each other. "You like being this close. Admit it."

Huntley responded by pressing his lips to mine, and everything around me shut down. I wrapped my arms around his neck as he slid his arms around my back, pulling me as close as humanly possible.

His kisses were warm and soft, lightyears ahead of that last guy I dated. There was a heated comfort to every single one, bringing me to a true and happy place. A place I wanted to drown myself in for a little while longer before I knew we'd have to part.

Maybe I didn't need a full-fledged relationship, but I didn't want to lose Huntley in my life. I think I had found my person, even if we wouldn't become a serious thing for a few years. I was just happy to know I'd found him, and one day we could start something truly magical.

For now, a few steamy kisses here and there would have to suffice.

Just for now.

ACKNOWLEDGMENTS

First and foremost, thanks to Disneyland for bringing me so much joy as a kid. I grew up about fifteen minutes away and had annual passes. In jr. high and high school, my friends and I loved hanging out there. No matter how crazy things were, the second I stepped into the park and smelled Main Street, everything exploded in magic, and all the crap outside the gates melted away. It was just ... home. It was also back in the '90's so not nearly as crowzy at is now (crowzy = crowded + crazy).

Thanks to everyone at Monster Ivy (Mary, Cammie, & Michelle!) for all your hard work and efforts. It's a joy being linked to such an awesome publishing company. You always help take my book to that next level, which the readers and I truly appreciate.

Chad, thanks for showing me true love does exist. You're my person, and I think I knew it the very first time I saw you. I still remember that day vividly, along with our first kiss, the first time you said, "I love you," the day you got down on your knee and asked me to marry you, and being across from you on our wedding day promising time and all eternity. I love you with all my heart and soul.

As always, thank you Dr Pepper for fueling my writing. You make every day better.

ABOUT THE AUTHOR

Sara Jo Cluff grew up in Yorba Linda, California, right next to the Happiest Place on Earth (aka her second home). Now she resides in Utah with her husband Chad, and their crazy cats.

She loves creating stories from scratch and seeing where the characters take her. When she's not writing, she's hanging out with her husband, watching Netflix, reading, or doing jigsaw puzzles.

She's a proud #PepperPack #Ambassador for the Most Delicious Beverage on Earth: Dr Pepper.

Visit her website at www.sarajocluff.com, and follow her on Instagram, TikTok, and Twitter: @SaraJoCluff.

Loved Taylor's Outrageous Vow?

Enjoy this sample of Monster Ivy's *The Kiss List*, also by Sara Jo Cluff!

I needed a license plate frame that said, "I'd rather be kissing." Because, honestly, if I could be doing anything right now, it would be kissing.

Which was why I pressed my freshly glossed lips against my boyfriend's somewhat dry lips. They wouldn't be dry when I was done with him. Dylan didn't hesitate—he pulled me into his lean chest, and our lips moved in perfect harmony like Pentatonix. After being together for over a year, it all came naturally.

We were on the leather couch in the front room of my house, me in his lap, his firm arms wrapped tightly around me, holding my body close, and his warm hand cradling the back of my neck. His long fingers drummed like they wanted to move, but he knew better than to let his hands wander. He'd get a solid smack across the cheek, like every time he'd ever tried.

I drew the line at kissing. A dark, thick line that wouldn't be going away any time soon, no matter how big of an eraser Dylan tried to use.

"Break it up." At Dad's deep voice, Dylan picked me up off his lap and set me down next to him.

Dad had one of those voices that no matter what he said, he came across serious, and slightly life-threatening. Add in his short-cropped military hair and huge muscles, and a lot of people stayed clear of him.

Dad didn't really care that much about us kissing. As long as we weren't alone in my bedroom, he was okay with it. But, obviously, it wasn't his favorite thing to watch.

"Hey, Mr. Collins," Dylan said, showing his dazzling white teeth and using his charming tone that made every adult smile. Except my dad.

Dad was in his 'at ease' stance, feet shoulder width apart, arms folded, and chin tilted up. He had on his hardly worn button-down shirt and slacks. The blue paisley tie was tied like it had been an afterthought. Mom would fix it when she got the chance.

Dad exhaled loudly through his nose—his calming technique—then turned his attention to me. "Camille, your mom and I need you to watch Seth tonight."

As if on cue, my little brother bounded into the room and put his hands on his hips. "Dad, I'm ten. I can take care of myself." He had his blond hair in a short mohawk and wore his favorite Minecraft shirt that was developing a few holes since he wore it so often.

Dad broke out in a fit of laughter, the rumbly sound making Dylan and me laugh as well. With his habit of opening the door for anyone, Seth couldn't stay home by himself, but Dad loved how grown up he tried to be.

"You all suck." Seth glared, his blue eyes too adorable to take seriously.

Dad's laughter cut off, and he slapped Seth upside the head. "Language."

Seth rubbed the back of his head, the glare intensifying. "Camille says it all the time."

I leaned my arms on the back of the couch and kneeled on

the cushion, my bare knees sliding on the leather so I could face them. "That's because I'm seventeen. I can get away with almost anything."

Mom rounded the corner of the hall, dressed in her typical form-fitting black dress, her blue eyes intently on her smart phone, her manicured thumb moving across it at lightning speed. She put my friends and me to shame when it came to how often she used her phone and how fast she could go. She was a teenage girl in an adult's body.

"Not true." Mom didn't take her eyes off the phone as she went into the kitchen and opened the fridge. She had a new case at her law firm that was occupying most of her time.

I held up a finger. "I said *almost*."

Dad snatched the phone from Mom's hand. She threw out her hands to retrieve it, but he just turned his back on her, a sly grin sliding onto his face. He loved to see Mom squirm.

"I was using that," Mom said with the same tone she used on Seth when he was misbehaving.

"I know," Dad said, dropping the phone into his jeans pocket. "But your clients will live until tomorrow. I promise."

Mom dropped her hands with a sigh. She opened her mouth, her eyes ready to challenge him, but instead, she grabbed a lime Diet Coke from the fridge, popped it open, and downed it.

"That's so impressive," Dylan whispered next to me.

I elbowed him, and he grunted, rubbing his stomach where I hit him. Mom didn't like anyone commenting on her "drinking problem," as Dad called it.

Dad pointed his thick finger at us. "Dylan can't be here."

I rolled my eyes. "Yeah, I know."

He told us that every time he and Mom left me in charge. He didn't like the thought of Dylan and me being alone in the house without them there. I once tried to argue that we weren't alone since Seth would be home. The intense glare that followed, with Dad's jaw pulled tight, and veins popping out basically everywhere, forced me to never bring that up again

Dylan kissed my cheek, leaving behind some of my lip gloss I'd given him earlier. "I gotta get home anyway. Have fun tonight, Mr. and Mrs. Collins." He jogged over to Seth and held his hand high in the air. Seth jumped up, slapping his hand against Dylan's, smiling brightly the whole time.

Normally, I hated seeing him go, and I'd beg him to stay just a little while longer. But as I watched his backside as he left the house, nothing flitted inside me—good or bad. I shook the random thought from my head. I was probably just tired.

Dad took the opportunity to come up behind me and slap the back of my head—his favorite thing to do.

"Not in my house," he mumbled.

"What? Looking at my boyfriend?"

He rubbed the top of my hair until it became a tangled mess. "Lusting after him."

I threw my head back and laughed so hard, I snorted. It took me a few seconds to calm enough that I could talk. "*Lusting?* Seriously, Dad? Gah. Will you please not use that word around me?"

Dad folded his arms, emphasizing his muscles. "If you stop lusting, then I'll have no reason to use it."

Seth had his small fingers in his ears and his eyes closed as he hummed the Star Wars theme song.

"Maybe we could grab an early dinner as a family before Dad and I leave for the party," Mom said, tossing her empty can in the recycle bin. She brushed back the blonde curls blocking part of her eye.

"Who has a party on a Thursday night anyway?" I asked.

Dad pointed his thumb at Mom. "Her weird clients."

Mom slapped his arm, and he huffed, smiling the whole time. A smile finally broke out on her face as well. Until she noticed Dad's tie, huffed, and stepped in to fix it.

When she finished, she went to Seth—still humming and plugging his ears—wrapped her arms around him, squeezed him tight, and pressed her lips close to his ear. "Food."

Seth took his fingers out of his ears, but couldn't lower his arms since Mom still had him in her grasp. He smiled wide, showing off his crooked front teeth. "Can we go to McDonald's?"

Dad scrunched his face, disgust filling every wrinkle. "No."

"You never let us go there," Seth said, flapping his hands awkwardly. Mom wouldn't release him, but he wasn't trying to get away.

"Because I'm being a responsible parent," Dad said. "I love you kids and care about your wellbeing."

I hopped over the couch, landing on the tile, shuffling closer to them and swaying my hips like a little girl. "Is that why you're going to take us to Chick-fil-A?"

Dad wiggled his eyebrows, his smile splitting wide. "You know it."

"What's the difference?" Seth asked, holding his palms up. "They both have chicken nuggets that are delicious."

"Oh, Seth." I squeezed his cheeks since Mom held him in place and he couldn't do anything about it. "One day your taste buds will develop, and you'll know the difference between gross and delicious."

Mom kissed the side of Seth's head, avoiding his Mohawk. "I personally love McDonald's chicken nuggets. Maybe we could go there, and your father and sister can go to Chick-fil-a."

Dad held up a hand. "We eat as a family." When Seth pouted, Dad sighed. "They're right next to each other. You two can bring your food over and eat with us."

Seth tried to pump his fist but couldn't move. He grunted. "Mom, you're making it hard for me to do anything."

"I know," she said, rocking him left and right.

Dad caught my eye, and I nodded. Seth saw our interaction and squealed, trying to wiggle away from Mom. "Stay away!"

With wicked grins, Dad and I swarmed in on Seth and tickled him while Mom held him in place. Seth squirmed and giggled, his eyes closing tight.

"Stop!"

We kept on tickling, getting his sides, armpits, and stomach. When I ventured down to his feet, he kicked out his legs, smacking his foot into my cheek. It hurt a little, but it was all too funny for me to care.

"Stop!" He laughed. "I'm going to pee my pants!"

Dad immediately stepped back and threw up his hands. "I don't want to clean that up."

Seth danced where he stood, so Mom let him go and pushed him toward the hall. He took off running, his socks sliding on the tile as he neared the bathroom. He already had his pants unzipped.

I leaned over laughing, clapping my hands. Tears pricked at the corner of my eyes. It didn't take long until Mom and Dad were laughing uncontrollably like me. Seth came out of the bathroom glaring but couldn't help laughing when he got a good look at us.

He threw his arms wide. "Glad I can entertain you guys. Can we go now? I'm starving, and those chicken nuggets aren't going to eat themselves."

Dad patted Seth's shoulder and turned him toward the front door, but then spotted Mom on her phone, probably emailing a client. He glanced at his jeans pocket, looking both annoyed and impressed that Mom had somehow wrangled it free. He opened the door, and they were about to step outside before I spoke up.

"I'm thinking Seth should probably put some shoes on," I said, pointing at his socked feet. What would they do without me?

Dad looked down at them. "Huh." He rubbed Seth's shoulders. "Hurry before I beat you to the car."

Seth plopped down in the entryway and scrambled to get his shoes on. Dad kept jerking like he was going to take off toward the car, causing Seth to whine. When he finished with the laces, Seth flew to his feet, past Dad, and out the door. Dad had to sprint to keep up.

"Mom, can I go to a concert with Dylan next weekend?" I asked. The best time to ask her for things was when she was preoccupied. Which was actually most of the time.

"Uh huh," Mom said, her eyes glued to her phone. We walked out the front door, and I locked it since that would be another thing they'd forget to do.

I could tell her anything, and it wouldn't register. "It's one of those wild ones. Lots of drugs, clothes coming off and such."

"That sounds fun." Mom opened the passenger door of the car, her thumb moving across the screen of her phone.

"Also, I'm an assassin."

Mom pressed send on her phone and smiled up at me. "That's nice, dear." She got into the car and closed the door.

With a sigh, I joined my crazy family in the car and wished for once that Mom would pay attention to us during dinner. But I never liked to get my hopes up.